Every One of Me

Lynette,
To the books
you don't see coming
+ never forget.
— Jessica Wilde
xo

Every One Of Me

By: Jessica Wilde

Front Cover Image by iStockPhoto.com
Back Cover Image by Shutterstock.com

Cover Designs by Jessica Wilde

ISBN-13: 978-1493758302

To my husband, for his love and support and for distracting our baby girl long enough for Mommy to 'get some writing done'.

To my beautiful baby girl. One day - in the far, far away future - I hope you find true love.

No regrets.

Every One Of Me

By: Jessica Wilde

Dissociative Identity Disorder (DID):

Also known as multiple personality disorder (MPD), is an extremely rare mental disorder characterized by at least two distinct and relatively enduring identities or dissociated personality states (also known as 'alters') that alternately control a person's behavior, and is accompanied by memory impairment for important information not explained by ordinary forgetfulness.

Co-consciousness:

The ability to communicate with other personalities (alters) in 'real time', to hear what they think/feel about things, and sometimes to see what they are doing when they have executive control.

Prologue

This had to be a dream. It didn't feel real and there was no way I could possibly be in a situation like this. This just… wasn't real.

"Hold her down! Careful with her head! Where's that Diazepam?"

I felt firm hands on my arms, legs, shoulders, and stomach and when I opened my eyes, there were several people around me that I didn't know and each one of them looked nervous. When I realized they were trying to hold me down, I relaxed my muscles and heard them all take a breath.

"W-What's going on?" my voice was hoarse and the words were painful coming out. I looked around the room for some kind of explanation and all I saw were a few plaques on the wall behind me and a chair that had been tipped over before someone grabbed my head.

"Ms. Marshall?"

A man was standing above me with a syringe held tightly in his hand. I nodded and my eyes darted between the needle and his face. I needed to wake up. This couldn't be good. I felt so… detached. Like I was watching all of this happen from far away, but I wasn't.

"My God, I've never seen a switch that… that fast."

"What switch?" I tried to tug my limbs away from the stressed out nurses on top of me, but none of them budged. "What the hell is going on? Why am I being held down?" I felt my heart pound against my chest like a hammer when I realized I couldn't remember. My stomach twisted violently and I snapped my mouth shut and closed my eyes, willing myself not to vomit.

"Ms. Marshall, we were talking and you shut down. When I asked you what was wrong, you became belligerent and tried to attack me."

The doctor didn't seem too freaked out by what he was telling me. In fact, he seemed to be a little more excited than I thought was appropriate, but his voice was calm and matter of fact. His expression told me everything.

"Did I… was anybody… please tell me I didn't hurt anyone." I started to panic and my gasps for air were hindered by the guy with his arm across my ribs.

"You can release her, now."

They all pulled away and it felt like a house was just lifted off of me. I sat up, but didn't make an effort to stand or move away. I was too freaked out and my body felt drained.

"I'm assuming you have no recollection of anything that has happened over the last ten minutes. Do you remember coming into my office for your session?" He was crouched down beside me and had capped the syringe. I knew it wouldn't stayed capped for very long. There was no other option if I was unpredictable.

"I remember talking to you, yes. I feel like it happened, but I'm not… I don't think I…" I couldn't even finish my thoughts. I felt fragmented, torn apart. I hated that feeling.

"Would you prefer to sleep this off and regroup later?"

I knew what he meant. I hadn't been working with him for very long, but from the very beginning, I knew I had to trust him. I didn't take too long to think it through. "I think it would be best to sleep this off, Dr. Deacon. Oblivion sounds nice right about now." I wiped under my eyes, but the tears I thought were there must have held back. How long had it been since I cried last? Oh yeah, that's right. When I left.

He smiled at me and nodded in agreement. I felt the prick of the needle, then… sweet nothing.

Chapter 1

Tessa

"So, what now?" Benny asked as she tapped her pen on the back of her chair.

"No idea," I replied. I stuffed the last of my clothes into my crappy suitcase and shrugged. "I guess I'll just take it a day at a time. Keep busy with Mom. Maybe… get a job."

She scoffed and quirked an eyebrow. "Really? A job? You better just stay here then because I don't think the world is ready for you, T."

I tried to smother the laugh that ascended up my throat, but it was no use. Benny knew how to make me laugh in the most brutal way. She may be right, but I was too determined to try and integrate my life among the living. I looked over and saw her tapping the side of her nose, something she did when she was planning on bringing up an uncomfortable topic.

I spoke up before she could. "I think the world has had plenty of time to prepare for me, Benny. Plus, the nurses are starting to make me nervous and Dr. Deacon told me the psychiatrist back home was the best for me." She grunted indifferently and started tapping her pen again. "I think he's just scared that I might make one of his precious nurses break a nail," I added.

She laughed loudly and nodded in agreement, her curly blonde hair bouncing off her cheeks. She had the brightest blue eyes that saw things others could only dream of. I was going to miss her terribly.

~ 4 ~

Bennett June Randolph and I had been roommates for the past nine months in 'The Facility', or behavioral health center if you want to get technical. To us, it was easier to think of it as just 'The Facility'. Better for our minds I guess. She had been in the system for a year before I met her and was being treated for her manic bipolar tendencies. She blamed her disorder on her parents giving her B.J. as her initials. Apparently she got a lot of shit for it in school and ended up getting in a lot of fights, and not just the yelling kind of fights. Actual physical, rip-out-your-hair-and-tear-your-face-to-shreds kind of fights. After a lot of therapy, she realized that her initials had nothing to do with it. It was just a means of figuring it out. Although, she will still put the blame on her parents anyway, just to make herself feel better.

Honestly, Benny scared the shit out of me when she went dark. Her few and far between episodes were like watching a nuclear explosion happen right in front of your eyes followed by every war movie ever made all rolled into one huge feature. Intense.

I'll never forget the day I met Benny, although I won't ever truly remember the circumstances. All I can remember is waking up strapped to my bed with her staring down at me and telling me I was 'one tough cookie'. When she realized I didn't remember anything, she replayed everything for me. Actually replayed it, as in she took me to the session offices and acted out every part I played in the whole incident.

"Craziest fucking thing I have ever seen," she shouted. "You were like a tiny, white Incredible Hulk only you weren't really fighting or anything. You were seriously tearing those girls down with words. Words! Those nurses didn't have a chance," she had said animatedly and threw her hands above her head triumphantly.

When I first arrived at this cold as death clinic, I was under the impression that I had some type of selective amnesia. I only recently found out it was much more than just memory loss and mood swings that only those around me at the time witnessed. I wasn't insane and I wasn't delusional. I just had a problem shaking off a few extra companions that decided to show up at unwanted times. Not that there were any *wanted* times anyway. Benny was the one to help the docs figure out what was really going on because she was the one that, at some point, got to have a conversation with… everyone else.

Let me get us out of this desolate building and everything will come together soon.

Benny was my only friend. She had been by my side for nine months and I'll never be able to make it up to her. I planned on trying, but I had a few things to take care of first.

I zipped up my suitcase and looked around the room to make sure I hadn't forgotten anything. There wasn't much in the desolate space. It was the opposite of a college dorm room, as it should be. This wasn't college life, this was simply the consequences. My life had been anything but simple before I ended up in The Facility. It sounds kind of creepy, but that was the only name any of us liked to call it as I said before. Makes it sound like some kind of secret organization who experiments with people making them superhuman or something. It's easier that way. I had come to enjoy the simple life I had here and was almost regretting my decision to leave, but Mom needed my help and I needed a doctor who could help sort me out. That doctor happened to live in my hometown of Denver Colorado where my brother was currently engaged to a woman that my mother just couldn't handle anymore and needed someone to work interference. This wasn't really the main reason I was going back. I missed my family and I had wronged them by taking off five years ago.

"So..." Benny sang and continued to *tap tap tap* her pen. "You think you are going to see him?"

"Who?"

"Oh, don't play dumb with me, T. You know who."

I looked down at the bed and studied the few possessions I had, trying to avoid eye contact. "Hope not."

"Ha!" she exclaimed and shook her head. "Sure."

A month after we became roommates, I had made the mistake of telling her the biggest reason I left and she never let me forget it. She thought it was stupid of me to just try and forget about my best friend, thinking it would make his life easier. The fact that I still loved him didn't convince her to be nice about it either. Charlie was still very much a part of my life whether I liked it or not.

"Tessa? You all packed up, dear?" We both turned to our open door and saw Judy, the discharge coordinator standing in her ridiculous bunny and carrot scrubs. She always looked so colorful and even though it was normally against the rules to wear anything but solid colors, the bosses made an exception for her. She always argued that what she wore made the first impression on anyone who walked in the front doors and the people who usually walked in the front doors were the ones in need of some color. Really, she was the administrators wife so no one dared to enforce the rules with her. Plus, she was probably the sweetest lady you would ever get lucky enough to meet. Standing at a solid five feet with streaks of gray shooting across her jet black hair and eyes as blue as the sky, she was a force of nature that no one wanted to change.

"Yeah, Judy. I'm ready," I mumbled and dragged my suitcase off the bed with one hand while cradling the shoebox full of the last year in the other.

"Great! I'll meet you up front. Don't keep her too long Benny. Her mother just finished up the paperwork and is anxious to see her." Her crooked finger was aimed at Benny who had the nerve to look incredulous.

"Of course, Judy. I wouldn't dream of doing anything other than protocol."

I snorted just as loud as Judy did and watched her walk away faster than she should be capable of.

"Well, T. I wish you the best, but honestly, I give you a month before you come back. You'll miss me too much," she smirked.

I wanted to laugh at the attempt she made to avoid an emotional goodbye, but I couldn't. I had a lump in my throat that was setting up camp for the last ten minutes and I couldn't seem to swallow it down. She was right. I was going to miss her desperately and I had no idea how I was going to get my life in order without her there to help me. I used to have control, or at least I thought I did. After what I had been through the last year, control was all but forgotten.

She must have noticed the moisture in my eyes because she hopped up from her chair and wrapped her arms around my shoulders. "Let the girls know I'll miss them, too. But not as much as you, Tessa. I love you, babe."

"I love you, too. Be good," I said and released my suitcase to wrap my arm around her.

"Yeah," she scoffed, "I'll do that."

When she pulled away, her eyes were as wet as mine, but she refused to let the tears fall. She tried to avoid getting emotional as much as I used to. She was just better at it. "I'll visit soon. I'm mad I won't be there to see Charlie's face."

I rolled my eyes, "I'm sure he doesn't even live there anymore. He was always desperate to get out of town. Why would he stay?"

She grabbed my suitcase and started to wheel it out the door. "For you," she said with an innocent smile.

My heart stopped for a few seconds at the thought, but when it started back up, I pushed the image away. Even if he did, I couldn't invade his life. Not with all the baggage I had with me.

***

My mother, Sarah Marshall, was probably just as sweet as Judy was, if not more. She had a way of becoming your most cherished friend with just a smile. She was waiting patiently at reception, bright sun dress covered in tiny flowers, her brown hair pinned up just the way I always remembered, and her brown eyes glistening with tears of an emotional reunion. Benny had a harder time saying goodbye to her than she had with me and for a minute, I was pretty jealous. I couldn't blame her though. I loved my mother and I knew she loved me, which made the apology I was about to attempt that much harder.

We were in the back seat of the cab on our way to the airport when I grabbed her hand and started to speak only to stop when she cupped my cheek and smiled.

"Don't be sorry for *anything*, Tess. You did what you had to do. I love you and I'm proud of you." Then she kissed me on the cheek and laid her head on my shoulder. "Save it for someone else, though," she muttered under her breath, but I pretended not to hear her.

I wasn't ready to make that apology and I knew I never would be. It would involve being face to face with the one person I couldn't be with and the only person I had ever truly wanted to be with. I was a mess, though, so I accepted the truth a long time ago. Didn't make it any easier, but I had never really dealt with easy so… I would be fine.

We arrived at the airport with no less tension between us. Mom hated flying, but she refused to let me travel home alone. After boarding the plane and settling in, she gave in to telling me the real reason she came to get me on the other side of the country. I couldn't help but feel a little relieved that she hadn't changed a bit.

"She's horrible, Tess. A real live-" she paused to look around and lowered her voice, "*bitch.* She is the spawn of everything evil in this world, but I can't say that to Trevor. It will only push him away and I would rather keep an eye on how things are going. I think she may be drugging him or something. Or she brainwashed him. I just don't see a nice man like Trevor marrying that… thing," she said and shivered in disgust.

My brother had recently gotten engaged to a girl that my mother didn't approve of, as you can tell. Well, I don't think anyone would approve of her because she was just awful. She was a senior when I was a sophomore and I saw firsthand the horrible things she had done. I couldn't imagine she had changed at all. But she was gorgeous and my brother was shallow. Always had been. I told Mom I was probably not the best one to be screening her requests, but after talking to her over the phone a few times, I knew Mom wouldn't be able to keep her cool much longer and I couldn't let her lose Trevor.

"I think you coming home will be the best thing for him. He'll get some time away from Ellie and maybe see that he would be happier without her. She is always bickering at him and telling him he is an idiot and that his friends are worthless," she sneered.

"Seriously? I wouldn't think Trevor would put up with that," I replied.

"Yeah, well, she makes a point to show off her breasts when she is talking, so I don't think he really even hears a word she says." She took a sip of her water and patted my leg, reassuring me not to worry too much and that I am who she needs right now.

The flight seemed to take forever and not just because I found it impossible to sleep, but because the one thing I was sure my mother would bring up, she doesn't. Where Charlie is and what he is doing. I am gratefully disappointed. It would be nice to know where he is at... so I can attempt to avoid him at all costs, of course. Not a word. She doesn't say a word about him except for that subtle hint in the cab on the way to the airport. For some reason, I feel like her *not* saying anything *is* saying *everything.*

By the time we landed in Denver, got off the plane, grabbed our bags, and found a cab, I was utterly exhausted and it was only seven o'clock in the evening. The ride home geared up the anxiety I already felt. Seeing all the familiar buildings and houses, the streets I used to roam with my friends when I was younger, the sandwich shop we used to frequent - it was overwhelming to say the least. As the cab pulled into the driveway of the house I grew up in - that hadn't changed a bit - I was practically gasping for the precious air I need to survive. Mom didn't notice. She saw my brother's red Toyota parked on the curb and immediately started praying that *the beast* didn't come with him. Unfortunately, two figures were waiting for us at the door and one looked very much like a woman.

My mother had already climbed the porch steps by the time I thanked the cab driver for helping me unload my suitcase. I looked up at the house and felt like I had never left. I know I said it hadn't changed, but damn.

The wind chimes I had made for Mom in the sixth grade were still hanging from the eave above the porch. The giant tree in the front yard was still there with three names carved into the trunk, one of which I didn't want to think about. Even the pieces of lumber that Trevor had nailed to the tree in an attempt to build a huge tree house for me, but never finished, were still there. Even the garden was exactly the same. Tulips and daisies. Pink and white only. The only change? The bottom porch step looked like it was about to crumble. I looked up at the window to my bedroom and took a deep breath.

Mom cleared her throat when she passed through the front door and I looked toward her. She seemed to be apprehensive about being together as a family again. It had been too long with so many unanswered questions. Tension was high.

My fault entirely.

Chapter 2

Tessa

"Hey stranger!" my brother said excitedly and wrapped me into one of his bear hugs. "So glad you are back, Tess. You have been missed."

I hugged him back tightly and took a deep breath in. His familiar scent washed over me and brought back memories of what my life was like before I knew where it was going. He always smelled like toothpaste and Old Spice and my smile widened when I realized that hadn't changed either.

"I've missed you guys, too," I muttered into his shoulder.

He released me from the hug but kept his hands on my shoulders and gave me a look that only a concerned brother would give his sister. "You okay?"

I nodded and gestured to my suitcase, "I'm great, but I would like to get unpacked before we get to all the heavy stuff."

He chuckled and moved an arm around the shoulders of the platinum blonde beside him. "Good, but first, Tessa, this is Ellie. My fiancé. Ellie, this is my little sister, Theresa."

I stretched my arm out to shake her hand as she assessed me from my head to my toes and then met my eyes with a genuinely fake smile before dropping her hand into mine and awkwardly shimmying it back and forth like this was her first handshake and couldn't figure out the physics of it. I smiled and tried to keep the sarcasm I was about to vomit on a tight leash. "Nice to meet you, Ellie. I hope you don't mind if I get settled in before getting to know you a bit."

"Nope."

That's all she said and I couldn't help but quirk an eyebrow. My mother cleared her throat from behind my brother, "Trevor, let her in for Hell's sake. She can't get settled out on the porch!"

I dragged my suitcase in and just as Trevor was about to grab it for me, Ellie snatched his arm and whined about being cold so he had to drape his arm over her shoulders again. I saw her move for what it really was. Not because I have a sixth sense about these things, but because she gave me an evil grin when I looked back at her. *Ugh! Great.*

Mom followed me up the stairs and into my old room. She always was a hoverer, but it couldn't possibly bother me now. I knew why she didn't want to leave the safety of my room. It was almost exactly how I left it. I slowly started unpacking and got a couple of things hanged before giving up and sitting on the bed next to her.

She sighed loudly and took my hand in both of hers. "I don't know what you have been through, my dear, and you know I would never ask you to take on more than you can handle here." She paused and then looked desperately into my eyes. "But I can't handle that bitch anymore. Is there any way you could run her off for me?"

I laughed for the first time since this morning and it felt so good under the circumstances. My mom just smiled and kissed my cheek. "Come on, let's have some tea and you can give us a synopsis before you go to bed. It's been a long day."

When I had spoken to my mother on the phone about coming home, she didn't ask any questions. In fact, when she first found out where I was, she just asked if I was okay and told me that she loved me and would support me in whatever I needed to do. I loved that about her. Her priority was me, not the crap, and even though I know she was worried about me and was probably heartbroken that I left her, she still loved me and apparently forgave me for everything.

Over the last year, I had stayed in contact with her and told her some of the issues I was taking care of, namely the therapy and anxiety I had been going through in trying to figure out what was happening to me. It took a year to come up with a firm diagnosis and when I had told Mom it was worse than I thought, she said there was nothing we couldn't handle together. She said she had been a witness to my 'affliction' several times, but I had been unaware that anything was happening. Like I said before, I thought it was selective amnesia and maybe the things I couldn't remember were a result of stress or that I just didn't care. Things changed when others close to me started talking to me about things I did, but couldn't remember, or started calling me a liar. By the time I put everything together, I was too upset to think clearly and too worried about the things I could possibly do to the people I loved. I had already hurt my best friend, what would I do to my mother or brother? So I left.

Unfortunately, I left without a word until I was gone for three days and realized they would send the police out looking for me if they didn't know I was okay. Yeah, I know. Stupid of me, but hey, I was a little stressed and a little freaked out. I wasn't really thinking clearly. I had called Mom and told her not to worry too much and that I had to do this on my own and I would be in contact with her to let her know I was still okay. Obviously, it wasn't that short of a conversation and there was a lot of drama and other things said, but in the end, she said she understood and that's all that mattered to me. The contact I told her I would make ended up being a postcard every month or so for four years with a phone call on Mother's Day and a letter for Christmas. She took it all in stride even though I knew in my heart I was tearing out her soul a piece at a time.

I just couldn't face them.

Now that I was back, I had to give them some answers. One of the promises I made to Mom over the phone that last time was that I would tell her and Trevor everything and trust them to support me and be there for me no matter what it was.

Now, I know what you are thinking. How could someone leave their family like that and not tell them *anything*? Well, like I said before, the last year was really the only progress I made and by then, I had told them where I was and the general idea of what I was doing.

We all gathered in the living room with my mom's herbal tea and chocolate chip cookies. I was hoping that Ellie would be gone by the time I came down stairs. She was sitting close to Trevor on the loveseat and looked like she couldn't give a shit less about what was going on. Mom gave me a knowing look, but didn't say a word.

Trevor was looking at his phone with a grimace and quickly looked up at me when I sat down in the recliner across from him. He tapped something in his phone and shoved it back in his pocket looking unsure of himself, which he never was. When he gave me a nervous grin, I chalked it up to being anxious about what I had to say.

"Sooooo," he said lazily, "what's up, Tess?"

I looked down at my hands and frowned. My brother was never one to beat around the bush and I knew, from my frequent talks with Mom, that he was concerned about me in an angry sort of way. I never thought he would be happy about my disappearing the way I did, but for a while I pretended like me taking off didn't matter to him.

It's not like we were never close or anything. In fact, we were *very* close. We were the kind of siblings that hung out with each other. He took me along quite often whenever he would go with his friends. At the time, I thought he was doing it for Mom. Now, I think he did it just for me. Some people thought we were fraternal twins at first. We looked a lot alike except his eyes were hazel. Mine were brown. We both had the same firm chin and rosy cheeks, dark eyebrows and dark brown hair. He was very handsome and could have any girl he wanted. He was also tall and had built up more muscle since the last time I saw him.

My brother always took care of me when we were younger. He was protective and annoying a lot of the time and chased off a lot of boys that may or may not have had good potential, but in the end I was grateful for his interference. I think, because the majority of my childhood was fatherless, he felt like he should take that position in my life. Sounds pretty unreasonable for a boy only a few years older to take up that responsibility, but I don't think things would have gone so smoothly if he hadn't.

After he graduated from high school, he was confident in my ability to survive without him. That and I always had Charlie looking out for me. I really think he just wanted to spend a while partying it up since he didn't get that chance while he was taking care of me and Mom. I don't blame him at all. But come on… he is engaged to *that?* Something must have seriously gotten embedded in his brain because never in a million years would I ever picture my big brother Trevor with someone so… uh, bitchy is not the right word. Think much, *much* worse. And this was all decided in the few seconds I spent in her presence. Not a good sign.

They were all waiting patiently - well, most of them were - for me to begin. I took a deep breath and a sip of tea before I started the speech I had been caught rehearsing in front of the mirror several times by Benny. She never laughed or made fun of me, she just gave me a sympathetic nod and would give me a few pointers here and there. I missed her already and knew if she were there, she would have my back and throw in a few jokes here and there to lighten the mood.

"First of all, I'm sorry for disappearing the way I did. I know that doesn't fix anything, but I want you both to know that I regretted leaving… I just *had* to." Trevor nodded and my mother just smiled at me. I loved them both and worried about what me being back would do to them, but I kept going. "As you know, I had realized that something was going on when more and more things I couldn't remember were brought to my attention." Thoughts of Charlie made me pause and swallow past the regret and shame. He was the one that had been worried enough to really get me to listen. "I also realized that I had hurt people without even knowing it. I couldn't just sit around and wait for something to happen that would hurt you two, so I left. I don't expect you to understand that, I just hope you accept it, because I can't change it."

Trevor flinched and reached into his pocket again with an apologetic smile. His eyes flicked to me briefly when he looked at the screen and he typed quickly and jammed the phone back into his pocket before giving me his full attention again. I noticed Ellie was busy examining the color of her nails and probably trying not to roll her eyes. Her platinum blonde hair was pin straight and her eyes were like a mix of poop green and yellow barf. Sorry, only way I know how to describe them other than evil. She had a nice chest, but I wouldn't call them nice enough to distract someone from her ultimate bitchiness. That's just me, though.

"Anyway, I moved around a little bit for several years. I had a few different jobs and made a few friends at first, but I kept noticing things that didn't make any sense. I would wake up one morning and see things around my apartment that I had never bought. Things that I would *never* buy. People around me called me by a different name and when I would try to correct them, they would be so confused and upset, like I had offended them or … I don't know." I ran my fingers through my hair and grasped at the little courage I had left. I described some of the things I discovered and what some of the people said I did.

"A neighbor of mine confronted me one morning and told me I needed to get some help. Apparently, I had made quite a scene the night before and I had no recollection of anything. I'm embarrassed to say that it took as long as it did for me to admit that I couldn't just deal with it on my own. That's when I called you, Mom. I was already in Massachusetts at the time and the day after my neighbor told me that, I went straight to the first doctor I could see and was checked into the behavioral health treatment center later that day." I winced recalling that first day. The doctor had been so overwhelmed with what I had told him that he immediately contacted 'The Facility' and got me into the inpatient program. I told them I didn't have the money or insurance to pay for the program, but the doctor that was taking over my treatment said not to worry. They were overly interested in my problem and were willing to negotiate.

"So, you have been in a mental hospital for the last year?" Ellie asked, letting us all know that the only thing she heard was 'behavioral health treatment center'.

I shook my head and breathed through the simmer of anger I felt. "You could call it a mental hospital if that helps you understand, but it was really a treatment center for people who are trying to get help for something they can't really control. None of us were really considered mental patients."

She shrugged as if it made no difference that her fiancé's sister might be offended by her words. I made the decision to just ignore her until I went to bed.

"And? Did they help? Did they figure out what was wrong?" Trevor asked.

Mom had been sitting quietly with her hands in her lap the whole time I had been speaking. She gave no indication that any of this was stressing her out or that her daughter might be considered a freak. I described some of the things that were discussed with my doctor along with some of the therapy I had gone through, then I just couldn't speak about it anymore. "I don't really feel like getting into everything tonight. A lot has happened, but I want you to know that I am continuing to receive the help I need and will hopefully find a way to control what is happening." I looked my mother in the eyes for several long seconds, then turned to Trevor and did the same. "I have been diagnosed with dissociative identity disorder."

There was silence for a few heart beats before Ellie decided we all needed to hear her voice. "And what is *that*?" She looked slightly disgusted, but when she looked at Trevor and saw his expression - which was one of confusion and shock - she looked a little amused.

I wanted to punch her stupid perfect little nose that I had no doubt was the result of plastic surgery. I spoke firmly and narrowed my eyes at my target, "It's another way of saying I have multiple personality disorder."

Unfortunately, I didn't get to see her reaction because the loud knock on the front door made all of us jump in surprise. Trevor looked at me nervously and I glared back at him. He knew who that was and he knew I wasn't going to be happy about it. My stomach lurched when my mom gave him a stern, but knowing glance and hurried to the door.

My heart rate jumped and I tried to force my body to get up and run like a bat out of hell to the safety of my bedroom and barricade the door. My body wasn't cooperating, though, and I was too busy doing the breathing exercises I had been taught to go through when I felt a build-up of stress. I couldn't see the front door from where I was sitting. The wall separating the living room from the foyer just blocked the recliner I was sitting in. If I really wanted to see, however, all I had to do was stand and move back about three feet.

Trevor hadn't taken his eyes off of me and Ellie was back to looking at her nails. The deafening sound of the doorknob turning and short squeak of the heavy door being pulled open almost burst through the little control I had.

Trevor took a deep breath, "I'm sorry, Tess. He just--"

"Where is she?" I heard the deep familiar baritone coming from the front door and was on my feet before I could stop myself.

"We just got home not even an hour ago," my mom said quietly.

Two more steps and I would be in full view, and yes, my feet were already going. I could now see my mother's small frame blocking everything from the shoulders down of the one man I was not prepared to see, but strangely, had seen every single day for the last five years every time I closed my eyes.

"Sarah, please. I have to see--" His words stopped abruptly when he looked up and saw me in the doorway. His brilliant green eyes roamed over my face before taking in the rest of me. He exhaled sharply as if he had been holding that particular breath for far too long. His face was still familiar, but more masculine with a stronger jaw line and a darker complexion. His eyes were as green as grass in late spring and his hair was still the perfect dark brown I remembered. His nose was just slightly crooked like it had been broken and his lips, the part of him I had always tried to forget, were… still his. Soft, full, and powerful. "Tess," he whispered.

My knees almost buckled hearing my name on those lips, but I was stronger now. I could control my reactions to him. Right? My shaking hands were trying to convince me otherwise. It was like the last five years had never happened and I was still the same eighteen year old girl who pined after her best friend in secret and became incredibly skilled at hiding the way she felt. I thought I would have been a crumbling mess from the lack of practice, but surprisingly enough, I was still standing strong.

Then my mother moved out of the way and I got a look at the rest of him. I had to grasp the door frame for support. He used to be skinny. Not scrawny, but skinny and kind of boyish. But in the last five years, he had become a man and had obviously been working out. A lot.

His shoulders were much wider than I remembered and I couldn't recall his t-shirts hugging his torso quite that deliciously before. I could tell that his stomach was ripped from where I stood and I just knew, without seeing, that if he were to take his shirt off, he would have that glorious V at his hips and his jeans would hang just right.

I saw all of this in a matter of seconds, but my perusal was halted when he took a few large strides toward me and his arms wrapped around my waist and lifted me off the ground, crushing me in a hug meant for lovers, not strangers.

Best friends turned strangers. That was what we were, now. My Charlie was a stranger because my heart wouldn't be able to handle anything else. His strong hold on me tried to convince me otherwise.

Chapter 3

Charlie

"Tess. I can't believe it," I murmured against her neck and inhaled deeply. I shuddered at the slam of her familiar scent. She had always smelled like sweet mint and rain. Good to know some things hadn't changed. Her dark brown hair was a lot longer now and she was slimmer than I remembered, but her eyes were the same. Chocolate and caramel and just as compelling.

Five years. It had been five years since I had last seen or talked to her and the hole I had felt in my chest since, kept reminding me of what she had left behind and what she had taken away. Now, with my arms wrapped around her, that hole didn't exist. It was filled completely and for the first time in five years, I felt like I could breathe.

"You're here. You're really here," I said, setting her on her feet and pulling back just enough to see her face again. Her cheeks were flushed and her lips parted when I took another close look at her. She was always much shorter than me with the top of her head just reaching my shoulders. I never really liked tall girls, probably because they were so different from Tess. She was no more than 5'4"and now that she had apparently lost weight, I felt like I could pick her up and tuck her in my pocket. She still had curves to die for, though, and I had died many times over the years watching every one of those curves gracefully move.

Her expression was pained as she stepped back and pulled out of the hold I had around her waist. "What are you doing here?" she asked shakily.

Her words sounded cold, but her face said something completely different and I knew what she was about to do. She had done it so many times when we were younger. She thought she was good at acting cold or indifferent, but she had really sucked at it. Still did. I always acted like I didn't know any better just to humor her. I liked seeing the relief on her face when she thought she had successfully tricked me into thinking what she wanted. Not this time, though. I couldn't let her push me away. I *wouldn't* let her.

I was too in love with her to let her go again.

"Tess, it's been five years. What do you *think* I'm doing here? Trevor said you were home so I came right over." I glanced over at her brother as she turned and glared at him, and he just had to look sheepish and innocent enough to make me forget how mad I had been at him. He and Sarah hadn't told me anything over the years. Well, Sarah hadn't said anything. I got Trevor to talk a few times, but only because I could do some physical harm to him. I had texted Trevor to ditch the bitch and come over for a drink and when he replied that he was reuniting with his long lost sister, it took me a good ten minutes to understand what he meant. I told him I was on my way and he made a lame attempt to stop me by saying *'not your best idea'*.

Tess backed up a little further and looked down at her hands. "Well, I was just heading up to bed. I've had a long day. Goodnight."

Then she was gone. Up the stairs and out of sight and the hole that had been filled, cracked open again. I stared after her in stunned silence and it took all my strength to stay where I was. I must have looked pathetic because Sarah stepped forward to give me a hug and she looked like she was about to cry.

"I'm sorry, Charlie. She just isn't ready. She has been through a lot and I don't think any of us can expect her to be very social right now." She looked up at me and patted my cheek. "Don't worry, though. She will come around. Come on, let's sit."

"I told you it wasn't a good idea, man. She isn't the same girl she used to be and I don't think she ever will be," Trevor said quietly.

"I know that, Trevor," I replied. "I just didn't think she would treat me like a total stranger. You know how close we were. I just couldn't *not* come over."

He leaned forward with his elbows on his knees and rested his chin in his hands. "She was telling us what was going on when you showed up."

I snapped my head up to look at him. "And?"

He looked over at his mother and back to me before shaking his head. "I'm not sure what would be appropriate to tell you, man."

Sarah stood quickly and walked into the kitchen. She looked like she was about to be sick and I wanted to follow after her. Over the years, she had become a second mother to me. Well, technically she was the only mother to me. Mine had remarried and taken off to Europe to spend the rest of her life traveling and being oblivious to the life she left behind. Tess and Trevor's mom had made sure I was a part of the family. After Tess left and Trevor went back to college, she needed someone to take care of and I was here every day for months.

I scrubbed a hand down my face and tried to wipe away the memory of those few days where we had no idea what had happened to Tess. Sarah was a mess and Trevor was furious with me. He thought I was the reason she took off, that I had hurt her in some way.

Tess and I had been best friends since the fifth grade when Michael Stower had knocked her down and dumped a bucket of sand on her head at the playground during recess. I kicked his legs out from under him, shoved his face in the sand, and told him if he touched her again I would make sure he ate nothing but sand every day for the rest of the year. I helped her clean the sand out of her hair and she hugged me and said thank you. She had the prettiest voice out of all the girls in school and I had always wanted to talk to her, but was too shy. After that, we spent every recess together and I made sure no one messed with her. I was a scrawny kid, but I could fight if I needed to.

We were inseparable all the way through high school and even though it tortured me to watch her go on dates with other guys and hear about who she thought was cute, I always answered the phone and listened to her excited voice tell me all about them. Senior year was different. Her summer boyfriend broke up with her the day before school started because he didn't want to be 'tied down' when he could be having fun and going out with other girls. She came over to my house in tears and I held her for hours while she told me all the things she had liked about him and kept asking why no one wanted to be with her.

I made it my goal that year to show her how much she meant to me. I had been in love with her since I first saw her at recess in the fourth grade when I had been the new kid who had just moved into the neighborhood. She was playing hop scotch with her friends and her long braid bounced up and down on her back, hypnotizing me. I attempted to talk to her several times, but there was always someone who got to her first. Until the day I saved her from Michael.

Senior year, I didn't go out with any other girls, not that there were a lot of girls that really wanted to go out with me. I had only ever been on three dates and those were girls from church whose mothers were friends with my mother and talked me into taking them to a dance. I wasn't the guy I was now. I was shy and reserved, only really opening up whenever it was just Tess and me.

When Sarah got the call from Tess after she had disappeared, Trevor had to hold me back from snatching the phone away. He ended up punching me in the face and sitting on my chest to keep me down. He had broken my nose, but I hadn't noticed all the blood. His mom hung up the phone in tears and told me that there was nothing any of us could do to get her back. We had to let her go.

I don't think I had ever cried before that day and I know I hadn't cried since. That was the day my heart was ripped out of my chest and nothing but a gaping hole was left. I lived for the monthly post cards and the only reason I woke up every day was the hope that she had sent one early and it would say where she was so I could find her.

I begged Sarah to let me talk to her that first Mother's Day that she called, but she wouldn't let me. That's when she told me that she had made Tess a promise to never speak of me. She would stop sending post cards if I was ever brought up and Sarah couldn't stand the thought of not knowing if she was okay. I stopped asking anything about her after that, only finding out she was safe when a new card would come in the mail. I started fighting then, doing mixed martial arts and competing underground and buried myself in my training. I stayed busy, traveling around the country for fights but always came back. Trevor graduated and moved back to be close to his mother and help take care of her.

I started taking care of both of them when I won my first championship. Sarah never asked for anything, but I sent her a check on the first day of every month no matter where I was and made sure she cashed it. She really didn't have a choice. She would lose the house and everything else without my help.

"Don't take it too personal, Charlie," Trevor said, breaking the uncomfortable silence. "Tess is back. That's what matters. There's time to fix things."

I nodded reluctantly and looked into the kitchen. Sarah was sitting at the dining table with her head in her hands. "What do I need to do?" I asked him.

"I don't know. Give her some time. She's been on her own now for years and I don't think she has really accepted what is going on with her," he replied.

Ellie scoffed, "How could anyone accept that? She's unpredictable and shouldn't be anywhere but in a mental hospital."

I stood abruptly and couldn't stop the words coming out of my mouth if I tried. "Don't you dare speak about her that way. You have no idea who she is and you have no right to--"

"That's enough!" Sarah shouted from the kitchen.

Ellie started talking as if nothing had happened, "Forgive me for being cautious about being in the same room as a freaking psychopath!"

A crash sounded from the kitchen just before Sarah appeared in the doorway looking more menacing than I had ever seen her. "Get out of my house!"

Trevor snatched Ellie up by her arm and dragged her to the door. "This is a shock for all of us, Mom. Ellie just isn't used to drama like this. I'll take her home and be back in a while, give us all a chance to cool down."

I shook my head as he walked out the door. The man was dense. Never in a million years would I marry someone who spoke about my sister that way, if I had ever had a sister. Something had to be done about that, but right now, the focus was Tess. We watched them leave and I forced my feet to stay where they were and not let them take me up the stairs to Tess.

"Charlie, come here, sweetie." Sarah tilted her head to the kitchen and went back in to sit down. I took the seat across from her and sat silently. "How was the fight, dear?"

I had gotten back into town two days ago and distracted myself with training, so I didn't get a chance to call yet. "I won. Got another coming up next month in New York."

"Congratulations, you don't look like he got in any punches." She smiled and studied my face, checking for the usual scrape or bruise.

"Not this time," I said. "New guy who was too cocky. I knocked him out forty five seconds into the first round." I cracked my knuckles and stretched my fingers, feeling the stiffness from a day of training on the bags. I had been working harder than ever for the last couple weeks knowing that Tess was planning on coming back, I just didn't know *exactly* when.

"You were cocky once," she chuckled. "Your first fight sent you to the hospital. I don't think I have ever seen so many bruises on one person before." She had come straight to the hospital after Trevor told her what had happened. She started yelling at me the second the doctor walked out of the room. I couldn't help but laugh when she said she would do twice the damage if I ever let another one of those 'big lugs' take me down like that again.

"I'm less cocky now."

Her smile faded and I had to look away. She was such a strong woman and was there for me when I needed her. She needed me now and so did Tess.

"She needs you, Charlie. More now than ever before," she said gently. "Just be patient."

I sighed and nodded in agreement. "I've been patient for five years, Sarah. I would wait for her for the rest of my life. I won't let her go again. You know that."

"Yes, I know." She took a sip of her tea and closed her eyes. "When you first realized something was wrong… what was it that told you she…?"

I rubbed the back of my neck and peered down at the old table that had been in this kitchen since before I was born. It was worn down and scratched, much like we all had been over the last few years. Tess had been wearing thin before any of us really knew something was wrong.

"I chalked up the first episode to her being drunk. We were sophomores and had gone to Danny Danko's birthday party. You remember that? We told you we were staying with friends overnight at the lake, but we really were just too drunk to come home."

She shook her head in amusement. "I knew you were drunk when you called me and told me she had already fallen asleep. You were slurring your words so badly, I could barely understand you."

"Serious? And you never said anything?"

She chuckled, "No, Charlie. I knew you wouldn't let anything happen to her. And how was I supposed to stop you. You both were already drunk and I had no vehicle to come and get you. Trevor had taken the car to that same party."

"Yeah, well, we thought we had you fooled. Tess was terrified of disappointing you, though, and swore never to do that again. I never saw her drink anything with alcohol after that night. Especially after she woke up the next morning and couldn't remember anything. We thought it was because of the drinking, but after what happened that summer, I realized it was more than that."

She hadn't even remembered going to the party in the first place. She was freaking out when she woke up in the back of my station wagon next to me instead of her own bed. I told her what had happened and she couldn't remember anything at all. Didn't even know we had gone to the party in the first place.

"I really knew something was wrong when later that summer we had gone to the lake together and she hadn't remembered even going with me," I added quietly.

"Yes, I remember that. I noticed something was off earlier that week. She was acting so strange. Not her usual relaxed self. She was so jittery and loud. I remember her pointing things out that she would have never pointed out before, like a zit that Trevor had or a shirt that didn't look good on me. I finally had to tell her she couldn't go out until she fixed her attitude." Her brow furrowed as she remembered.

"What's going on, Sarah?" I couldn't take the mystery anymore. I couldn't do anything until I knew what was happening with Tess.

She took a deep breath and said, "She'll probably kill me for telling you, but she is too stubborn to do it herself." She stood and walked to the sink to rinse out her mug, then braced herself on the counter and stared out the window. "She has dissociative identity disorder, Charlie. Multiple personalities. I don't even know how to help her. I'm her mother and I can't help her."

I didn't know what to say and I couldn't wrap my head around what I had just been told. I just sat and listened as Sarah told me what she knew.

Trevor walked in about thirty minutes later and apologized for what Ellie had said. "She's not really familiar with any of this stuff so she didn't know what she was saying," he said.

I was starting to believe Sarah's suggestion that he really was brain washed. That or he just didn't think he deserved anyone better. I was there when he and Ellie first started dating. She wasn't so bad at first. They had known each other back in high school, but were in different groups and never really spoke to each other until he came back from college and saw her in town. They went out a few times and we all hung out occasionally without any problems. It was when I brought them out to L.A. for one of my fights that I noticed she was putting on a show for him.

Trevor had gone to sleep in the extra room of the suite we were staying in and she came out into the living room where I was settling up some of the schedule with my team. We all got to talking and she said some things about Trevor that surprised me. Things a woman shouldn't tell her man's best friend. When my team left, she tried to convince me to have a drink with her. When I refused, she started coming on to me and tried to kiss me. I shoved her away and let her know exactly what I thought of her before heading into my room and locking the door. The next morning, she had already gotten to Trevor and tried to convince him that I had tried to get her to have sex with me. The only problem with that plan was that she didn't know about Tess.

I had been with a few women over the years. I was in a career that gave ample opportunity for me to be with someone with no strings attached. After my first win, I had discovered how easy it was to find a woman to help distract me from what I really wanted, but couldn't have. Trevor had previously been with me on one of those occasions that I was especially ignorant about who I was taking back to my room. He stopped me and dragged me back home to his mother who then told me that she had spoken to Tess a week before and she knew where she was. I broke down and finally said out loud what they had known all along. I was in love with Tess.

After that, Trevor knew I didn't have it in me to be with anyone else. But instead of calling Ellie out on her lie, he played it off as a misunderstanding and left it all but forgotten. I still didn't trust her and made sure I was never alone with her. Ever. There was no convincing him to step back and really see what was happening in front of him either. She flirted relentlessly with other men when Trevor wasn't watching and played dumb when she insulted anyone he considered friend or family. I knew she had cheated on him several times, but I had no way to prove it. We were just going to have to wait until she slipped up and got caught. It made me sick. I wanted to wring that woman's neck, especially after what she said about Tess.

Tess.

Seeing the look on her face over and over again in my mind made the fist around my heart squeeze tightly. She was determined to do whatever it took to keep me at a distance and after hearing about what had happened over the last five years, I understood why she would, I just didn't understand why she would think I could love her any less.

Obviously, she still didn't remember that I had told her my feelings for her and she had told me the same things. That was years ago, and next day it was like nothing had ever even happened. That's when I told Sarah that I thought something was wrong. She made me promise not to say anything to Tess until she spoke with a therapist. For the entire junior year of high school, she went to a therapist under the impression that it was for the occasional anxiety she had been feeling. She always complained about it and said her mom was always overreacting about everything she did. It killed me to not tell her, but I told her it wasn't going to hurt anything and convinced her to do it for her mom.

When she spent an entire week after one of her appointments acting strange and moody, I begged Sarah to let me talk to her about her so called 'blackouts', but I promised to wait. She didn't want Tess to be tortured for the rest of high school because of something she couldn't understand. We thought it was suppressed memories from when she was little and living with an angry drunk for a father and maybe it was causing the anxiety and everything else. I didn't believe that entirely, but I didn't know of any other explanation. I researched everything I could, but everything I found seemed too farfetched at the time.

After we graduated, I thought things would work out with us and there hadn't really been very many incidents our senior year. She was carefree and full of life. She stopped seeing the therapist and everything got better. We planned on attending college together and I was looking forward to finally having a way to be with her. I wish I would have kept my mouth shut until we moved away. She wouldn't have had the chance to run.

Now, knowing what had been really happening to her for most of her life - I just couldn't get my head around it. Was she on medication? Was she safe living at home? Would me pushing myself back into her life make it worse?

I had so many questions, no answers, and no idea what to do next.

"Just love her, Charlie," Sarah had said before I walked out the door. "Love her and don't let her push you away."

So there I was, pulling into my driveway and replaying the promise I had made to her and to myself over and over again. "I'm not going anywhere, Sarah. And neither is she."

Chapter 4

Tessa

I opened my eyes and squinted at the bright light shining in through the crappy blinds hanging over my bedroom window. Charlie had given me dark red curtains to cover it years ago and I had ripped them down before I left and stuffed them into a box with everything else that reminded me of him and stashed it in the attic. After waking up to the annoying brightness, I promised myself to either go find them or buy some new ones right away.

Life would certainly be different here. I had gotten so used to my routine with Benny. I needed to create a new one to keep me busy and keep my head on straight. No use diving right into the drama I knew was waiting for me.

I brushed my teeth, combed through the tangles in my long hair, and pulled on a robe before walking down to the kitchen for some breakfast. Trevor was at the table drinking a huge cup of coffee and reading through the sports section when I walked in. He must have gotten up early because he was dressed and ready to go and he lived a few miles away.

"Morning, T. How did you sleep?" he asked warily.

"Great! Slept like a baby," I lied, and he knew it. It took me hours to fall asleep since I was straining to hear Charlie's voice the whole time he was here and then trying to forget my reaction to him hugging me the rest of the night. I had probably only slept a few hours and I was going to pay for it later.

"Uh huh, I bet you did," Trevor said looking quite amused. "Brought you a muffin from town and there's fresh coffee in the pot."

"Oh, no coffee for me. Makes me crazy," I said sarcastically and it made him wince. "Have a sense of humor, Trev. It's the only way to survive this."

"Yeah, well I don't think the world is ready for your sense of humor, T." He shook his head, but I saw the corners of his mouth twitch as if he were struggling to contain a smile.

"Interesting. My friend, Benny, said that exact same thing."

His head snapped up from his coffee cup and he looked panicked. "Benny? Who the hell is Benny? He better not be some boyfriend we don't know about."

"Calm down, Trev. Benny is a girl. She was my roommate back in Massachusetts," I said rolling my eyes at him.

He scrunched his face up and looked confused, "Why does she have a guy's name?"

I smiled, thinking back to the first conversation I had with Benny about her name. Trevor would be flat on his ass right now if she were here. "Her full name is Bennett, she just prefers Benny. Says it helps weed out who she can trust."

"Huh?"

"Don't worry about it," I said and took a huge bite of the chocolate chip muffin Trevor bought for me. It was delicious and exactly as I remembered. I used to get one of these every Sunday with Charlie. He would get the lemon poppy seed and we would trade back and forth since neither of us could really afford to buy both for ourselves. I shook the memory away and took another bite. I had to keep those thoughts at a distance.

"I like your hair. It's really long," Trevor mumbled.

"Thanks! I'm glad I haven't woken up to see it chopped off. It's been forever since I've had it this long."

"What do you mean by that? Why would you wake up to it chopped off?"

I sighed in frustration, realizing he still didn't know the full extent of who I was now. "One of the alters hates it long. She usually chops it. Hates having anything hanging on her neck. I think Dr. D convinced her to just pull it up into a pony tail instead of trying to cut it. Benny told her she looked like a freak with it short and it looked better in the pony tail anyway."

"Um, okay? I'm so confused," Trevor said and looked a little paler than usual.

I explained to him that an alter was one of the different identities I had. "I have two alters that I know of, each with a distinct personality and her own name. They even have their own postures, gestures, and way of talking. I have videos and recordings if you would like to see."

He couldn't seem to come up with the words for a response so I kept talking. "I'll just explain everything to you now so you can get it over with. It's a lot to take in."

He nodded, so I continued.

"The switch that usually takes place is for Lydia. She is the alter that reveals herself the most often. Her name is Lydia Cooper, she is about thirty two I think. She has a higher voice than me and stands up a lot straighter than I ever would. Sometimes I like to think she grew up in England around royalty or something. She thinks that is pretty hilarious." He hadn't moved an inch and his expression was still shock. "Like I said before, she hates the long hair and she is really opinionated. She's nice, but will tell you if you look like shit without blinking. You'll know she's out for sure if I start telling you dirty 'knock knock' jokes. She's pretty funny if you ask me. Just to warn you though, she will hate Ellie. Benny had a hard enough time with her and she is the coolest chick I have ever met."

"Why would she hate Ellie if she can get along with Benny?" he asked slowly. His voice was a little shaky, but the color in his cheeks came back and he seemed to be relaxing the more I spoke. That or he was just so completely lost that he decided to not even try catching up.

"She hates girls, says they piss her off. Especially girls who have a flare for the dramatic and are high maintenance."

He nodded, "Well, I guess that makes sense. Ellie is a little dramatic sometimes."

I rolled my eyes again, but he didn't notice. Maybe he really was brain washed. "Anyway, I think you would like her. She's got some issues, but is more like me than you would think. At least, she is now from what Benny and Dr. Deacon told me. I don't mind her too much except for her problem with my hair."

He cleared his throat and took another gulp of his coffee. "And the other… um, alter?"

I shifted in my chair a bit and took a cleansing breath. The other one made me nervous. "She's… different. I don't switch with her that much?"

"Switch?"

"Oh yeah, 'switching' is when the identity reveals itself and takes over. It can take seconds, minutes, or days to happen. Depends on what's going on, I guess." I shrugged my shoulders and took another bite of the muffin.

"And when you switch with her?"

"Her name is Camryn Garrett, she is in her early thirties. We figure she only shows up when I'm really upset about something. She is kind of my defense against that stuff I guess. From what I hear, she is very protective of me."

"She doesn't sound so bad," he said and quirked his eyebrow. He could tell I was nervous, but didn't call me out on it.

"Well, she is… bad I mean. She can be a real bitch when she wants to be."

He watched me closely for a minute while I avoided eye contact. He was taking this well, but I could tell he wasn't sure of what to say about it. "And you only have the two?"

I nodded, "That I know of. That's one of the reasons I came back. There is a Dr. Geoffrey who practices here and is really experienced with this stuff. He does a lot of psychotherapy that he thinks might help me learn to live with… all this. Hypnosis and stuff."

He stood and walked over to the coffee pot, pouring a full mug and took a few sips before turning back to me. "Have you already tried that? In Massachusetts?"

"Yep. Both of them are pretty responsive to the hypnosis. Dr. Geoffrey seems to think we can find out my triggers a little more specifically the more we talk to them and maybe get a little more in depth about the 'why'. We are going to try to work at integration or just some type of communication between us. I'm not co-conscious, or aware, of what is going on during a switch. The alters are aware of me, but not each other unless they are *made* aware. I don't know, that's something I will start working on once Dr. Geoffrey gets a little more experience with me and what my case is. I haven't been at this very long, so there is a possibility of someone else showing up. I can't think about that now, though." I took the last bite of the muffin and crumbled the wrapper between my hands.

"You seem to be taking everything… really well."

I patted myself on the back for my Oscar worthy performance. I was suffering, but no one needed to know that. I woke up every day feeling unpredictable and frustrated. "I have to, Trev. What else can I do? There's no cure. I just have to deal with whatever comes and try to keep away from any triggers. This isn't some simple thing I am dealing with here. I don't have a control switch or anything. If anything bad even comes close to happening, I'll go back."

He stumbled and almost dropped his coffee, spilling it all over his hands. "What do you mean you'll go back?"

I just shrugged.

"You can't leave, Tessa. Not now."

"Why not?"

A knock at the door stopped him from saying anything else and he hurried out of the kitchen cleaning his hands off with the towel. I pulled a glass down from the cupboard then pulled the milk out of the fridge. I was in the process of pouring myself a large glass when that smooth deep voice came from the doorway making me spill milk all over the counter.

"Good morning, Tess."

I spun around and met that green gaze that I saw every time I closed my eyes. The sound of the milk dripping to the floor was the only thing I could hear except for the steady pulse in my head.

"I'm sorry. I didn't mean to startle you," he said and hurried over to grab some paper towels to clean up the mess.

"What… what are you doing here?" I pressed and cursed myself for stuttering.

His lips turned up into a sly grin, "I believe I answered that question last night, Tess. Why wouldn't I be here? My best friend, who took off five years ago leaving everything and everyone who cared about her behind, just came home."

I cringed and felt like I had been slapped in the face. He immediately looked apologetic, "I'm sorry. I shouldn't have said that. I understand why you left. I just…"

I snatched the paper towels from his hand and started cleaning up the spilled milk and avoiding as much eye contact as possible.

"You couldn't possibly understand," I muttered under my breath. I wasn't quiet enough, though, because he responded immediately.

"You are right. I don't understand, but I want to." He was standing right behind me as I rinsed my hands and tossed the paper towels in the trash can under the sink. I could feel the heat radiating off of him and a shiver ran up my spine. And not the bad kind either."I don't know all the reasons you took off and I don't know everything you have been through over the last five years. But I want to."

I couldn't turn around to face him. I was terrified of what I might see. I knew if I saw his face, I would crumble to a pitiful lovesick mess right at his feet and I wouldn't have any problem with it. His hand rested on my shoulder and I had to grip the counter tightly to keep myself upright after feeling the familiar current run through me and the air in the room thicken significantly. "Please don't, Charlie," I whispered. "I can't… do this."

His hand fell from my shoulder and I nearly cried out at the loss. Without looking at him, I turned and walked out of the kitchen just as Trevor walked in looking confused and awkward.

"You ready, Charlie?" he said.

I took the stairs two at a time, making my way to Mom's room. I paused at the top of the stairs and listened to my brother comfort him. Charlie's voice was quiet, but held the determination he always demonstrated, "I'm not giving up, Trevor."

The sting of tears threatening my eyes was a major wakeup call for me and I realized right then that regardless of how logical it was for me to avoid the emotions he caused, there was no possible way I could avoid Charlie without suffering any internal damage.

I opened the door to my mother's room and saw her sitting up in bed with a laptop in front of her. I knew, before she even gave me the guilty look, that she was searching Google.

"Find anything interesting?" I asked, flashing her an amused grin.

She pulled off her cute old lady glasses and shrugged, "A few things, but mostly stuff that makes little sense to an old woman like me."

I shut the door and climbed onto the bed next to her. "You're not old, Mom, and I'm no expert, but I might have some information for you."

She closed the laptop and smiled as I snuggled in close to her. "Hit me with it."

I proceeded to tell her everything I had explained to Trevor. She took it a little better than he did and even threw out a few jokes. By the time I had explained everything to her, answered her questions, and told her what the plan was, it was lunch time. Trevor had come back from where ever it was he had gone with Charlie with his arms full of ice cream and cheese pizza.

"Compliments of Charlie Mackenzie," he said when I grabbed a slice.

I paused with the slice midway to my open mouth and narrowed my eyes at my devious brother.

"Don't look at me like that. I was ready to come home. He was the one who forced me to drive to the store for him. Shoved all this in my arms and told me to say 'Hi'." He held his arms up in surrender and backed away from the table. "He would have brought it in himself, but he wasn't sure how well that would be received seeing as how you have pretty much built a wall around you."

I scowled at him, but it didn't hold for very long. He was right.

I looked down at the slice in my hand with a pang of regret, wondering if maybe… I pulled a chunk of cheese away. When I saw the tiny pieces of bacon mixed in with the sauce, I about lost it. "He remembered?"

My mother looked at me like I had grown a second head. "What? What is she talking about, Trevor?"

Trevor smiled at her and shrugged, "Ask Tess." Then he walked out of the kitchen and out the front door.

"Theresa? What's going on, sweetie?" She sat down next to me and peeked at the piece of pizza sitting unsteadily between my shaking fingers like it was a grenade and I had just pulled the pin.

"Bacon in the sauce," was all I could get out. She looked hilariously confused, but shrugged and pulled a slice out for herself. I didn't even have to look at the ice cream to know what kind it was. I knew he wouldn't have forgotten that. I hurried out of the kitchen and was pulling open the door with the pizza still in my hand and saw Trevor backing down the driveway with Charlie sitting in the passenger seat looking at me with a bright smile. Surprising myself, I smiled back and lifted the pizza in my hand with a thumbs up in the other. He gave me a thumbs up in return and I watched them drive away.

It was a simple thing to someone who didn't know us well. The thumbs up was my attempt at *keeping* things simple. I really wanted to wrap my arms around him and hold on tight.

I headed back into the house with that same smile plastered on my face and ran into Mom in the door of the kitchen.

"You look happy," she said with a mouthful of pizza. "Care to share?" She was grinning knowingly, even though she had no idea what made me so happy. All she knew was that Charlie was the cause and that made her feel triumphant. She looked so young with that grin on her face and that flicker in her eyes and I felt a weightlessness that I hadn't had in a long, long time. It was good to be home.

I plopped down in a chair and took a bite of the delicious pizza while Mom grabbed a couple spoons and pulled out the chocolate chip cookie dough ice cream. "When we were younger, I used to always wish that pizza was made with tiny pieces of bacon mixed in with the sauce. Whenever we got pizza together, I would ask them to make it special like that, but they always said no."

Mom looked at the pizza a little closer. "And there is bacon in the sauce now?"

I nodded, "Charlie convinced the pizza place to do it for me a few times and I always made such a big deal out of it. I didn't think he would remember that."

She laughed and scooped out a spoonful of ice cream before setting the carton down in front of me. "Oh, sweetie. I think you should know that boy remembers everything about you. You were inseparable and he… that man adored you. Still does. You were best friends."

I shook my head and scooped my own giant spoonful. "We were always *just* friends, Mom. Best friends, but just friends."

"And now?" she asked.

I picked up my slice of pizza and thought back to all the times I thought maybe we could be something more, but never thought he would go for it. He was always so supportive of me going out with other guys, always there to listen. He was protective, but didn't seem to be interested in me that way. Now? A lot of things had changed, but he was still able to make my knees weak. "I don't think it would be wise to go back to that, Mom. I have too much baggage and too much to worry about for myself." I looked up and met her gaze. "I don't want to end up hurting him," I added, "or being hurt."

She folded her arms across her chest and pursed her lips, obviously pondering something serious. "Well, dear, I think he has other plans. Plus, you need a friend."

"I have Benny. Speaking of which, I need to call her." I took a bite and pulled the crappy cell phone out of my pocket that Mom had gotten for me before picking me up in Boston.

"Theresa." My mom's voice was firm and I knew by the way she said my full name, she was about to say something important and I cringed slightly knowing her words were going to cause some sort of epiphany or something that would make me see reason. "Just… think about it, okay?"

She kissed the top of my head and left with the carton of ice cream in hand. I smiled after her knowing that thinking about it was all I was going to be doing.

Chapter 5

Charlie

I couldn't think about anything but the smile on Tessa's face as we drove away from her. The rest of the afternoon was spent formulating ways to see her. Trevor must have slapped the back of my head ten times before I told everyone that I was done for the day. He was sparring with me for the day because my coach was out of town and he was extremely annoyed with my lack of concentration.

Being home didn't help either. I was there five minutes before I finally grabbed my keys and drove over to the Marshall's, anxious to see Tess. Sarah answered the door and instead of letting me in, she stepped out onto the porch and shut the door quietly.

"I need your help with something," she whispered and looked inside the side window to make sure no one was watching.

"And what would that be?" I asked, bemused and a little curious about why she was so nervous. She was known to manipulate certain situations to turn out the way she wanted them. Tess always said that her mom could predict the future. I knew it was just good planning.

"Tessa needs a little nudge. I have a bunch of old photo albums with pictures of you both and I think it would be a good idea to bring them out," she informed me and looked back into the house quickly.

"Okay…? Um, what do you need *me* for?"

She slapped my shoulder, harder than she usually did, and narrowed her eyes at me. "Ow, jeez!" I rubbed my shoulder to get rid of the sting. "That actually hurt, Sarah. Have you been working out?"

She started laughing, but caught herself and slapped her hand over her mouth to silence it. "You stop that, Charlie Mackenzie. I need you to come by while she is looking at them. I think it would be good for her to see the two of you together... the way you were. Maybe it will help put some things into perspective." She wrung her hands together and looked at me pleadingly. "I wouldn't do it if I thought it would hurt in the slightest."

"I see." I rubbed my chin thoughtfully and let her squirm for a few seconds. When she realized what I was doing, she made a move to slap my arm again. "Okay, okay," I chuckled and put my hands up in surrender. "I'll be there. I promise. I don't know that it will change anything, but I'll be there."

"Good. I'll let you know when. Now, you can come inside." She turned swiftly and hurried through the front door, leaving me to follow in her wake. I planned on taking things a little slower with Tess. Let her get used to the idea of having me around her again, but my patience wasn't very saintly and now that I was thinking of what we used to be to each other, all the memories we had together, I was wearing a little thin.

"Charlie?"

I turned when I heard her sweet voice coming from the top of the stairs and took a breath. She was... God, I missed her. "Hi, Tess," I said breathlessly before clearing my throat and giving my voice a little more power. "I, uh, I was hoping I could get a minute with you... to talk."

She blinked several times before responding. "Oh. Um, I was just about to head out, but I guess I can sit for a minute." She looked nervous, tired, and like she had the weight of the world on her shoulders even though she did everything she could to hide it. She started down the stairs, arms folded over her stomach like she was holding herself together and I almost dropped to my knees in front of her and begged her to let me take some of the worry, some of that burden.

"What? Where were you going?" Sarah interjected.

"Nowhere in particular," she muttered and rolled her eyes. "Just out." Probably anywhere that was far away from where I was.

Sarah looked like she wanted to say something about that, but I spoke before she could, "Would you mind if I took you somewhere? Or tagged along?"

Her eyes widened and the few seconds it took her to respond felt like a lifetime. Her answer surprised me, but I wasn't about to complain. "Um, I guess. I haven't driven in forever, so it might be better if I just went with you anyway." Her submission was reluctant, almost as if she had been defeated in a battle of wills without the actual battle. The hurt I felt at her reluctance quickly dissipated.

I tried not to let my smile take over my entire face, but I was struggling. It was hard not to feel like this was Christmas when I was ten and she had just given me the newest bike out on the market. "Great!" I had to clear my throat after my voice squeaked like a fifteen year old boy. "Let's go then."

Sarah waved excitedly when I opened the door for Tess and I shook my head at her to let her know she was over doing it. She didn't really seem to care, she looked like she was about to break out in a dance, rocking side to side excitedly. That woman was something else and I loved her for it, but sometimes she didn't know how to tone it down.

Tess climbed in the car before I could really get to the passenger door and open it for her. She smirked when I grunted in frustration, but I just gave her my best smile and winked. That always seemed to do the trick when we were in high school. Things hadn't seemed to change in that aspect. Her breath hitched and confirmed that she was still very much attracted to me.

I drove the short distance to the dock where we had always gone for peace and quiet. It was almost sunset and the view would be perfect. I almost decided to head somewhere a little less romantic, but changed my mind when she continued to look out the window without saying a word to me. I would need all the help I could get.

We parked in the empty lot and I turned off the ignition. She was out of the car and walking before I could open my door. She wouldn't make it easy, but I never expected her to. She hadn't known my feelings for her, but she never made it easy to come out and tell her either.

I followed her to the end of the dock and watched her look out at the water with a lost and empty expression. When I stepped next to her, she ran a hand through all that long dark hair and closed her eyes with a deep breath.

"Thanks for the pizza and ice cream. You didn't have to do that," she said without looking at me.

"Yes I did," I replied.

She looked down at her feet then sat down and let her legs hang off the edge. I plopped down next to her, but kept several inches between us. Inches that felt like miles to me. The wooden planks creaked and tilted as we sat in silence and looked out over the glistening water. I was surprised there weren't imprints of our asses in the exact spots we were sitting. We had done this countless times before and tonight, it felt as if no time had passed since the last. The sound of the water lapping against the dock always put us in a trance. She had her eyes closed, listening, and I took the opportunity to study her face that was even more beautiful than before. She wasn't the eighteen year old girl I was so infatuated with. She was a woman now.

"I'm sorry I've been so horrible, Charlie. I just don't think it's good for you to be involved with me at all." Her voice was soft , but firm and I was pulled from my thoughts by the words that felt like a punch to my gut. She was staring down at the water now and seemed like she was making an effort to look at anything but me.

"Why don't you let me decide what's good or bad for me. I'm a big boy, I think I can make the tough decisions on my own." Her shoulders slumped and her feet stopped swinging back and forth. "Hey."

Finally, she glanced up at me and the dejected look in her beautiful eyes was like a knife in the chest. "I didn't mean that to be rude, Tess. I'm serious, though. I'm not worried about whether it's a good idea or not. I just want to be with you." *As more than just your friend.* I didn't say the words, but they hung in the air between us and I hoped she had heard them somehow.

She looked away just as the moisture in her eyes started to collect. "So, I'm told you are a fighter now."

The sudden change in the subject didn't surprise me. She was always one to avoid any extreme emotion and knowing how easily something like that could stress her out now, I understood. "Yeah, I got into it a few years ago. Liked the work out it gave me and the excitement. I was hoping to get into the UFC, but this underground stuff is a little more laid back. Better to get some experience. Then I might sign a contract and take the next step." I shrugged noncommittally. I wasn't pushing for a serious career anymore. It was more of a distraction. Something that kept my mind off of what

I really wanted but could never reach. Now? Well, she was right next to me and nothing else really mattered anymore.

"Do you get hurt a lot?" she asked leisurely, but the concern in her voice betrayed her attempt at being casual.

I felt a little satisfaction that she was worried about me, but didn't tease her about it. "I used to, but not too bad anymore. I do well enough to avoid that."

She nodded tightly, but her eyes looked relieved at my answer. "That's good."

I couldn't take it any longer, she was breaking my heart by acting so distant and trying to sound indifferent when I knew she really wasn't. I had to ask her the question that had been on repeat in my head for five years. "Tess, will you tell me why you left? The real reason. Please."

She must have been anticipating my question because she didn't even flinch. After several long and agonizing moments, she closed her eyes and took a few more deep breaths, calming herself. "I don't want to," she finally said.

I ran a frustrated hand through my hair and tugged to distract myself from the impatience I was starting to feel. I couldn't go into this thinking it would be simple… at all. "Well, like I said before, I would really like to understand. I just… I wish you trusted me enough to be honest with me."

"I *do* trust you, Charlie."

"It doesn't seem like it, Tess," I snapped and wanted to smack myself for being such a dick. "Listen, I don't want to argue about it, I just wanted to talk to you without you running off."

She looked at me again and my relief was palpable, I hated not seeing her eyes. "I already apologized for that," she stated firmly.

I frowned. Couldn't really help it. It wasn't an angry frown. It was more on the sad side of frowns. I was devastated that she had been through so much and I wasn't there for her. I would do anything to make it up to her. I had tried to find her. Felt like I was looking under every rock I came across to find her and when I didn't… I couldn't handle it. "I looked for you, Tess."

This made her flinch and her eyes widened while her breathing picked up its pace. "What?"

"I looked for you when you were in Kansas, after you finally let us know you were alive. The caller ID showed that area code and I left the next day. Spent a week asking around and showing your picture to anyone who would stop to look at it. I finally came back after my mom threatened me, then I started at the university. After a year of classes that I couldn't concentrate in because I was too busy worrying about you, I dropped out and started training to distract myself. I held my breath between post cards, Tess. To find out if you were safe. Just to hear from you."

I couldn't make myself stop babbling. I needed her to know how she left me, how much she meant to me.

She had looked away when I mentioned college. We were supposed to leave together and experience everything college had to offer *together.* That had always been the plan, but she left. Obviously, it meant as much to her as it had to me.

"I promised your mom and brother that I wouldn't go looking for you again and I would try to make a life for myself. I got into the underground fighting and ended up winning the championship. It was a lot of money and I couldn't think of anything better than to take care of your mom and always hold onto that last thread of communication with you. Even if you wanted nothing to do with me." I could remember how desperate I was to hear from Sarah and hear that she was okay. That nothing bad had happened and there was still a chance of seeing her again.

She still hadn't spoken so I kept going. "Your mother is good at keeping secrets, Tess. The only reason I found out she knew where you were when you called her a year ago was because your brother had to use it to stop me from--" I caught myself and shook my head, "doing something stupid. They weren't able to stop me from looking for you again, though. They wouldn't tell me exactly where you were, but I knew you were in Massachusetts. You aren't an easy one to find, Tess. But I tried."

And now that I had her back, I wasn't going to lose her again.

Her eyes flickered with something I couldn't identify, then filled with tears. "I didn't know, Charlie. I had no idea what leaving would do to everyone." She was choking on a sob and spoke quickly, "I thought I was doing the right thing."

She fell against my shoulder and I wrapped my arm around her and pulled her close. Her tears soaked my t-shirt and I only held her tighter, welcoming anything that was her. Seeing her cry was always torture and it didn't happen often. "I know, Tess. It doesn't matter anymore. You're here. That's all that matters to any of us, now." I took a deep breath of relief. Holding her in my arms, her putting herself there… it was like the weight that was pressing down on me for five years was lifted and I knew that it didn't matter why she left, just that she was back. "You don't have to explain anything, Tess."

The sunset filled the sky with purples, oranges, and reds, reminding me of that night so many years ago when we both sat in the same spot, watching the same type of sunset, under completely different circumstances.

"I know that my mom told you," she said on a sigh. "I don't know why I thought she wouldn't. You and my family have obviously stayed… close."

"She didn't say much about it, but yes, she told me." She tensed and I tightened my arm around her and discreetly buried my nose in her hair while she rested her head on my shoulder. I inhaled the sweet smell of rain and saw a glimpse of the memories we shared and thought of how many we missed out on. I couldn't go back in time and change things, but I could spend the rest of the time we had making up for it. Making new, better memories.

"And?" she asked softly.

"And… it doesn't change anything for me," I replied.

"That's… good."

I heard her relief even though she tried to hide it. It gave me hope.

***

I walked her to the door when we got back less than an hour later. Nothing else had been said except for a few obligatory statements made to be polite. I wanted to press her for more, make her tell me everything so I could *feel* that she trusted me, but I knew doing that would only end in an argument. I would just have to continue to be patient.

"Thank you, Charlie. I'll see you around, I guess," she said hurriedly and stepped up to her front door.

See me around? Definitely. "Can I take you to dinner on Friday?"

She stumbled a bit before turning with her arms crossed over her chest. "I don't think that's a good idea… for me. I can't lose focus, Charlie."

"It's just dinner, Tess. You need to eat. I just thought--"

"I know what you thought and I'm sorry. I just… can't right now. Thank you again and have a good night, Charlie." She rushed inside and shut the door leaving me thoroughly speechless and confused in the darkness of the porch. After what happened at the dock, I hadn't expected her to still be so determined to shut me down.

I thought I could do this on my own, but it was looking like Sarah would get to take over soon if I kept striking out, and I knew I would keep striking out. So did Sarah. Tess was Tess and she was stubborn and overly logical about everything. And even though it was causing me to become desperate, I loved her even more for it.

"Great," I muttered and stomped back to my car. Looked like another night of tossing and turning and trying not to picture Tess next to me with her hair spread out across the pillow... I pulled out onto the road and made my way to the gym ready to work out some built up frustration.

Theresa Marshall was a woman worth waiting for and I was good at waiting.

Chapter 6

Tessa

My first session with Dr. Geoffrey on Thursday was awkward and frustrating to say the least. Being the matron saint of patience everyone knew I wasn't, I wanted to start making progress right away, but the doctor spent the entire appointment asking me questions about my friends, my family, my hobbies, and everything else that seemed to be irrelevant to what we truly needed to be doing.

He kept telling me that informing the other alters about my needs, and vice versa, would help. I kept reminding myself that he was the doctor and I needed to trust him, but my determination to figure out how to live with this overpowered everything else. Dr. Geoffrey noticed my frustration, but made no attempts to change the course he had set for the day. This made me want to shove that stupid silver pen--

"I want you to make an appointment to see me Monday, Ms. Marshall. I know you are anxious to get started on integration, but this kind of thing takes time, and integration may not be the answer. I don't want you to think that things will fall into place with a few sessions. It could take years." He walked me out to his scheduler and spoke slowly so I would have no choice but to accept his words. I was already aware of everything he was telling me, I just didn't like it. It wasn't a quick fix and that's what I wanted. My life had been upside down for too long and I was desperately trying to turn it over and find some kind of harmony.

"Is it okay for me to get a job?" I asked.

"That's up to you. It might be a good idea to get a hold on things before you take on that responsibility."

I should have known better, I still wasn't completely comfortable on my own, but I'm a stubborn woman. Ask everyone I know.

"We can see how responsive you will be to my hypnosis on Monday and go from there. Until then, try to stay positive. Once I have established a form of communication with your alters, we can move on to the three of you communicating on your own."

He shook my hand and left me standing in front of a middle aged blonde who looked like her face was going to split in two from the size of her smile.

I didn't see how me communicating with the alters was going to help anything. Not remembering a switch, to me, was a blessing in disguise at times. I felt bad for the people who were co-conscious with their alters. Mine could party together as much as they wanted, but I wanted nothing to do with it. Even though, in the back of my mind, I knew I was being more destructive by thinking that way, I didn't care. I had to do this so I could move on with my life. From the look on Dr. Geoffrey's face today, though, I had a feeling I would be changing my way of thinking very soon.

"What time of day is best for you on Monday, Ms. Marshall?" the receptionist asked in a high pitched, way too sweet to keep me from wanting to smack that smile off her face, voice.

"Stay positive," I muttered to myself. "Stay positive and don't let people get to you."

"I'm sorry, what was that?" she asked and leaned in closer to me.

"Morning, please."

***

Charlie stopped by each day, further convincing me that I was fighting against a force that was even more stubborn than myself. He was always relentless, but my God, he was like ten times worse now. We didn't talk much except for the usual topics of conversation everyone shares with a long time acquaintance. I asked him about fighting, how his mother was doing and who her new husband was. I didn't really allow him to ask any questions and at first he was noticeably agitated, but continued to let me steer the conversations. They were short and sweet and always ended with me remembering that I had something important to do and leaving the house. I never had anything to do, I just couldn't continue to be in his presence and not throw myself at him.

Years of suppressed attraction added to five years of separation? That equaled uncontrolled physical and emotional… feelings. I couldn't afford those kinds of feelings. Not when I knew things would go bad, eventually.

He just kept showing up every day and continued from where ever we had left off. It made me start to waiver and I almost wanted to get a job now just so I could avoid him.

Mom was no help no matter how much I begged her. She didn't want me to work and said that I could use my savings if I wanted, but it wasn't necessary.

"I lost five years with you, dear. I want to make up some of that time."

She also kept trying to trick me into leaving the house with Charlie. Out of nowhere, the milk she had just bought the day before was gone or she needed another block of cheese or we ran out of toilet paper and the perfect pair for the job was Charlie and me. I found a brand new giant package of toilet paper in the hall closet under some coats and ended her little game by Sunday. I figured all that milk had been poured out into the sink, but I didn't need to confirm it with her. She would never admit it.

That didn't mean she stopped trying to come up with another trick.

My appointment Monday was no less frustrating. We talked about triggers, stressors, and what kinds of things I could do to prevent them. After showing me a few exercises that were similar to Dr. Deacon's, he decided to spend the last few minutes of the session putting me under hypnosis.

I didn't remember any of it, but when I came out of it, he seemed overly excited and confident that things would go smoothly from here on out. Hopefully. Apparently, he had spoken with Lydia. She seemed to think this whole thing was just spectacular. I scheduled another appointment for Thursday with Miss Happy Pants and was on my way.

I told Mom all about the session when we went out for lunch and what do you know? We ran into Charlie Mackenzie, of all people. Mom always wanted to be an actress and I know why she never made it in the business. She was awful at it. Her surprised face looked like… well, not a surprised face at all. More like a cat-caught-the-canary-and-pretended-to-be-surprised-that-he-did-it face. Charlie was better at it. I just glared at the two of them and let them play out their little skit. After taking the last bite of my sandwich, I finally looked up to see Charlie watching me with a smug grin. When I rolled my eyes at him, he just shrugged and tilted his head toward Mom. His way of saying *'she made me do it'*.

I didn't see him again until Thursday morning before my appointment. He came to pick Trevor up for training and caught me in the kitchen in my tank and sleep shorts… oh yeah, with no bra. Now my breasts aren't really a slave to gravity, but they still haven't really decided so I am self conscious about them. I was in the middle of using a sharp knife to cut up some fruit and couldn't cross my arms in front of me fast enough to block the girls.

Actually, that's not true. I honestly just froze at the sight of him. He looked incredible in his dark jeans and white t-shirt with his hair all messy like he just rolled out of bed and didn't touch it. No one should look that good in the morning. It's almost a crime. I didn't even remember being without a bra until my eyes moved back up to his and those greens were staring down a little too far. Before I could drop the knife and cover myself, he had already turned away and muttered something unintelligible about finding Trevor somewhere else. I didn't miss the pink in his cheeks as he walked out the door and the smile that spread across my face was unexpected.

Oh, he was still so cute when he blushed.

Dr. G went over a few protocols with me for the first few minutes of our session. He talked about safety issues and procedures that his staff would have to abide by should anything happen that would be a risk to myself or anyone around me. He obviously was a fan of my old chart from The Facility. Benny always said that thing would follow me around for the rest of my life and eventually would end up in People magazine or be published into some kind of crazy novel for people to drool over. I had finally walked out of the room when she asked me to promise to sign her copy before signing anyone else's because it would be worth more that way.

God, I missed her.

"Let's begin then, shall we?"

He always spoke so formally and it made me feel like I needed to be sarcastic, but I resisted the urge.

"Okay," I replied.

"Are you comfortable, Ms. Marshall?" he asked smoothly.

"Yep."

"Alright, just like we did on Monday, I want you to settle in and take three deep breaths when you are most comfortable."

I relaxed my muscles beginning with my toes and moving up my body until my neck was no longer holding my head up and I sank into the plush leather of the chair. He spoke for a few seconds, directing me into a deepened relaxed state. The last thought I remember was how I wish I could do this to myself at night and just block everything else out. Then I thought that might not be a good idea since I got my best thinking done while lying in bed staring at the ceiling. Then I thought about the things I thought about while lying in my bed and how strange it was being back in the home I grew up in and everything that happened as I grew up in that house…and I started to feel that disconnection I hated.

Next thing I know, I'm opening my eyes to a couple guys holding me down in the chair and Dr. Geoffrey inches away from sticking a needle in my arm.

"It's me, Doctor! It's Tessa!" I said like I was pleading for my life.

He paused and studied my eyes before nodding at the guys still pinning me down and taking a step back. "Well, then we have a few things we need to discuss." He handed off the syringe and ran a shaky hand through his hair. He was always so controlled, so the slip surprised me.

I shook the surprise away and reminded myself that he was the professional who was going to help me through this, but he was still just a man. A human being who probably had seen a lot in his years, but who could still be a little shaken. Disturbed. Maybe even shocked. "Hit me with it. What happened?" I rubbed my forearms and saw the red marks from one of the guy's fingers. *That's gonna bruise.*

"I met Camryn."

My head snapped up, bruises forgotten, "And?"

"She is very… I don't know the word," he said and rubbed the back of his neck. I hadn't ever seen him be anything but proper and formal. He always knew how to describe everything with words I had to look up when I got home.

"Creepy? Bitchy? Maybe even a little psychotic?" I supplied. "Those words seem to be the ones used the most."

"I would say she was more unpredictable. She seems to enjoy making other people squirm before she decides to lash out. She doesn't seem to be very agreeable either. We will have to find a different way to ask her about her needs and make her feel safe to see if we can get her to work with us," he stated and reached into his shirt pocket, pulling out his prescription pad. He scribbled something and tore off the small square of paper and handed it to me.

"What's this?" I couldn't make out any of the letters he had written down. Typical.

"I think it would be a good idea to take it easy for the remainder of the day," he said quietly and moved behind his desk. "I attempted to get you out of the hypnosis, but she took over completely."

"You want me to spend the rest of the day drugged up? Is this some kind of sedative?" My tone was angry, incredulous. When he made eye contact with me, I immediately regretted getting so upset. He had obviously just experienced something rare and a little frightening by the look in his eyes.

"Ms. Marshall, we just forced a switch that the alter had no way of controlling and she didn't like that, so she adapted. It almost ended in someone getting hurt." His fierce look told me he was a little more upset about what happened than he was letting on. "Since we have just started your treatment, we don't know what will happen now. We have to anticipate that Camryn will be… around. Especially since the look on your face shows more stress than you need right now."

It made sense. Dr. Deacon had only pulled Camryn out on accident and I always ended up coming to in my bed with Benny staring down at me with awe plastered all over her face. The Facility had people constantly watching out for us. People around that were trained to handle situations that got out of control. Plus, they always had some kind of drug on hand that could take down a small elephant in a heartbeat.

I was 99.9% sure that Mom had no training or drugs like that sitting around the house.

"Okay."

"Okay?" he asked, surprised by my easy acceptance.

"Okay, I'll spend the rest of the day high as a kite if it means no trouble for my family," I murmured.

"Well, you won't necessarily be high as a kite. In fact, what I am prescribing will knock you out for a good amount of time. Don't take it until you are somewhere safe where you can lie down." He smiled and gestured toward the door. "Let's schedule a session for Monday. In fact, I think it would be a good idea to see you every Monday and Thursday, indefinitely."

I nodded in agreement and stood slowly. "Sounds like a plan, Doc."

***

"What if you don't wake up?"

My mom was not on board with the medication. In fact, I had spent the last ten minutes trying to calm her down and stop her from marching into the doctor's office and knocking him out. She was pretty strong these days so I had no doubt she could get past me if she really wanted to. Now, she had tears in her eyes and was looking at me like I was on my death bed.

"Mom, calm down. Believe me, I've been given medications a helluva lot stronger than this one and as you can see, I always woke up. It's just a precaution," I explained. I had already told her all about the session, leaving out the parts about two large men holding me down and making sure to cover up the bruises already surfacing. She took it pretty well until I told her about the medication I was given.

"Fine! But I swear to God, if you don't wake up, I'll shove every last one of these pills down that so called 'doctor's' throat," she used her quote fingers which I found absolutely hilarious, "and give him a taste of his own medicine. Literally!" I was shaking with laughter and had to clamp my lips together to try to keep it inside.

"This isn't funny, Theresa!" she shouted.

"It's a little funny," I said holding up my thumb and forefinger less than an inch apart and started shaking again, "I don't think I've seen you use quote fingers so much in my life than I have the last couple weeks. "

"I did not use quote fingers!" She glared at me, but I saw the twitch at the corner of her mouth. She was fighting a smile and it made me happy.

I wrapped my arms around her and squeezed her tightly, still laughing. "Okay, Mom."

"Wait a sec! I just got an idea." She clapped her hands excitedly with the bottle of pills still in her hand, making them rattle. "Ellie is coming for dinner tomorrow night. Do you think we could crush some of these up and put them in her drink?"

"Mom!" I snatched the bottle out of her hand and held it behind my back.

"What? You know it's a good idea," she rolled her eyes with her hands on her hips as if she were scolding me.

It was. It was probably the best idea she had ever had, but I didn't want her to go to jail, and I didn't know if it might actually kill the bitch. It *was* a good idea, though.

Mom shrugged and casually stated, "We can talk about it later."Like the decision was still on the table.

I opened the bottle, dumped out a small white pill, and handed it back to her to lock up in the safe at the back of her closet. "No." Then I popped the pill in my mouth and took a long drink of water out of the glass she handed me.

"Later," she repeated with a big smile, then she walked out of the room.

I took off the cardigan I had put on to hide the marks on my arms. I wasn't upset or resentful about them. I would rather end up with a few bruises than hurt someone or myself even worse. I pulled back the white comforter on my bed and climbed in. The pharmacist said the drug would start to work after a few minutes, so I stared up at the ceiling and waited. Charlie kept popping into my head and pissing me off more than usual. I thought of that morning's braless encounter and felt the embarrassment all over again.

I tried to picture Benny's face in my mind and closed my eyes. I would miss waking up to her and seeing the silly expression on her face before she dove into telling me what I missed. She could talk for hours if you let her, and I usually did. She would always start by asking, "Who the hell are you today?" She usually started every day with that question and I didn't realize how much I looked forward to it until I moved back home.

For some reason, that question kept me grounded. Probably because the only answer I ever remembered giving her was "Tess, who else?"

I started to feel the heaviness take over my body and I welcomed it for the first time in a long time. I hadn't ever *taken* a sedative willingly until today. I usually woke up and found out that I had been given one by way of needle. Benny occasionally had to calm me down when I woke up. She agreed that it sucked to be knocked out, but convinced me it was necessary sometimes. She would describe in detail everything I did just before being sedated anytime she was there to witness it, which was often. It was hard to believe her. I just couldn't see me doing those things or saying the things I had apparently said.

She started keeping a calendar for me and marking my switches on it. She said it was just for fun, but she knew how much it helped me. She said it helped the alters, too, whenever I would switch, which had been quite often at first. I always felt better after looking at the calendar and seeing more boxes without marks than with marks. Sometimes I thought Benny helped me more than any of the doctors or nurses. She accepted everything about me and I think that's why we were allowed to be roommates for so long. She was just her and I was just me, and it worked.

Just before I sank into oblivion, Charlie's blushing face came into my mind again and I admitted that I wanted to see him again, but only for a minute.

Honestly.

Chapter 7

Charlie

Please be wearing a bra, please be wearing a bra.

I had repeated this request about sixteen times before I knocked on the front door of the Marshall's. Don't get me wrong, I would love to see Tess like that every day. She was beautiful in the morning with her hair all over the place and her clothes all jumbled. However, it was frustrating as hell when there were other people around and she wasn't ready for me to go all caveman on her.

Sarah opened the door with a frown and all my senses perked up. "Good morning, Charlie. It's good to see you again."

"Is everything alright?" I asked, stepping forward and looking around the house for anything suspicious.

"Yes, everything's just fine," she muttered and stomped toward the kitchen.

"I don't believe you, Sarah." She was easy to read as Tess had always been, but Sarah leaned a little more on the dramatic side when she was upset about something.

She stopped abruptly and shook her head as she turned around. "She's still asleep!" Her arm shot out and pointed up the stairs. "She took that pill at five o'clock yesterday and she is still out like a light. I told her I wasn't comfortable with it, but noooooo, she just had to take it. 'It's just a precaution' she says!" It was always weird when Sarah used her quote fingers, I'm sure Tess got a kick out of it and normally I would have busted up laughing, except I was still stuck on the word 'pill'.

"What pill?" I asked, making no attempt to control the volume of my voice.

She threw both arms in the air and turned back into the kitchen. "Some stupid sedative or something that the doctor told her to take."

I rushed in after her so I could ask the questions racing through my head. "What sedative? I thought she wasn't going to take anything. You told me she was determined not to. Didn't want to be out of it all the time. Are you telling me she changed her mind?"

"No, Charlie. Apparently there was some kind of incident at her appointment yesterday and the doctor wanted to anticipate it happening again." She was tossing around the dishes in the sink and I was just waiting for something to shatter. "She said something about making sure that she doesn't hurt herself or anyone else. Why would she be worried about that, Charlie? Has she hurt someone before? Did she tell you anything like that?"

My stomach was twisting around violently and my chest felt like it was in a vice, "No, Sarah. She didn't say anything like that. She hasn't really told me much."

I remembered, though.

I remembered when she had hurt someone else even though it wasn't a big deal. I remembered how hard it had been to hold onto her and calm her down. I also remembered how scared she had been afterward without even realizing what had happened.

I knew all of this because it was me she had hurt. It was an accident, but I came out of it with the worst black eye I had ever gotten. I never told anyone about it because I knew Sarah would end up taking her back to a therapist and Tess would fight it. So I had kept my mouth shut.

"I tried to wake her up a couple hours ago, but she didn't move," Sarah said. "Maybe you could try. I don't know what to do. I can't just let her sleep. Can I? I don't know how long it's supposed to affect her." She was starting to panic.

I put my hands on her shoulders, "Shhh, Sarah. You need to calm down, okay?" She took a few deep breaths and nodded. "Those doctors know what they are doing and Tess is too logical to do something stupid. I'll go see if I can wake her up, okay?"

"Okay, thank you." She turned back to the dishes and started scrubbing, shoulders stiff from worry but accepting my offer with full trust. I was grateful she trusted me so much, but it put the pressure on me to make sure I didn't let her down.

I made my way up the stairs and had to take some deep breaths myself. It wasn't like Tess to take something so strong for no reason. I had to keep reminding myself that she was more familiar with what was going on than the rest of us and was the only one with… with…

My thoughts trailed off when I opened her door and saw her lying in the middle of her bed, sheets tangled in her long legs and hair spread out over her pillow. The way I wanted to see her in *my* bed. She looked so peaceful and content, I didn't have the heart to even try to wake her up. Maybe it was better that she slept like this for a little longer. She had been so tired lately, according to Trevor, and it was nice to see her face without a trace of worry or stress.

I walked further into her room, which hadn't been changed at all since she had left five years ago. I had spent so many nights in that bed wondering where she was and if she was happy. Sarah had needed someone to chase away the silence of an empty house, so I had stayed over frequently. It was hard not to when the closest I could get to Tess was this room.

I started to pull the covers over her body, forcing my eyes away from her legs, when I saw the bruises. In the middle of each forearm was a clear outline of fingers, dark and purple. I felt an anger that I hadn't ever experienced before and I the urge to shake her awake and demand to know who hurt her so I could strangle him to death was almost too overwhelming. I sat down on the bed next to her hip and lifted her arm to study it more closely. I hadn't been wrong. It was the outline of fingers and from the size, it *had* been a man who made these marks. My temper flared hotter at the confirmation and my heart felt like it was going to beat out of my chest.

"I'm gonna kill him," I growled. I had no idea who it was, but I was going to kill him.

Tess stirred and rolled toward me. I couldn't let her sleep any longer, I needed answers.

"Tess, wake up." I put my hand on her shoulder and shook her lightly.

She groaned and tried to turn away, but I shook her a little harder and spoke louder, "Tess, you need to wake up, now."

Her eyes fluttered open and for a moment, she looked incredibly happy to see me which, under normal circumstances, would have caused me to kiss her senseless, but not now. She blinked a few times and her expression morphed into anger. I didn't care. I was already livid.

"You mind telling me where these came from?" I lifted her arm and pointed to the bruises.

She ripped her arm out of my hand and sat up with her back against the headboard still trying to wake up. "What the hell are you doing in my room?" Her voice was hoarse and groggy, so incredibly sexy that I almost forgot what I was so upset about.

"Your mother was worried that you were sleeping too long," I replied steadily.

"So you thought it was okay to barge into my room and shake me awake? Did she not explain to you why I was sleeping in the first place?" Her eyes were wide with annoyance and her chest was rising and falling heavily with the rapid breaths she was taking to calm herself.

I don't think she realized that her shirt had ridden up a little and the soft skin above her shorts was in full view. I glanced down for a moment and not so successfully stifled a groan before my eyes returned to hers. I hoped the heat I could feel in my gaze was mistaken for anger instead of the stifling desire I felt for her.

"She did, it's Friday now, Tess. I wasn't going to wake you up once I saw you. But I noticed the bruises on your arms and thought it would be a good idea to let you explain. Obviously, your mother doesn't know about them or she would have told me." I crossed my arms over my chest and glared right back at her. Barely. I really wanted to kiss her.

She huffed and started to climb out of the bed. Her leg brushed mine and I held myself steady when the current of electricity buzzed up and down my leg. "It's none of your business, Charlie. I don't have to explain anything to you."

"It becomes my business if someone hurts you!" I shouted.

She pulled on a sweater and started for the door. I was more than livid now, if that was even possible. I couldn't control the tightness in my chest and the thought of someone hurting her felt like I had been punched in the stomach with no hope of ever getting another breath. I watched her stop in the doorway and turn back to see that I wasn't following her.

"You need to leave my room, now," she said in a low voice.

I looked down at my hands before lifting them to my head and running my fingers roughly through my hair. My shoulders felt stiff and my entire body was clenched tight. I took a slow and steady breath, still aware of her eyes on me and still feeling the lasers I knew she was trying to shoot into my skull. My blood cooled to a simmer and I felt the anger seep away as I focused on what my ultimate goal was. I didn't want to give her a reason to push me away.

"Tess, please," I whispered. I couldn't risk her hearing the anger I knew still lingered in my voice. It would only make her more guarded and I couldn't lose any of the ground I had gained over the last week.

She didn't say anything, but her posture relaxed slightly and her face softened.

"I can't stand the thought of someone hurting you." I looked at her arms now covered in a sweater, but all I could see was the hand print I knew was there. "Please. Tell me those aren't… if someone did that out of… just tell me." I was stuttering and felt like I was going to explode from the helplessness coursing through me. I hadn't protected her before and I made a promise to myself that I would make up for it. I needed that.

She sighed and looked down at her feet. I kept my eyes on her, pleading over and over inside my head for her to just trust me.

She walked back to the bed and sat down next to me with her head in her hands. "It wasn't intentional, Charlie. It wasn't someone trying to hurt me." Her voice was small and full of sadness, pain, and confusion.

"Then, how?" I carefully picked up her arm and pushed up the sleeve of her sweater to reveal the purple marks. I ran my fingers over them lightly and welcomed the familiar hum I always felt when I touched her skin. She didn't pull away or flinch as I touched her and I realized that in some way, she did trust me.

"It was during my session. The doctor had to have these guys, who I'm assuming were nurses or something, help hold me down. I guess I was fighting pretty hard." She let me hold her arm in my hands for a little longer before pushing her sleeve down and moving it into her lap. "Mom would freak out more than she already has, Charlie. She is pretending to be unaffected by all this, but I know she is having a hard time. This would push her over the edge and I can't let that happen."

"She is worried about you, Tess. We all are. We are all trying to understand."

"I know." She fidgeted with the buttons on her sweater and looked ready to cry, but she was trying so hard to hold it back.

The sound of footsteps in the hall made both of us snap our heads toward the door. We looked back at each other at the same time and her eyes were pleading with me to keep quiet. Before I could give her any indication of what I had decided, Sarah walked into the room.

"What is going on up here? It's about time you woke up, Theresa! You scared the hell out of me. I don't think you should take those pills again." She was back to panicking and looked at me for support.

I had to get out of there before I pissed them both off all over again.

"She's just fine, Sarah. Woke up without any problems. We were just discussing a few things before I had to leave." I stood quickly and made my way to the door. "I've got a few things to do today."

"You're coming back for dinner, right?" she asked desperately. Before I could respond, she started to panic. "Don't you dare think you can get out of it. Tessa and I are going to need all the help we can get with Ellie being here."

"I'll be here, Sarah. I promise." I looked over at Tess one last time and then turned to leave.

"Charlie?"

I stopped and turned back to that sweet voice, hopeful. When I met her eyes, they were happy and grateful. Her smile, however, was sad and I knew she was cursing herself for being so cold, but she hadn't done anything wrong. "Yeah, Tess?"

"Thank you," she said softly.

I just nodded, too afraid that my voice would betray the emotion I was fighting desperately to control. Sarah looked confused, but I didn't stay long enough to find out if she asked any questions. I almost ran to my car and by the time I pulled out onto the road, my heart had slowed down enough to dull the pulse that had clouded my head. I couldn't go another day without telling her.

She deserved to know. I *needed* her to know. I just didn't know how she would take it.

***

My head was in the clouds again. Rob, my coach, kept yelling at the top of his lungs for me to keep my hands up. He hadn't done that since my first week in training. It just wasn't in me today. I couldn't stop thinking about the bruises on Tessa's arms and my concentration was toast.

I had called them both to meet me at the gym after I left the house. I told them I needed to let off some steam. They kept telling me I just needed to get laid, which made me think of Tess all over again.

After two hours of hearing nothing but complaints about my stance, my jabs, and the lack of energy behind my kicks, I threw up my hands and told them I was done. Trevor kept smirking at me and it took everything I had not to punch it off his face.

"See you at dinner," he yelled from the door.

I didn't respond and dropped down onto the bench in the locker room to unwrap my hands. I had a fight two weeks from today and if you had asked me two days ago if I was ready for it, I wouldn't have hesitated in saying yes.

Now?

Not so much.

If I had to fight the guy right now, I would end up a bloody mess lying in the corner and hugging my knees.

I climbed into the shower and started scrubbing the stickiness of my sweat off of my body. I imagined seeing the guy who had made those marks on Tessa's arms and immediately saw red and felt my muscles twitch. Guess I would just have to use that at the fight.

The hot water ran over my back and I took some calming breaths to try to relax. I saw Tess lying in her bed with her long dark hair flared out behind her. I imagined running my hand through it and feeling the softness between my fingers. Her hair had always been so soft and silky for as long as I could remember. The only times I ever really got to touch it was whenever we were watching a movie and she laid her head in my lap while I combed my fingers through it or when she was crying in my arms over some jerk who broke her heart. Needless to say, we watched a lot of movies together. But I couldn't do anything more than touch her hair. We were friends and nothing more.

Didn't stop me from hoping.

Before long, steam had blanketed the room and I was in the middle of a fantasy I had played out hundreds of times before.

Tess would open her eyes and roll toward me with a smile and I would lightly stroke her face. I imagined her closing her eyes while I ran my fingers over her full lips and she darted her tongue out to taste me. I would drop my head and brush my lips against hers until she gasped and reached out to pull me closer. That's when I would run my hand down her side, grazing my thumb over the side of her breast before continuing down to grasp her hip and pull her into me. She would open for me and let me run my tongue against hers slowly until she couldn't take it anymore and her kisses got hungrier and she pressed her body against mine, feeling how much I wanted her and moaning because she wanted me just as much.

I opened my eyes and looked down. "Damn it all!"

For the millionth time since Tess got home, I had a problem to take care of. It didn't take long since I played out the rest of my fantasy that I had perfected in my imagination over the years. Normally, I would feel a little disappointed in myself for letting my mind go that far. This time, I wanted to bang my head against the shower wall because I knew, without a doubt, seeing her tonight would make it that much worse.

I shut the water off and quickly dried off. Tonight would decide my fate. If she rejected me, I would pack up and leave, find a new town, a new coach, a new friend. Maybe even get a dog to keep me company. I would have to because there was no other way I could be around Tess without self destructing.

I dressed in the dark jeans I knew she liked and a black t-shirt and prepared myself to live without Tessa Marshall so I wouldn't have to pick all the pieces up later. I would never fall out of love with her, but I would have to learn to cope.

"I'm so fucked."

Chapter 8

Tessa

I went for a walk after Charlie left and Mom disappeared into the attic. I hadn't expected Charlie to not say anything. In fact, I thought for sure he would have. He always did the right thing even when we were kids. I should have told Mom what had really happened at my appointment, but I didn't want to risk her being even more stressed out about what she still didn't understand. It only stressed me out more and we were trying to lessen my amount of stress, right? Well, that's what I kept telling myself to chase away the guilt. She was going to find out sooner or later. I just wasn't prepared for sooner, yet.

When I walked back into the house, after spending over an hour wandering the streets and walking around the lake, I saw that Mom had been busy. Several boxes were scattered around the living room. They were all opened, but nothing had been taken out of them.

I heard Mom humming to herself in the kitchen, probably starting dinner, which, by the way, I was dreading. I hadn't really spent a lot of time around Ellie and the time that I was around her was spent trying to focus on not imagining throwing her across the room and ripping her stupid hair out of her stupid head. She was awful and Trevor couldn't take his eyes off her chest. The sex *must* be great because no one was that tolerant.

I wasn't looking forward to hearing her argue with him about the guest list for the wedding or that the food my mother had slaved over was too salty, fattening, or dry.

Trevor was going to have a rude awakening one day and I prayed I was there to witness it. The woman was just evil and manipulative and hiding something. We, as in me, Mom, and Charlie, all knew it. We just had to wait.

Poor Trevor.

I walked past the boxes without taking a second glance and into the kitchen to see what help Mom needed. I always enjoyed cooking with her. She may be over protective and motherly past the point of irritation, but she was my best friend and I had always gotten along with her. It helped that she was always there for me no matter what and I regretted every day that I had left her the way I did. I know she had forgiven me, but I still felt like I needed to earn it.

"Hello, dear. How was your walk?" she asked, looking up from the pot she was stirring.

"It was good. Refreshing. Sorry about staying asleep for so long. I know that worried you." Figured I'd get right to the point.

"Oh, sweetie. Thank you, but you don't need to be sorry. I let my worries get the best of me and I should have trusted you to know what you were doing. I just can't help it, you know?" She gave me a hug and kissed my cheek before returning to the boiling pot.

"Yeah, I know."

"Good. So, you ready for tonight?" Her voice seemed higher and a little shaky which immediately signaled that she was planning something.

"What are you up to, Mom?" I asked and narrowed my eyes at her.

She scoffed and tried to look innocent, but like I said before, she was a horrible actress. "Nothing, dear. I'm just… I want you to be prepared for Ellie, that's all. She is going to make the night hell and I just want to make sure you are ready for that."

"Mmm hmm, yeah right."

She just smiled and winked, knowing there was nothing I could do about what she had planned. I had already committed to having dinner with *everyone* tonight, meaning Charlie. She had been planning this dinner for the last few days so I couldn't back out now.

"Will you help me with the chicken, sweetie?" she asked.

I rolled my eyes and moved to the fridge, "Of course, Mom. Anything for you."

She laughed loudly and then we cooked. I chopped chicken for her famous Chicken Alfredo and started on the French bread that was to be buttered and set aside to bake at the last minute so it would be fresh. When I started on the vegetables, she slyly brought up the boxes that I hadn't asked about.

"So, I was going through some stuff in the attic and ran across some old pictures. The ones you took in high school for the yearbook committee?"

"Ugh, seriously? Those were awful. I was the worst photographer they had." I chuckled at the memory of my advisor looking at most of the pictures wondering what they were. I told them many times to just let me format everything and design the pages, but they didn't have enough photographers so they didn't have a choice.

Charlie used to tease me about it whenever he helped me organize and label the pictures. He ended up taking a lot of them for me so the people in them could actually be seen.

"Oh, you weren't that bad, dear," Mom said hesitantly.

"Ha! Yeah I was."

"Well, regardless, I found them all. You should go out there and go through them. It would be good to remember all the good times you had." She hadn't looked at me yet which made me all the more suspicious. She was good.

Since no one else was really around, I decided it was safe and left the kitchen to rifle through some boxes. The first one I went through were of Trevor on the football team and all his trophies and plaques. Nothing interesting for me.

The next box was full of papers and assignments from my whole school career that Mom had filed away and written little notes about. She was good with stuff like that. Every time we gave a speech or performed something in front of an audience, she took pictures and wrote down everything that happened and how proud she had felt. All of that was neatly organized in several thick binders and labeled accordingly. I had to laugh. Maybe one day I would be motivated enough to do that for my kids.

Then I thought, *how could I possibly have kids if I can barely manage myself.*

I started going through another box to distract myself from the very idea and pulled out a few photo albums. As I started turning pages, the memories came flooding back to me and I was giggling at the ridiculous poses Trevor and I used to make for pictures.

Mom came out a minute later and sat beside me, laughing and telling me the details of each picture. Her memory was like a steel vault. Whatever got in, never came out.

I picked up another album which consisted of my high school years and there they were, the awful pictures I had taken of Trevor or Mom or Charlie. Heads were cut off, faces were blurry, and some of them were unrecognizable. Of course, Mom had written down who or what it was right beside each picture. I turned the pages and saw some of me and Charlie standing on the beach by the lake, wrestling on the couch, or sleeping out on the back deck. He used to stay over a lot during the summer when his mom went on her vacations and some of my best memories were of those late nights. I used to tell him my deepest, darkest secrets on nights like that. I smiled at that memory. He had been everything to me. My best friend, my shoulder to cry on, the one person I could always be myself around. I had been so in love with him, but never had the courage to tell him for fear of ruining something so important to me.

It was in the past now. You can't change the past.

I turned the page again and saw a picture I didn't recognize. Two figures were standing at the end of the dock where Charlie and I always used to go. They were wrapped around each other, sunset in the background, making the figures into a silhouette so you couldn't make out the faces. The taller figure was leaned down kissing the smaller figure on the forehead. It was so romantic and I felt a tingle in my spine looking at it.

"Who are these people?" I asked, running my finger over the figures in the center.

She didn't say anything for a few seconds until I looked up at her to make sure she heard my question. Her eyes were wide and anxious. "You don't remember at all?"

I shook my head, "No. Did I take this of Trevor and one of his girlfriends or something? I don't think I would have made it look that good."

"Tess, that's not Trevor." I looked back down at the picture and tried to make out the faces. I couldn't, but the shape of them looked so familiar and the tingling in my spine spread into my chest. Then my mother softly said the words that changed everything. "That's you… and Charlie."

I froze as the surge of panic creeped over me. "What?"

"That's you and Charlie, dear. You both had gone to the lake earlier that day and when I came to pick you up, that's what you were doing." She looked down at the picture again and sighed. "I couldn't help myself. It was so beautiful, I just had to capture the moment." Her voice was quiet and she was speaking slowly like she was trying to calm a frightened animal. In the background somewhere, I heard the front door open and close and a deep voice. Trevor had shown up, but I didn't dare look up. I was engrossed with the picture in front of me

My heart pounded against my chest like a sledgehammer and I shook my head. "How can that be? These two people look like they are… in love. Charlie and I never…" I looked back at her and the look on her face was full of pain and regret. "Mom? This can't be me and Charlie. I would have remembered something like that. You know I would have!"

"It's us, Tess."

That voice.

I looked over and saw that it wasn't just Trevor and Ellie that had arrived. Charlie was standing in front of me with his hands shoved in his pockets looking like he just stepped out of "World's Sexiest Man" magazine. He looked cautious as I met his green eyed gaze. The flicker in his eyes told me he was telling the truth.

"I don't understand," I said, looking back down at the picture. "I don't remember this. Charlie, I would have remembered something like this." My eyes went blurry from the threat of tears, but I quickly blinked them away and put the album down on the coffee table like it was a bomb ready to destroy everything I ever knew. My hands were shaking and my mind was racing, trying to dig up the memory that would have stayed with me forever.

If Charlie had ever held me like that before, I would have locked it up inside my head and never let it out. It would have been the best day of my life. It would have meant happiness for the rest of my life. Whatever happened… I had no memory of and I wanted to run away from the implication that there were other things I didn't know, didn't remember.

"It's us. I know now why you don't remember," he said softly and knelt in front of me, pulling the album off the table and holding it up to study the picture. He touched it lightly running his finger down the image of the smaller figure and grinned. "That was the scariest and happiest day of my life."

I felt like I was having an out of body experience. Like I was looking down from the ceiling and watching the scene play out in front of me. My face looked ridiculous and Mom looked like she was about to pass out. I ignored the image of Trevor and Ellie standing off to the side because she was doing what she always did, studying her nail polish.

But Charlie. Charlie was something else. He was gorgeous kneeling on the ground in front of me and looking down at the tender moment in his hands. He looked happy.

I could barely take in a breath and realized I was gasping loudly for air when my mom put her hand on my back and rubbed up and down. "I… I don't… what happened? Tell me… please." I clutched my chest and kept staring down at Charlie.

I had to get a hold of myself. *Deep breaths, clear head, don't switch, don't switch, for the love of God, don't switch.*

He nodded and glanced at my mother. "It's time, Sarah, but I think we need to be alone."

She stood quickly and ushered Trevor and Ellie through the kitchen and to the back deck before I could process what he had said.

"Time?" I breathed.

"Yes. It's been too long." He shook his head and irritation flashed over his face. "I want you to know that I begged your mom, *begged* her, to let me tell you. She made me promise, though. I keep my promises, Tess." His hand had moved to my knee and he squeezed gently.

"I know that," I said confidently. He did keep his promises. Every single one of them. Never made a promise he wouldn't keep and it's one of the reasons I loved him so much.

"We had gone to the lake late that morning," he began nervously, "and spent the day swimming and just doing whatever. No one else was out there and it was really the first time we had ever been completely alone out there. You wore this white bikini with pink polka dots and I couldn't take my eyes off of you all day." He paused and looked back down at the picture for a minute before closing the album and setting it aside.

He moved closer until my knees were pressed against his stomach and grasped both of my hands in his, lifted them to his lips and kissed my knuckles softly. My stomach fluttered and I fought the urge to close my eyes. Charlie was always a touchy feely kind of guy, but the way he held my hands, the way his warm lips moved over my knuckles, it was almost too much.

"I had been in love with you for years, Tess. I told you that day," he said huskily.

I felt my eyes widen and my mouth gape open. "You did?" I could barely hear my own voice as I processed the one thing I had always wanted to hear him say. *He had been in love with me?* How could I have missed that?

He nodded, "Yes, I did. I told you that ever since I saw you in the fourth grade playing hopscotch with Amanda Jones, you had me wrapped around your finger. I told you that the day after Michael Stower pushed you down and I saved you, I found him and thanked him for being a jerk because it meant I got to be your friend, then I punched him in the nose and told him that if he was ever a jerk to you again, I would do more than make him eat sand."

My lips twitched, begging me to let them form a smile, but I refused them. I couldn't take my eyes away from the green ones that were holding me in place. His jaw flexed and his throat contracted as he swallowed.

"I told you that it killed me every time you went out on a date with some jerk, but that it killed me even more when that jerk broke your heart, like it wasn't the most precious thing in the world. I told you that I would do anything to make you happy and I wanted to be the one to make you happy for the rest of your life." He dropped his head and gripped my hands tighter for a moment before he twisted the ring on my middle finger around over and over again. "And when you told me that you had felt the same way and that you were just too scared of ruining our friendship… and that you loved me, too… I *promised* to love you forever."

I let the tears that I had been holding back for so long finally fall and dropped my head into my hands. Defeated. How in the world could I forget something as beautiful as this man telling me all those wonderful things? How could I forget finally working up the courage to tell him how I had felt for so long? Then I thought of what *not* remembering meant for him.

"Did we… What happened next?" I asked breathlessly.

He hesitated and shut his eyes tightly as if he were trying to get through the pain he was feeling. "I kissed you. We kissed… a lot." He opened his eyes and I could see the memory flicker through them. "We held hands, we held each other. Talked about our plans. A couple hours later, we watched the sunset and your mom picked us up and took me home. You walked to the door with me pretending you had to get something from my house and we kissed goodnight."

The tears fell faster and harder. How could I forget that? We only had a couple of hours together and my mind wouldn't even allow me the memory of such a short period of time. The loss ripped through my chest.

It had to have been Lydia who got that time with him and apparently, she had known what was going on inside my head. Or she felt it, too. It was something she would have done either way, I'm sure. It *had* to be her. Or I had been too deep in the middle of a switch I had no idea I was having.

I felt his hand cup my cheek and swipe away a tear with his thumb. His hand was so warm and strong and it only made me feel worse. "I'm so sorry, Charlie," I said through a sob. "I'm so, so sorry."

"Shhh, Tess. You didn't do anything wrong. You couldn't do anything about it. I'm sorry you don't remember, but I'll never be sorry that it happened. I found out that you loved me that day." He lifted his other hand to cup my other cheek and continued to swipe my tears away. "Right?"

I nodded, slowly.

His eyes were filled with relief and hope, but there was a trace of fear that lingered and I knew there was more for him to tell me. More that I probably wouldn't like.

"Tell me what happened next, Charlie. When did you find out that I didn't remember?" I wrapped my fingers around his wrists and held him to me tightly. I didn't want him to pull away before I knew everything. His touch was the only thing keeping me grounded at the moment.

He sighed and his eyes grew dim, but he didn't pull his hands away. "I came over the next day. We had planned to go out on a date, as a couple. When you came to the door… God, you looked so beautiful, but so confused. I thought you were messing with me, trying to tease me, but when I realized that you were actually getting upset that I kept saying we had plans, I knew." He dropped his hands and grabbed both of mine resting them in my lap. "You had acted that way once before after we got drunk at Danny Danko's birthday party."

Memories came slamming back to me, "I remember waking up with a hangover, but not remembering how I got it."

He nodded and continued, "I thought it was just because you got drunk, but after the lake, I realized that there was too much about that night you didn't remember. And the similarities… you were so blunt that night at the party, so talkative and loud, so unlike you. You had acted so strange all day and it was the same that day at the lake. It was more subtle, but thinking back to it, I could see the similarities. There were lots of people at the party wondering why you wouldn't respond to your name. You kept telling them you weren't Tess. We all thought it was just you being funny."

"What happened when you realized…?"

"I looked up everything I could find on every kind of amnesia there is. Everything that matched up to how you were behaving just seemed too farfetched to be true. I didn't think it was possible and I didn't really believe that kind of thing existed." He glanced over at the kitchen door, then got up from his knees and sat beside me on the couch, still clutching my hands. Our eyes locked and I felt a buzzing in my arms, traveling to my chest. "I talked to your mom, told her that some things had happened between us, but you didn't remember any of it. I told her I thought something was wrong and that we should talk to you about it.

"She made me promise to wait until she could find you some help. She was sure it was all because of the anxiety you were having about school and everything else. You were having a tough time, Tess. We all saw it. You were just too stubborn to admit it." He slowly caressed his thumb in tiny circles on the back of my hand, making the buzzing sensation stronger, but not unpleasant. My reactions to him should not have been surprising by now, but come on… who feels this stuff with just a simple touch?

"That's when she sent me to the therapist?" I remembered how against it I was and how Charlie convinced me to go.

"Yeah. We were hoping he could somehow find out some answers for us, but again, you were stubborn. Then things got better… mostly."

"Mostly?"

He shrugged his shoulders, "Well, I don't know if anything happened when you were with me, but there was one other time that you… well… don't remember."

There were lots of things I didn't remember. Classes and tests, parties and shows. I left because I realized it was more than just being stressed. I was losing my mind. Charlie waited for me to run through my thoughts until I was ready for what he said next.

Something I knew I didn't want to know.

But I *had* to know.

Chapter 9

Charlie

I knew she had no desire to hear about that night, but she wanted answers, and I was going to give them to her in the hopes that she would give some to me. Mainly, one.

"What happened, Charlie?"

I was still holding onto her tiny hands. Her skin was so soft, softer than I remembered, and her eyes were a beautiful rich brown and still glistening with tears. I hated seeing her cry, but everything about her afterward seemed so vulnerable and open. I wanted to kiss her more than I wanted to take my next breath, but that would be taking advantage of her and she was still so confused and scared.

"You remember, a few weeks later, that morning we woke up in your bed?" I asked.

She went stiff and squeezed my hands briefly before nodding. "I fell asleep during the movie."

"Yeah, but not really," I replied. When she didn't respond, I reached out and swept a piece of her hair behind her ears, the same piece that always fell in front of her eyes. "We had talked about an assignment in school, your father came up in our conversation and you shut down. I wasn't sure what to do so I just started a movie thinking it would get your mind off of things.

"When I realized you weren't watching the movie, I started to ask if you were okay. You just sat there and stared at me with this look on your face… I didn't know what to say or do. Your eyes looked so dark and angry and I got nervous. I thought maybe you were mad at me for not leaving or that I had said something I shouldn't have. I kept asking you questions, but you never answered me. You were just so cold and withdrawn."

I felt a shudder run through me picturing her face that night. She had looked like a completely different person. Not my Tess.

"Camryn," she whispered.

"Who?"

"Camryn," she said a little louder. "One of the alters."

She hadn't explained much to me herself, but I knew what she was talking about. "You still haven't told me anything about them, yet."

"I know. I'm sorry. I will, Charlie, but please finish telling me what happened? I need to know."

She was terrified, but I knew she wouldn't let it go. I kissed her hands again and heard the catch in her breath as I entwined our fingers and held her gaze.

"Out of nowhere, you started screaming at me, telling me I didn't know you and that I could never make anything better for you. At first, I thought you remembered me telling you how I felt and you were upset that I hadn't said anything more. Then you said something about staying away from you and that you wouldn't let me ruin you, that you wouldn't let me hurt you, like he did."

From what she had told me when we were kids, her father was a mean bastard. He was a drunk and an absolute asshole. From what Sarah had told me, he always spoke to Tess like she was nothing and that she would never become anything. She told me that the first time she saw a bruise on her arm, she kicked him out of the house and never saw him again.

He had never touched her sexually, but he had done enough to make her miserable for a long time. I remembered how reserved she had been when we first became friends. She was jumpy and constantly apologizing for the most ridiculous things. It took a few years for her to realize that, with me, she could just be herself.

"I tried to calm you down, but you were hysterical and then you punched me in the eye. Hard. I saw stars for a few seconds before you came at me again."

"Oh my God!" she covered her mouth with her hand and started crying again.

"No, Tess. Please don't cry. It wasn't *you.*" I held her face between my hands again and pleaded with her.

"How could I do that to you? It was still my body, my mind. How could I do that to someone I loved?" she sobbed.

I pulled her to me and she pressed her face into my chest and fisted the front of my shirt. It was the first time since the day she couldn't remember that she admitted, out loud, she once had feelings for me. The feeling was indescribable

I couldn't go any deeper with her and still have a chance of coming out alive, not unless she was there with me.

"Finish, Charlie," she sobbed into my chest. My shirt was wet with her tears, but I held her firmly against me.

"Okay." I took a breath and tried to remember ever detail about that night. "I got my arms around you, just like this, and held on to you for what seemed like hours before you calmed down. You never cried, but you finally started breathing normally and all the muscles in your body shifted. Next thing I knew, you were asleep in my arms. I couldn't leave you after that. Your mom was helping Trevor move in to his apartment at college, so she wasn't coming back that night."

"You held me all night?" she asked and sniffed.

"I did."

"And the next morning, when I asked you about the black eye? You told me it was an accident." She wasn't accusing or resentful that I had misled her. She sounded grateful and relieved.

"It *was* an accident, sweetheart. I knew you didn't mean it." No way was I going to let her feel guilty for something she had no control over. For something none of us understood.

She raised her head and pulled back out of my arms. I let her, even though it went against every cell in my body. She looked down at her hands and then dropped her head into them, twisting her fingers in her hair and massaging the sides of her head. Her eyes squeezed shut and she let out a long breath. Minutes went by as I watched her rub her head and breathe over and over again, like she was trying to contain some kind of explosion.

When she started to speak, I felt a strange relief that she was still with me. "I need some time to process all of this."

Not what I wanted to hear at all, and I barely succeeded in holding in my cringe. I couldn't force her to accept anything or even really absorb everything I had told her. She knew that her mind had been experiencing this disorder for a long time, but she didn't realize how far it had gone until now. She had to feel some kind of betrayal from all of us. We had kept everything from her thinking it would only protect her, but it only made it take longer for her to find the help she needed.

She stood and started packing up the box of albums slowly, taking in deep breaths here and there and shaking out the tremble in her hands every few seconds.

I stood and handed her the album on the coffee table. "I'm sorry, Tess. It shouldn't have taken this long to--"

Her hand went up to stop me. "No, I'm not mad, Charlie. I'm just… trying to put it all together. I already had plenty to talk to my doctor about, this just adds to it and seems a little more… significant." She stepped forward and wrapped her arms around my waist, hugging me tightly.

I wrapped my own arms around her tiny frame and pressed my cheek into her hair, inhaling that minty rain scent and finding myself even deeper into her and not wanting to come up for air.

"Thank you for telling me, Charlie." Then she pulled away and started toward the kitchen. "We better get the rest of them before my mom's dinner is ruined."

She was trying to keep her emotions in control. Her jaw twitched and her fingers kept fidgeting with anything she could get them on. Knowing that she really did love me back then was enough for tonight. It was *her* that said it. Not an alter. Her.

I could hold on to that until she was ready to talk again.

"Will you explain things to me tonight, Tess? About the alters?" It was a shot in the dark, but I had to ask. I had to trust that she would let me in now, let me be a part of what she was going through.

"Of course. Let's go eat and I'll explain everything I've learned. I'll blow your mind with the shit I've been told," she said with a wide, forced smile.

I smiled back and followed her into the kitchen. "You already blow my mind every day."

She laughed loudly and leaned in so I could hear what she had to say, "Then I'll blow Ellie's mind, but I'm sure it won't be that messy. I don't think she's got much in there."

We both laughed as we made our way to the back door and found Sarah sitting on her hands and straining to keep them underneath her. Ellie was talking about something to do with gardening and what Sarah could do to improve hers. They looked up at us when we walked out and Sarah about jumped into our arms.

"Oh, wonderful! Let's eat!" she exclaimed, then scurried into the kitchen and put the bread in the oven.

Trevor grunted, "It's about time. I'm starving."

Before any of us could retreat into the kitchen, the psycho slut made her voice heard, "Well, I *was* hungry until I smelled what was cooking. I don't know how you eat that stuff, Trevy. You're going to get so fat if you aren't careful."

I glanced at Trevor to see his reaction, and was granted the usual one. He was just staring down her shirt and had his hand on her ass. "I'm not going to get fat," was all he said back to her. Not "I think my mother's cooking smells delicious" or "maybe you should leave and never come back", either of which I would have been content with.

Because he didn't say anything else to her, Tessa's instinct was to step forward and say it herself. I knew this because it was what I would do in the same situation. I wrapped my arm around her shoulders and immediately steered her into the kitchen. She glared at me before her face softened and she smiled mischievously.

"You think you can stop me every time, Charlie?" she asked innocently.

"Nope, I'm just too hungry to let you tonight. Maybe next time, huh?" I winked at her and sat down at the table across from her so I could see her face.

She threw her head back and laughed. It was the most beautiful thing I had ever seen and from the look on Sarah's face, it hadn't happened often enough since she had come back home.

This was a good sign.

***

Over the next week, my relationship with Tess started to remind me of how it used to be. She beamed at me whenever I came over and talked to me like she used to. The last five years had still happened, though, and we both were very aware of the time we had lost.

Our friendship was mending, but that wasn't all that I wanted from her and she knew it. Nothing more had been said about that night or how we felt, now or in the past. Tess explained everything in detail to me, about the alters, the time she spent moving around, and Benny.

The last thing she said before I left for home was, "Think long and hard about whether or not you can live with this, Charlie. It's not something that will ever go away. Especially if I can't figure out…"

I just said, "I already knew that and I've already decided. I'm just waiting for *you*."

She seemed to like that response and smiled shyly. I loved that smile.

We spent some time each day together and she had even stopped by the gym to see what all the fuss was about with Trevor and my training. She only stayed a few minutes and watched me spar with my coach. Then, after saying a quick goodbye and making an excuse about running errands she left with a full body blush. At least, that's what I imagined it was, but I really only saw her face and neck flush red and her eyes angle down to avoid eye contact with me.

Trevor said she was probably just turned on, and coming from him, well it was weird, but I tried not to think about that. I had enough fantasies to last me a lifetime, one more would just dissolve all the control I had left when I was around her.

It was Thursday night and she had just gotten back from her session with Dr. Geoffrey looking glum and frustrated. I had been fixing a door hinge for Sarah and didn't plan on catching her while I was there.

"How did it go?" Sarah asked the second Tess walked into the kitchen.

She paused when she saw me, then smiled a greeting before opening the fridge and pulling out a water bottle. "It was okay. Disappointing. I don't know." She took a gulp and let out a breath while staring at her feet. "I guess I'm just losing what little patience I have."

"Oh, sweetie. I know you want things to move along, just keep working at it. You are doing so well," Sarah praised and hugged her daughter firmly before leaving the kitchen, but not before throwing me a sly wink. You would think, knowing my intentions for her daughter, Sarah would stick around when Tess and I were together. Isn't that what moms did? Chaperoning and all that?

Not Sarah. She wanted us to be alone as much as possible, it seemed. Something about years of tension coming to an end.

Tess turned back to me and saw me staring at her. "Hi."

"Hi."

"So, Mom thinks you are some kind of handyman, too?" she teased.

I shot her an arrogant smile, "Well, I *am* pretty handy these days. She doesn't really trust anyone else either."

"That's understandable. She told me the other day that she called a plumber last year to fix a leaky faucet and swears up and down that he was flirting with her the whole time." She smiled and took another gulp of her water, "I know for a fact he wasn't, but I would rather her call you anyway."

I felt a surge of pride warm my chest. A quick idea ran through my mind about breaking a few things around the house before I left, then I would get a call to come back. That was stupid, though. Right? Well, stupid or not, I was still undecided about it. Then I processed what she said about the guy not flirting with Sarah and asked, "How do you know he wasn't? Your mother is a good looking woman."

"Well, since the plumber she called has been completely gay since junior high, it wasn't that hard to figure out," she smirked.

My mouth gaped open and a thousand memories came rushing back to me, "She called Samuel Anderson."

She nodded.

"You are telling me that Sammy Anderson, star quarterback through all of high school, breaker of skank hearts for even longer than that, and also the only guy who has ever beat Trevor up, is actually gay?"

She smiled at me playfully and, regardless of the topic of conversation, it made all my muscles shift and blood rush where I didn't need it.

"Yep."

I tried to concentrate on what she was telling me, but lost the ability to speak for a minute or two. I hoped she couldn't tell how much she truly affected me and that it was just the result of shock from this new information. "Well, good for him. That must have sucked trying to hide it all those years." Just like it sucked trying to hide my feelings for her all those years.

"I called him out on it in the eighth grade and he spilled everything. Made me promise to keep it quiet until he was ready, but I saw him last week with his husband. They are great together, too. Really happy. His husband, Mark, is actually from Boston and used to live near the facility I was…" She paused and took another drink of water, her eyes shifting around to avoid mine. "I'm actually surprised Mom hasn't figured it out, it's not like he is keeping it a secret anymore," she said casually and moved to the door I had just fixed to examine my work.

I felt a warmth rush through me with the comfortable silence I had longed for. Years ago, we used to just sit together, not talking or doing anything, and it just felt right. It was something I had missed. Her shoulder brushed against my chest as she turned to look at the door.

The sudden close proximity of her body with mine made all my muscles jump and more blood rush away from my brain. Not good. I needed that blood up there so I could focus on being a gentleman. Or I needed to get out of there before I did something she wasn't ready for, but before I could really do anything, my mouth started flapping.

"Come to dinner with me tomorrow night," I blurted out.

She hesitated, still looking at the door, then took a deep breath and let it out slowly before turning those dark chocolate caramel eyes my way, "Okay."

I blinked several times, worried that the blood wasn't going to come back at all, and I was in the middle of a fantasy. "Okay? Really?"

She chuckled and folded her arms across her chest, "Well, yeah, Charlie. Unless you really don't want me --"

"No! I want you to. I'm just a little… surprised," I said quickly, and before she could change her mind I packed up my tools and said, "I'll pick you up at six." I had to resist throwing a fist in the air in victory. It was difficult, but I held back.

When I turned back to her, she was grinning with her arms folded tightly across her chest. I leaned toward her slowly, wanting more than anything to wrap her in my arms and kiss the hell out of her. Maybe one day soon, but not today.

When my face was just inches away from hers, she stopped breathing and her eyes glazed over. That was confirmation enough that she wouldn't smack me afterward. When my lips touched her warm cheek, she relaxed and didn't pull away.

"I'll see you tomorrow," I whispered near her ear, then turned and walked away.

I reached the front door and heard her finally take in a breath and mutter, "God, help me."

I was smiling until I got to my car and sat down, then I realized that even though I won this round, I was just setting myself up for torture. Being close to Tess, close enough to finally show her that I wanted her, but not being able to *truly* show her yet, it would probably kill me. The noticeable bulge in the front of my pants glared back at me when I looked down. Just thinking about kissing her was enough.

It was going to be a long night.

Chapter 10

Tessa

"Please tell me you are wearing something that shows your cleavage." Benny sounded like she was about to have a heart attack. I had spent the last ten minutes telling her what had happened with Charlie so far and when I told her he kissed my cheek, she about lost it. She always told me that she could feel the sexual tension between us and she hadn't even met the guy.

"God, Benny! I don't even own a dress let alone something besides pajamas that would show anything like that," I said, holding the phone against my shoulder while I rifled through my closet.

"When is he picking you up?"

I looked at the clock, it was only two in the afternoon and I was already a mess. Why did I agree to do this? It would only make more stress for me. "At six?"

"Holy shit! You don't have much time, T!"

"Yes I do! I have four hours. It won't take me that long to get ready," I balked.

"Except for the fact that you have to go shopping, like, right now! And you have to send me pictures for approval AND it's *Charlie* for hell's sake! Now get off the phone with me and get your ass out of the house and to whatever kind of dress store you can find because there is no way I am letting you go out with the guy you have been in love with since the fifth grade without looking like sex on a stick!" She was gasping for air by the time she finished her rant and I was gasping for air from laughing so hard.

"I miss you, Benny," I said between breaths.

"Aw, my sweet little psycho, I miss you, too. I'm going to come visit next weekend okay?" She sounded nervous about telling me, but she had no reason to be. My heart about leapt out of my chest with excitement.

"Yes! Please do." I paused. "Wait! Does that mean you are checking out?"

She laughed loudly, "Hell yeah! I am checking out tomorrow, but I got a few places to visit first. Then I'm flying my cute ass over to you and staying with you for as long as you'll have me, *then* we are going to look for a place. That is, unless you are already tangling the sheets with Mr. Mackenzie."

I gasped and felt my face go hot, "Benny!"

"Don't write it off just yet, T. True love doesn't come around more than once in a lifetime and you know it," she said sternly and I had no argument to give her. She was right. I was just too much of a coward to admit it.

"Okay, enough of the fairytale bullshit. You've got a dress to find. Call me when you're ready and send some sexy pictures. Bye." Then she was gone.

I was chewing on my thumbnail, wondering how the hell I was going to find something nice in just a couple of hours, when Mom walked in with a smile that could crack her face in half. "Nervous?" she asked and quirked her eyebrow.

I nodded and started taking deep, cleansing breaths. They weren't helping. I couldn't stress out or I wouldn't make it to dinner, someone else would. *It's just Charlie.*

It's Charlie.

"Well, get some shoes on and let's go. Benny texted me and told me to use force if I had to."

I smiled and scurried around my room looking for my sandals. What would I do without these people in my life?

***

Mom was snapping pictures with my phone while I posed in my new date dress. It only took about an hour to find it with Sarah Marshall taking the reins. She had an eye for this stuff.

We ended up finding a charcoal satin cocktail dress that was sleeveless and stopped just above my knees. The V neckline was lined with tiny clear beads, and yes, it was showing a bit of cleavage. I had left my hair down but curled some waves into it. It was heavily layered so it already looked like I had spent some time on it. After applying a little make up and pulling on the silver heels Mom lent me, I looked in her full length mirror and tried to catch my breath.

I looked *good.*

Benny called a minute later full of compliments and advice. I thanked her for the compliments and ignored the advice since it was mostly where to put my hands when he kissed me or how to 'accidently' show a little more leg than was necessary to distract him.

Mom was in tears with laughter, hearing everything because she had put her on speakerphone. I was just trying not to sweat.

Two minutes before six o'clock, there was a knock at the door. We were still up in my mother's room and I had just said goodbye to Benny. I checked myself in the mirror again while Mom ran down the stairs first. She was opening the door when I started down carefully since the heels were a little much for me.

"Oh Charlie," she gasped, "you look so handsome!"

"Thanks, Sarah. Is Tess about re--"

His words halted when he caught sight of me. Benny would be proud. Mom stepped aside to let him in, but he didn't move. I felt a simmer in my veins when I took him in.

He was dressed in dark jeans with a black dress shirt with white pin stripes and a white undershirt peeking through since he left the top two buttons opened. His hair was still a little shiny from a recent shower and styled messily, like he had just ran his fingers through it and tugged like he did when he was nervous. It looked so sexy and my knees about buckled at the sight of him. In his hand was a small bouquet of brightly colored daisies. His other hand went to the door frame, like he was holding himself up.

His eyes moved leisurely from the top of my head to my toes and back up and I felt his approval in every inch of skin. "Wow," he breathed.

Mom clapped her hands and stepped toward me to give me a quick hug. She kissed my cheek and whispered, "He's a goner," then walked up the stairs in a rush.

He had finally stepped inside the house and shut the door. I felt a tingle run up my spine when he looked at me again and his green eyes ran down my body a second time.

"You look… wow. Gorgeous, Tess," he said and pushed a hand through his hair, then rubbed the back of his neck. He *was* nervous, which made *me* nervous, which made me even *more* nervous because I was starting to sweat again. "Um, these are for you," he blurted out and offered me the flowers.

I couldn't stop the giggle that bubbled up in my throat as I reached for them. I felt like I was back in high school again and on my first date ever. "Thanks, Charlie. They're beautiful."

He just smiled shyly and shoved his hands in his pockets. "Is this as embarrassing for you as it is for me?"

I giggled again, but it came out as more of a snort. I clapped my hand over my mouth and nose and felt my face turn beet red. That was the opposite of sexy, Benny would be disappointed.

He just stared at me with a pleased grin, "You have no idea how great it is to hear that again." Then he stepped closer until our toes were touching and I had to look up at him, he had gotten taller and I felt so small standing so close to him. He reached down and grasped my hand in his, then brushed his lips across my knuckles. "This is what I missed. You've always been so beautiful and tonight is no exception… but you take my breath away when you are just *you.*"

I wasn't sure how to respond to that so I just kept staring at him hoping that the erratic beating in my chest wouldn't be heard over the heavy breathing I had no idea how to stop. Either way, I probably sounded like a complete lunatic.

"I know this may be pushing it, but tonight let's not pretend like we haven't been apart the last five years. I know it may be a little awkward, but there is no point in acting like you have been here all along. Nothing between us has really changed, but..." His voice was so deep and smooth, when he spoke.

I really don't think I heard everything he said correctly, but I think I got the gist of it. However, if he didn't want things to be uncomfortable, he was going to have to ugly himself up a bit because I couldn't guarantee I wouldn't spend the night staring at him.

"Okay," I finally said, "let's just let whatever happens happen and not worry about anything else but enjoying each other's company." I could do that, right? I mean, I really wasn't jumping ahead to the end of the date and wondering whether or not he was going to try to kiss me or if he would kiss me before he brought me home and if it would lead to us not coming back to my house and maybe going to his house. I wasn't doing that. At least, I was lying to myself about it, but I could deal with that.

Oh God, I was sweating again.

He was still holding onto my hands and had somehow gotten even closer to me so our chests were only an inch apart. His eyes were smoldering and I couldn't look away. When his fingers caressed my cheek and moved a piece of hair behind my ear, I felt a pleasant shock and leaned into his hand as he cupped my cheek. I felt his warm minty breath against my cheek as I moved my hand to his chest to hold myself up.

He leaned closer until our lips were just a breath away, both of us taken over by some unseen force and neither one of us fighting it.

I had always imagined how soft his lips would be and wondered if his kisses would be firm and confident, or soft and tender. I wondered how he used his tongue and where he would put his hands. I had been kissed a handful of times in my life. Most of which were in high school. When I was moving around over the years, one guy at a bar kissed me after talking to him for fifteen minutes and it was absolutely horrifying. I knew Charlie's kiss would change my life completely and there would be no going back after it happened.

Of course, since my luck isn't exactly up to par these days, I didn't get to find out. He had just taken the final breath of courage to close the distance between us, which felt like miles instead of millimeters, when drunk Trevor burst in the door with a giggling Ellie by his side, forcing us to spring apart like we had just gotten caught doing something naughty.

I could tell by the look on his face that Charlie regretted pulling away and the look he gave Trevor would have probably dropped anyone else, but Trevor just smirked and became his recent belligerent self. I missed my sweet brother, always shallow, but sweet brother

"Looks like we were just in time, babe," he slurred and Ellie stopped giggling when she saw our faces and knew what was just about to happen between us.

Unexpectedly, she shot me with a death glare. I had no idea why she would be angry with me for almost kissing Charlie. Then it hit me. She was jealous of me. Well, needless to say, this pissed me off. She had my brother on her arm and okay, yeah, he wasn't the most romantic guy or really the most thoughtful, but he took care of her and all she did was treat him like a lap dog. I was just about to give her a piece of my mind when I felt Charlie's hand on the small of my back, pressing me toward the door.

"Have a nice time, T," Trevor called as we stepped onto the porch.

Charlie was practically dragging me to the car and I was pretty certain steam was coming out of my ears. He helped me into the passenger seat and came around the front, watching me watch him. When he took his place in the driver's seat I couldn't hold it in anymore.

"I want to strangle that bitch."

He smirked, "That makes two of us."

"How does she have the nerve to look at me like that? Did you and her have something before she was with Trevor or something?" I shifted in my seat to get more comfortable. Not that I cared. What he did while I was away was really none of my business.

I didn't care.

Stop caring, Tess.

He hesitated, but didn't look away and this made me a little nervous. If he had been with that psycho before, I don't know what I would do. No, he would have never been that shallow. But then, my brother would have had to be interested to get with that woman in the first place and he was not *that* desperate. Was he?

"No, Tess. But when her and Trevor were first dating, she tried to make a play at me."

I gasped and whipped my head back to the house, then back to his face. "Does Trevor know that?"

He nodded somberly, "Yeah, he does. She tried to twist it to her advantage, but he wasn't stupid enough to believe her. Plus, he knew that I was still--" he cut himself off and started the engine. "He had no reason to believe her. But somehow, he stayed with her and she has gotten worse since then. He just doesn't want to admit it."

"Oh my God." I was fuming, mortified, and devastated all at once.

"Hey," Charlie soothed and grabbed my hand, "don't let them ruin our night, okay?"

I nodded, but couldn't get my head around how manipulative that woman actually was. "Okay." I took a deep breath and nodded again. "Okay, I'm okay now."

He eyed me cautiously, then shifted the car and pulled out to the street.

By the time we got to the restaurant, we were both more relaxed. The conversation started out with me asking questions about his training and him telling me about the different fights he had won, then it turned into laughing about the stupid things we used to do together and I was almost in tears when he came to a stop. I didn't realize how much I missed him. I used to laugh and smile so much with him and it was good to know we could go back to that after so much time. As we ate, it felt like we picked up right where we left off, except I now knew how he had felt about me all those years ago and I wanted to find out more. We were just finishing up dessert when he surprised me with a question I never thought he would ask.

"Tess, would you mind if I came to your appointment on Monday?"

I stared at him in disbelief for a few seconds too long. He looked down at his plate and moved some of his cake around.

"I mean, unless you are uncomfortable with that. I just thought it would be good to get a little more insight… I don't know, I just want to understand it better." He looked back up at me and waited.

I'm not sure what made me respond. Normally, something like this would have made me run for the hills and never look back. I mean, that was asking a lot of me. I had no intention of ever letting him or my family see a switch if I could help it which I knew eventually I wouldn't be able to, but still. I wasn't about to say 'hey, you guys want to see something crazy?' and go all switchy on them. And this? This was completely different. This wasn't a 'what if', it was a 'for sure' he would see it.

I know he had seen it before, but I wasn't aware of it thanks to everyone keeping secrets and I knew that a switch was very possible every single day I spent with him. I couldn't *truly* control them, but knowing it might not happen made me feel better. So far, things had gone well and I was learning to avoid my triggers.

"I- I don't know," I said quietly.

He just nodded tightly and took the last bite of his cake. He looked around the room, obviously a little embarrassed about asking and probably a little disappointed in my answer.

Here's the thing, though. As I thought about what it would be like for him to be sitting in that room and seeing something like that, I wasn't panicky about it, I guess I was just shocked that he actually was willingly putting himself there. I wanted him to understand and learn how to deal with me, but I couldn't ask him to do it. That was too much, too selfish.

"What about your training?"

He shrugged, "It wouldn't hurt to take a day off."

In other words, he *shouldn't*, but he wanted to come with me more.

"Charlie."

His eyes came back to mine and his smile was tight and forced, but his eyes… those beautiful green eyes were soft and I could see how much he cared about me.

"I don't know what will happen. I just… I don't want you to see something that will…" I trailed off, unable to get my thoughts together long enough to form a coherent sentence. What if I had a freak out or something and he got scared and took off?

His hand reached across the table and grasped mine. "Tess, there is nothing that could happen that would scare me off."

Okay, so now he was reading my mind or I had actually spoken my thoughts out loud.

The look on my face must have clued him into what I was thinking because he smiled, a genuine smile this time, and it was beautiful. His eyes brightened when he smiled like that and the green in them was so breath taking. He wasn't forcing it, but he was letting me know that I could trust him.

"Okay," I breathed. Might as well chase him off now than get any deeper and end up with a shredded heart, too. "Okay, come with me Monday."

He smiled again, kissed my hand and nodded. "Thank you."

"Don't thank me yet," I muttered.

I decided then and there that no matter what happened, I would hold onto the good things. I would hold on to what I felt every time he touched me. I would never let myself forget the happy memories we had made in the past, including the past few weeks.

I would *have* to hold onto those things, because for me, there wouldn't be anyone else. If I lost Charlie… I lost everything.

Chapter 11

Charlie

"You nervous?" Tess asked as we pulled into the parking lot of Dr. Geoffrey's office.

Yes. I was nervous, but I couldn't let her see that. She was already stressing out about it enough for the both of us. I was nervous about seeing her become someone else in front of my eyes, but I knew it would still be her. I was even nervous about seeing the process for it.

Hypnosis had always freaked me out. What scared me the most, though? Seeing her suffer with it. I know how frustrated she could get and after seeing her so upset about things she couldn't remember and blaming herself for all the things that had happened, I didn't think I could handle seeing her fall apart. She was barely holding on by a thread. I saw it in her eyes and in the way she avoided getting serious about this whole situation. She tried to find the humor in it, which I loved about her, but sometimes I think it weighed on her more than she let on.

"No, Tess. I'm not nervous," I said and was surprised by how steady my voice was.

"Good," she said and her voice broke on the word. "I'm terrified."

I wrapped my arm around her shoulders and walked her into the building. She relaxed and chuckled to herself. "I told Dr. G to make it interesting for you. He's an odd duck so we'll see what he has in store."

I stopped just outside the door leading to the office and turned her shoulders to face me. Her face was strained and tired. She hadn't gotten much sleep since I asked to join her today and I hadn't seen her since our date.

Sarah told me she thinks she had a switch over the weekend. She had been acting strange and stayed in her room almost the entire time. She didn't know for sure though and Tess refused to confirm it. So far, she didn't remember anything during a switch, I didn't think she would start to after all these years so I know she would have realized whether it happened or not.

I felt a hefty dose of guilt about it. If I hadn't asked to come, she wouldn't have been so stressed which was probably the trigger for whatever happened over the weekend. I would have to keep that in mind later on.

After I brought her home from dinner Friday night, she was fidgety and quiet. When I walked her to the door, I thought she was going to burst into tears, so instead of kissing her goodnight, like I had planned on doing the whole night especially after seeing her in that dress, I pulled her into my arms. She wrapped her arms around my waist and held on so tight, it felt like she became a part of me right then and there.

"Remember, Tess," I said in her hair next to her ear, "nothing will scare me off." She had pulled away to look up into my eyes and I made sure she saw how honest I was being. "Nothing."

She just nodded and rocked to her tip toes and gave me a peck on the cheek. I think we were both a little shocked, but she hurried inside and shut the door before I could do anything about it. I would have to talk to my coach about my reaction time lately. I felt like I was slipping a little.

Now that we were actually here, at her appointment, I was more than ready. I looked down into her chocolate, caramel eyes which were wide and glistening. "Nothing, Tess," I reminded her.

Her lips twitched before she nodded, more to herself than to me, then opened the office door.

Here we go.

***

Tess was right. Dr. Geoffrey was odd, but he was straight forward. He told me to prepare myself for anything and not to interfere if he needed to call for assistance. I looked over at Tess when he told me this and she was staring down at her shaking hands trying not to hyperventilate.

"Calm, Theresa. We don't want to trigger anything before we begin. Deep breaths, remember what your focus is," he said.

She immediately began to relax and looked up after a minute and stated she was ready.

"Alright, now, I think it would be a good idea to ease into this with Mr. Mackenzie here," he said and waited for her response.

"I agree," she whispered.

"Good." He turned his chair to face me and pulled out a small digital recorder, setting it on the small table separating me from Tess.

I was an observer so he had me sitting in the farthest chair away so I would remember to keep my distance unless he gave me permission. It was all a little intense for me, but he reminded me that since this was all very new between him and Tess still, we had to be cautious.

"Now, Mr. Mackenzie, before I induce hypnosis, I want you to listen to a piece of the last session. It will give you an idea of what to expect and it will also allow me to point out the switch when it occurs so you will understand what you will see today."

I nodded and shifted in the uncomfortable leather chair, the creaking sound reverberated through the room. He pressed play on the recorder and I could hear him speaking clearly through the small speaker.

Dr. G: "Theresa, are you there?"

Tess: "Yes, I'm here."

Dr. G: "How are you doing, Theresa?"

Tess: "I'm nervous. I feel disconnected."

Dr. G: "That is common. Remember when we talked about feeling like you were having an out of body experience?"

Tess: "Yes."

Dr. G: "Good. Now, Theresa, I want you to try to keep your mind open. You have informed me that you want to try and remember the switch. You wanted to see if opening that up will help you remember the switches in the past. Is that correct?"

Tess: "Yes."

She wanted to remember? This was after I told her about the episodes I was with her that she didn't remember. I felt a surge of hope. If she could remember… I couldn't finish that thought. What happened next made my stomach twist.

Dr. G: "I would like to speak with Lydia.(Pause) Lydia? Are you there?"

Tess: "What's up, Doc? You miss me?"

I felt my muscles clench. The voice was still Tess, but just barely. It was higher, sharper.

"Meet Lydia," Dr. Geoffrey announced with a smile, then folded his arms across his chest and continued to listen.

Dr. G: "Lydia, how have you been?"

Tess: "Oh, you know. Same as always."

Dr. G: "You haven't gotten into any trouble lately?"

Tess: "Ha! I'm always looking for an adventure, Doc. You know that. Ugh, is it hot in here? My neck feels so hot. I need to chop this crap off."

Dr. G: "Oh, I don't think so. Remember what Benny said about that. Just put it up into a pony tail, I'll tell Stacy to turn down the heat."

There was some rustling, the sound of the door opening and shutting and then silence. She must have moved around in her chair because the leather groaned. Then she was humming, but she started giggling and the leather squeaked again. There was a popping sound and then loud breathing.

"Lydia likes to mess with me a bit," Dr. G huffed and looked over at Tess who was resting her chin in her hands. "You'll see."

Tess: "Hey, Doc. Are you listening to this?"

She was whispering into the recorder and you could hear the smile in her voice.

Tess: (Heavy breathing in and out) "Dr. Geoffreeeeeyyyyy," (singing his name)

The doctor picked up the recorder and started to fast forward with a chuckle, "I was only gone two minutes but she moved around the room holding this and rambling on about why she thinks I need to go back to medical school. Then she says she hid my pen," he gestured to the empty silver pen stand on his desk, "still haven't found it."

Tess smiled, but didn't say anything. Then he put the recorder back down and let it play.

Dr. G: "Okay, Lydia, I think that's enough. I'll not wear this shirt to another of our appointments, if you promise not to cut your hair."

Tess: "Oh, thank God! That I can do. Just please, yellow? It looks awful on you, Doc."

Dr. G: "I'll keep that in mind. Now, we were talking about that boy you mentioned seeing several years ago. Have you seen him again lately?"

Tess: "No. Not in person. Tess has all the luck with that one. I have been dreaming about him a lot lately. God, he is so handsome. Greenest eyes you've ever seen." (Long pause and a loud sigh) "I miss him."

Dr. G: "Have you tried to communicate with Theresa lately? Maybe she can talk to him for you."

Tess: "Yeah right, she isn't ready for that. I don't blame her, but still..."

Her voice sounded sad and quiet. I looked over at Tess and she was looking back at me intensely. My heart sped up and I wanted to reach out to her. I knew they were talking about me and for some reason, it pleased me that the other parts of Tess remembered me. Cared about me.

Dr. G: "Thank you for being cooperative today, Lydia. I think we are done for now. I'll see you again soon. Would that be alright?"

Tess: "Sure, Doc."

Dr. G: "Good." (Long pause, then a few pen clicks) "Can I see Theresa now?" (Pause) "Theresa, are you there?"

Tess: (Loud sob, then muffled words) "I don't think I can do this."

Dr. G: "What happened, Theresa? What has you so upset, today?"

Tess: "What if he can't accept it? What if I spend the rest of my life trying to fill in bits and pieces and never really getting there? What happens if I switch on my wedding day and I can't remember it? Or if I have kids and... can't take care of them. What then? I can't keep doing this knowing that I'll be hurting the people around me. That I will be hurting him again. I can't hurt him again."

Dr. G: "That's why we are here, Theresa. To learn to live with it. To learn the triggers and to maybe one day bring it all together and understand how to adapt to taking care of several people at once. Or just make it a little easier. If you can accomplish that, it won't be so hard to help the people you love accomplish it as well."

Tess: (sniff) "I know."

He instructed her through a few more exercises with the hypnosis before he woke her up.

Dr. G: "Let's take a break for today. Next time will be a little more difficult. Take the weekend and just try to relax and forget about the worries in the future. Let's focus on now. We are going to attempt to find the root of this. If we can find a way to deal with the cause, maybe we can find a way to deal with the effects. Each alter has different needs and fears as you do. We need to figure those out."

Tess: "Okay."

Dr. G slowly picked up the recorder and switched it off. Then he pressed some buttons and the red light came on indicating it was recording.

"You ready, Theresa?"

She nodded then looked over at me, terrified and pale.

"Nothing, Tess," I reminded her.

Her face softened and she relaxed back into the chair and focused on Dr. Geoffrey.

"Let's begin."

It didn't take long until Tess had her eyes closed and the doctor said she was fully under. He waited a few seconds before addressing her again. "Theresa? Are you there?"

"Yes," she said lazily. She looked so peaceful and calm, then after a few more seconds, her eyes opened and the calm was gone. "I'm nervous," she said.

"Don't be, my dear. We are prepared for anything today."

She nodded and kept her gaze on him.

"Close your eyes, Theresa. I want you to think back to the first time you felt the disconnection." His voice was smooth and firm. He obviously knew what he was doing and it gave me a little more reassurance that what was happening, was okay.

"It's hard. It was a long time ago," Tess muttered and squeezed her eyes shut a little tighter.

"I know, Theresa. Don't rush it."

Her eyes snapped open and she narrowed her eyes. She wasn't looking at the doctor though. It was like she was seeing something else. "He was there. He was more clumsy than usual and he smelled like stale bread and rotten meat. I don't think he had showered for several days."

"Who is the man, Theresa?"

"My father. He hated me. I know he did. I always pretended to be somewhere else when he came home like that. Mom would yell at him and he would just stumble around the house."

Dr. G was scribbling on his notepad as she spoke, then looked up and asked, "The disconnection. Did you feel it then?"

She nodded, "It was the first time I didn't have to try so hard. I saw myself somewhere else and he started yelling at me, but I don't know what he was saying."

"How long did it last?"

"I don't know. I remember Mom coming into the room and making him leave. He came back without her, though. It felt like I was looking down at him. I saw him throw me into my bookshelf, then I don't remember anything until the next day when Mom was crying and lifting my shirt to see the bruise."

Her voice was hesitant, but she kept going. "My dad was walking out the door with a suitcase and she was yelling at him and telling him to never come back. He looked at me and I got scared again, but then… he looked so strange." Her brow furrowed like she was trying really hard to remember something. "His eyes got really wide and he practically ran out the door. He looked just as scared as I felt."

Dr. G kept scribbling on his note pad and waited. I was staring at Tess and my stomach felt like it was about to crawl up my throat. That bastard! She was only six years old when Sarah kicked her ex-husband out. I felt the anger build in my chest, but when Tess closed her eyes again and stiffened, I put it on hold. It was seconds. That's it, but everything about her changed.

The doctor cleared his throat and shifted in his chair. "Theresa? Are you still there?"

She opened her eyes and looked straight at him and glared. The look on her face was familiar and brought me back to that night so many years ago when I witnessed her shatter.

"Shit!" Dr. Geoffrey exclaimed and hurried to the door. I didn't expect him to be anything but a stoic professional, which told me that this new development wasn't expected or desired today. At all.

Tess stayed in her chair, stiff and looking like she was about to snap into a million pieces. Dr. G called out to a couple of people and all I heard were loud footsteps getting closer. My eyes never left her and the urge to go to her was overpowering. She was beautiful, but so cold and angry.

She turned her head to look at me and her eyes widened. They were almost black, so different from the beautiful caramel and chocolate I could stare at forever, and they focused on my face, pinning me to my chair. Her expression softened infinitesimally, but not enough to wipe the fury away. Then she stood and took a step toward me.

"Are *you* going to hurt me?" she growled.

Her question surprised me, but she didn't look scared of me or even the slightest bit worried if the answer would ever be in the affirmative. It was almost as if she were threatening me. I spoke slowly and quietly, "No, Tess. I'm not going to hurt you."

Dr. G looked back into the room when I spoke and looked stunned. "Maybe you should--"

I raised my hand to stop him from talking, but kept my eyes on Tess. The sudden movement made her jerk in alarm, but she didn't step any closer.

"I know you won't hurt Tess," she sneered. "I asked if you are going to hurt *me*?" Her voice was hard and low. Completely different from Tessa's. She took another slow step toward me, but I held still, worried that I was going to scare her if I moved. This was still Tess, no matter what, this was still my Tess.

"I would never hurt you, Camryn."

She flinched back in surprise at hearing her name, but recovered quickly. "Yeah, sure! That's what they all say, but they always lie. Go ahead and do it. I'd rather you hurt me than her. I can take it!" She tilted her head slightly, "You'll regret it, though," she warned.

I stood then, slowly and cautiously, and she stiffened. Her jaw twitched and her eyes narrowed again, but I saw something that she was trying to hide. Something that Tess could never hide when she was struggling to control her emotions, but Camryn didn't know that. Her lips trembled, so slightly that I would have missed it if I didn't know to look for it. She was about to break down.

"Camryn, I would never hurt you," I said sincerely. "You are a part of Tess… and I love Tess." I swallowed hard and inched closer, "I want to help you protect her."

"I don't need any help!" she screamed, looking more and more like she was going to fall to her knees. Looking further and further from the Tess I knew, but she was still in there.

I saw Dr. Geoffrey and two other tall figures in the doorway out of the corner of my eye. I prayed they stayed where they were or Camryn was going to lose it. She must have noticed because she whirled around and grabbed the chair she had been sitting in, tipping it over and letting out a scream that sounded more like a growl.

I just reacted. I moved toward her faster than I had ever moved before, and wrapped my arms around her. She struggled to get away, but I held her tightly against me. She jerked in my arms and tried to turn to face me. When I let her and looked down at her face, the look in her eyes tore through my chest. She was so scared. Panicked.

"Let me go!" she bit out, but the shake in her voice didn't help the fierceness of her words.

I buried my face in her hair next to her ear. "Never," I whispered.

Her whole body uncoiled and she leaned into me as if she couldn't stand on her own. I held her up and she buried her face in my chest, breathing deeply and trying to hold back the sobs rising in her chest. "I'm here, Tess. Baby, come back to me. I'm here."

Her sobs tore out of her and her knees buckled. I lifted her into my arms and moved over to the couch on the other side of the room, cradling her against my chest and rocking her back and forth with my face buried in her hair. Her hands came up around my neck and she clung to me.

"My God," I heard the doctor breathe.

But as far as I was concerned, it was just Tess and me. I kept telling her I was there and I wasn't letting her go, murmuring in her ear that everything would be okay. She cried for a long time. We sat there for over an hour before she fell asleep in my arms.

Dr. Geoffrey spoke a few words, attempting to release her from the hypnosis, but nothing changed. He left the room quietly while Tess broke down in my arms and hadn't disturbed us, so when he walked back into the room, I knew it was time to go. "She needs to come back Thursday and you need to come with her," he said from the direction of his desk.

"She needs a break from all of this," I replied hotly. "She is wearing down and this time won't be so easy to recover for her."

"Yes, I think she does need a break, but she doesn't want it."

"I'm leaving town Thursday morning." I ran my fingers through her hair like I had been doing since she fell asleep and looked up at the doctor.

"Then next week," he demanded.

I nodded, then stood with Tess in my arms, careful not to jostle her too much, and carried her out of the office. The nurses were all standing around staring at us until we made it to the door. She stirred when I put her in the passenger seat of my car, but didn't open her eyes. I realized at that moment that she must not have slept all weekend, worried about me coming with her. I had caused her more stress than I initially thought and I silently cursed myself for doing that to her.

Maybe she had been right about keeping me at a distance. No. We could get through this together. I just needed to be more attentive to what she needed from me. But she was *not* right about doing this on her own and I was not going to let her push me away because she thought I would be better off without her. No way would I be better off. We just needed to get through this, to understand it better and learn to live with it. I could handle it. But I wondered if *she* could. She was wearing so thin and I couldn't help but wonder if she was giving up.

For the first time in years, I felt the very real fear that I would lose her forever and I wasn't sure that I would actually survive it.

Chapter 12

Tessa

I woke up in my bed late Monday afternoon, panicked and disoriented. I scurried down the stairs to find Charlie sitting in the living room with my mother looking subdued. When he looked up to see me walk into the room toward him, he jumped up and hauled me into his arms.

I wanted to pull away, at first. I needed to know what happened before I let him get any closer to me, but in his arms, I felt strong and complete. He buried his face in my neck, inhaling deeply, and a flash of something came into my mind. I pulled back but kept my hands on his shoulders.

"Are you okay?" he asked warily.

I tried to focus on what I saw, what I felt, but before I could get a grasp on it, it was gone. It felt like trying to recall a dream that was forgotten the moment you wake, on the very edge of your mind.

I pulled out of his arms completely, shaking off the feeling that I had missed something extremely important. "What happened?"

He searched my eyes and his expression dropped, disillusioned. "You don't remember anything at all?"

I sat down on the couch and dropped my head in my hands, trying to play out everything in my mind. The last thing I remembered was listening to the recording, then relaxing into the chair while the doctor started the process we had done several times before. I remembered feeling nervous that I would do or say something that I would regret later or that one of the alters would do or say something to Charlie that would make him question everything he had previously known. I remembered feeling the worry build the closer I got to going under.

I shook my head and looked back to Charlie, hoping to hide my guilt. "Nothing after he started the hypnosis. I feel like maybe… I don't know."

Another flash went through my mind. An image of Charlie looking down at me determined, but it was foggy, almost like something I dreamed or…

Oh, God. Why did I have to agree to bring him?

Charlie sighed, but sat down next to me, close enough for his leg to brush mine. Mom was wringing her hands and looking like she wanted to burst with questions.

"Mom, go ahead and ask. I'll need to hear it, too."

She let out a short breath and sat in the recliner across from us. "All Charlie told me was that something happened that he couldn't really explain. I knew when he came in carrying you that it was something big. We've been waiting for you to wake up."

I looked down at my hands, straining to keep the question I really wanted to ask inside. Was he disgusted with me now? Was I better off leaving this place again and staying away?

I didn't feel like anything was going to change, I was completely disconnected from the person I used to be and I didn't feel stable enough or hopeful enough to go back to her. There was just too much in the way.

"Please tell me you don't have to knock yourself out again," my mom pleaded.

Charlie looked over at me for confirmation. He obviously didn't want that either. "I don't know, Mom. Did the doctor tell you anything?" I asked Charlie.

He shook his head and rubbed the palms of his hands on his jean clad thighs. "Nothing about any medication, but you were asleep already so I don't think it will be necessary. He did say that…"

He looked at me nervously and my stomach twisted. "What? What did he say?"

He took a deep breath and looked down at his hands, looking unsure of himself which was quite rare these days. "He said he wanted me with you the next time you go in."

My muscles went rigid and I felt my eyes squeeze shut so tightly, I thought my eyelids would fuse together. It was hard enough to let him come *this* time. I hadn't slept at all since the night he asked and I don't remember a lot of what happened in those two days since. All I remember is Mom looking concerned anytime I walked into the room.

"Charlie--"

"Wait. Don't," he said and put a hand on my knee. "I'm leaving town on Thursday for New York. I told him you needed a break and before you argue about it, he agreed even though he knew you wouldn't like it."

I felt that bitter nervousness that I hated so much. That feeling of regression, like I wasn't getting anywhere and I never would. I couldn't not go. If I didn't go, what would happen then? I could lose it. I couldn't lose it.

Another flash went through my mind when he squeezed my knee. His face looking down at me. I felt my heart go heavy like lead, then lift as I studied his face in my mind. My lungs squeezed tight.

I couldn't handle this.

"Tessa."

Charlie's voice was so soothing. Why did it have to be so soothing? I didn't want him to have any kind of power over me. I couldn't put him through that. It would take over his entire life. I didn't want him to have to learn to live with me, no one should have to *learn* to live with someone like that.

"Tess, please look at me."

I met his gaze and took a shaky breath.

"Will you come with me? To New York?"

I hadn't been expecting anything like that. I wanted to. I really did. I wanted to watch him fight, but I couldn't make myself say it. I couldn't let myself get deeper into him, I couldn't let him make me comfortable again. It was for his own good.

"Benny is coming this weekend. I need to be here with her."

"She can come, too. Trevor will be there. I can get you and Benny a nice room. You both can go shopping or just do whatever together. I think you would love it." He paused and his eyes studied mine, the green in them turning darker. "You need some time, Tess."

I shook my head and stood quickly, "I can't decide right now."

I walked over to the stairs and started to climb, trying to ignore the trembling in my knees. His voice made me pause.

"I'm not giving up. You know me better than that."

Tears flooded my eyes, but I didn't turn around. I couldn't look at him. Before he could say anything else, I hurried up the stairs and into my bedroom, shutting the door softly and throwing myself onto my bed. I needed to talk to Benny.

She answered on the second ring.

"What's up?"

"Benny? I need some help." I don't know why I was so breathless, but I could hardly fill my lungs and I was feeling pretty dizzy. Charlie was too patient, too willing to wait.

"Whoa, calm yourself. First things first. Who am I talking to today?"

The expected question wasn't as much of a comfort as it had been in the past. All it told me was that I hadn't been myself, and my heart tore apart a little more. "It's Tess. God, I hope it's Tess."

"What happened?" she asked, her voice filled with worry at my solemn words.

"I don't think I can do this, Benny. I feel like I'm being ripped apart and God forgive me for involving my family like this. And Charlie? He doesn't deserve this." Hot tears rolled down my cheeks and splattered on the comforter beneath me. I strained to listen to the space outside my door. No one had followed me up the stairs and I fought the urge to go back down and tell Charlie everything I felt and how scared I truly was.

"Okay, T. You need to take a few deep breaths and calm down. You sound hysterical and you are making no sense at all really. Your family needed you back. Charlie needed you back. What is so bad that you are regretting everything?"

"He saw me switch, Benny. With Camryn…"

Silence. Benny was never silent and the silence was almost deafening. It felt like a swarm of bees had just taken up residence in my head and *they* were hysterical. Not me. Are you kidding me? Theresa Marshall didn't get hysterical. Her alters did every once in a while, but not Tess. Not me.

"And?"

I took a moment to breathe in and out, to get myself together enough to tell her that I was screwed in every way. "I think I remember. I think I remember seeing him, but it was like it was through someone else's eyes… and… and I could feel how much I trusted him and how much she didn't… at first. Then, it was like something snapped in her. He pulled me out, Benny." I pressed my palm to my forehead and tried to push the dizziness away.

Now, I could feel him, remember him holding me and feel her reassuring me. It was like she was there with me, or I was there with her. Whatever it was, it felt like Charlie was the cause.

"So? Now what? You make him come with you again and see what happens, go from there. Maybe he will help you gain co-consciousness, that was your goal from the start. I know you hate to hear this, but cooperation with the girls is key. Are you telling me that you are going to put a restriction on the method? Avoid communication with the other parts of you just because you can? Cause that is just stupid and you know it." She sounded like she wanted to reach through the phone and slap me and at that point, I wanted her to do it.

"How can I do that to him, Benny? You were with me for months is all, but you didn't really have a choice. It worked because of that. What if I decide to cooperate with them and he is the only way to bring it together? I can't do that to him."

"Oh, you weird little psycho." Disappointment was dripping from her voice. "I had a choice, T. I could have checked out at any time. I stayed because of *you*."

And just like that, the dizziness faded, the buzzing stopped, and my lungs opened up. "What?"

She let out an exasperated sigh, "You heard me, T. You aren't forcing anyone to do anything. You aren't invading someone's life and you aren't burdening them with your problems. We all love you. Sarah loves you more than anything and would do anything for you. She's your mother for God's sake, how can you expect her not to? I love you like a sister, but like a sister who is the very best friend I have ever had. There is no way you could force that on me and you know it." She paused and let me soak in her words.

My tears stopped and warmth invaded my chest. I felt relief.

"And Charlie," she continued, "he loves you… God, he loves you like you wouldn't believe. Like you refuse to believe. That man… he was *made* for you. He was made for *this*, T. There is a reason for everything and he is the only reason you actually need to let yourself believe in."

We sat in silence again, but it was comforting for once. My shaking hand clutched the phone against my ear and I breathed in a new kind of air. Acceptance. I had been lying to myself all along. I didn't accept any of this before. None of it. I only accepted the loneliness.

Benny was right. There was a reason and now that I knew it, I could finally accept it. Everyone else already had. So, I made a goal, a strict one. I would find a way to talk to Lydia and Camryn. They had taken care of me all these years, not always in the best way, but still… I would have to try to take care of them.

"You still coming?" I asked softly.

"You already know the answer to that," she replied, just as softly.

"He asked me to go with him to his fight in New York. Says I need a break from all this."

She laughed loudly in my ear, "Never mind, T. That man was made for *me.* I think I might love him. He's smart."

I sighed as I felt a calmer warmth pass over me.

"Let it happen, Tess. Let him love you."

She didn't need a response. For some strange reason, she already knew I nodded in agreement.

"So, am I invited, too?"

I laughed and fell back onto my pillow. Just like that, the seriousness of our conversation took a turn and it was just me and Benny and no elephant in the room. "Of course, Benny. He wants to meet you. I think he has this idea that you will be on his side with everything and he needs all the help he can get."

"Well, he's right. I don't know his plan yet, but I'm on board with it. You better start getting used to it now. We all want what's best for you, especially when you have no idea what that is," she said with a smile in her voice. "Get all the details and tell me what to do from there. We are going even if I have to tie you up and drag you there myself. I got some shopping to do."

"I'll let him know." I heard footsteps on the stairs and decided to follow Benny's advice and *let it happen.* "See you soon?"

"Yep."

I hung up the phone and climbed off of my bed. The carpet in my room was as plush as it was the day my mother had it put in and I flexed my toes against the soft fibers. It was calming in a weird sort of way, feeling something familiar that wasn't a big deal, but really was in my mind. I closed my eyes and took a deep breath, seeing Charlie's face again as he held me close and brought me back. *Let him love you.*

I stepped to my door and turned the knob, opening it just wide enough to peek through. Mom was standing against the wall on the other side of the hall with her hands folded together. She looked like she was about to approach a wild and frightened kitten and any sudden movement would scare me off.

"It's okay, Mom," I said with a grin.

"He left. A few minutes ago," she blurted out, "But he said to tell you that you can take your time to decide. He will have two tickets on hold and will book the room anyway." She took a step toward me as I swung the door open a little wider and stepped through. "I'm about to beg you to go, Theresa, but I won't do it. He told me not to pressure you. This is me not pressuring you."

I smiled. A genuine smile. Mom was never one to hide what she was really thinking. Except for around Ellie. I think she was holding in a hell of a lot of stuff for Trevor's sake and it was wearing her down. I appreciated her non-subtlety and smiled wider, and that seemed to help her relax. "Oh, good. You are going then. I'm sure you talked to Benny and she is a smart girl. She wasn't told not to pressure you, so that's good."

"Mom."

"I'm sure she told you that it wouldn't hurt anything and that it would be a good idea for you to take a break and try to forget about everything."

"Mom."

She kept on rambling, ignoring me, "She would do that because she thinks like me. At least, I think she does. That's why I like her. And Charlie is going to like her, too. Especially when he sees how loyal--"

"Mom!"

She finally looked into my eyes and let out her breath. "Yes, dear?"

"I love you, Mom."

Her eyes glistened and I immediately felt guilty for making her upset. Then she smiled and I realized I had actually made her really happy. Those three words always made her happy. How could I have forgotten that?

"I love you, too. More than anything. We all do."

I almost laughed at *those* three words, 'we all do'. She had no idea that I counted two more than she did.

She wrapped me in her arms and squeezed me tightly, pushing away all the fear and worry and despair the way only a mother could.

As I thought about it, I realized I needed a little more time ruminating on this whole acceptance thing. It was giving me courage and I needed to bask in it a bit longer before I took off to another state far away with the one man I had ever truly loved. "I'm going to wait for Benny to come here first. She'll get here Thursday."

She pulled back and stared down at me incredulously. "But the fight is Friday night. You have to make sure you are there well before so Charlie can--"

"Don't worry, Mom. We'll make it. I just think I should wait for Benny to get here first. I know you probably don't understand, but…"

"I don't need to, dear. It's your decision, not mine," she said quickly and waved a dismissing hand in the air. "No worries, right?"

"Right."

This was a good decision. Benny could pep talk me into going to New York head first and she could give me all the advice I needed about how to talk to Charlie.

I could spend some time with Mom and talk to her about Charlie, too. Find out what had happened in the time I was gone. Things I hadn't asked about because I couldn't handle hearing them. Now, I could. Now, I wanted to know. I needed to know.

I would leave Friday morning and get there in time for the fight. I wouldn't be a distraction to Charlie. I wouldn't be a burden. Not anymore.

When I got back, I would figure this out. Right?

I clutched tightly to that hope. Too tightly.

Chapter 13

Charlie

"Their plane landed on time, Charlie."

Trevor's voice did nothing to reassure the worry I had been harboring for the past twenty four hours. In fact, what he told me only made me that much more concerned. Tess and Benny were in New York, had been for a few hours, but they hadn't contacted either one of us. I had been pacing the floor of my suite for the last hour and a half while coach was yelling at me to snap out of it and get ready for the fight.

When Tess had called me on Tuesday and told me she was going to come with me, I had almost burst with happiness and relief. Then she went on to tell me that she was going to wait for Benny to get into town and leave Friday morning, this morning, to be here in time for the fight. She also told me she thought it would be a good idea for me to concentrate on what I needed to do for the fight instead of going out of my way to spend time with her. Which is absolutely ridiculous. If anything, I was going out of my way to train for these stupid fights. Being with her was a basic need, like food and water. I felt like I needed every minute I could get with her to survive.

I only felt a little better when she told me she was fine and that she just wanted to spend some time with Sarah and Benny before leaving.

I tried to understand. I really did, but I sucked at it and I had been driving Trevor crazy. I talked him into letting me pick him up from Sarah's house on Thursday so I could drive us to the airport. He protested, but not near as much as he originally should have.

Thursday morning, he called all excited to make sure I was still planning on it. Apparently, he had met Benny a few minutes before and was intent on 'getting to know' her. He had already said his farewells to Ellie the night before and he mentioned something about her acting strange and not wanting to stay the night at his place. He had been distracted with it until Tess showed up at the house with Benny at her side. Then, I guess he just forgot.

When I showed up, I realized why. Benny was a looker and for a minute there I thought he was going to change his mind and wait to fly in with them.

When Tess introduced me to her, she shook my hand and winked at me. Tess rolled her eyes, which then made my jeans fit uncomfortably tighter and made me want to throw her over my shoulder and force her to come with me in Trevor's place. Benny's response to her eye roll was, "Oh come on, T. If you aren't going for it, why can't I?"

This was obviously her way of provoking Tess and to my surprise and elation, it worked. Tess made a point of removing Benny from my presence and pushing her back into the house with Trevor. I thought of the flush her cheeks got when she turned back to me and saw the smug smile on my face.

"If you think I have problems, they don't hold a candle to hers. Don't even think about it. She likes to flirt, but that doesn't mean you need to flirt back," she chided.

It shocked me that she would feel the need to talk me out of doing anything with Benny. Benny was not the woman for me.

"You have no reason to be jealous, Tess," I said with a knowing smile.

"I'm not jealous," she scoffed.

"You should be," Benny shouted from the kitchen, which then made Sarah laugh.

Tess rolled her eyes again and the tightness down below became almost unbearable. She was adorable when she did that. She was adorable when she gave Benny the middle finger, too.

"I'm not jealous," she repeated as if she was talking herself into believing it.

I reached out and wrapped my hands around her waist and pulled her in for a hug. Her arms automatically wrapped around my neck and I held her against my chest, being extra careful of the not so subtle bulge that was just an inch away from pressing against her. I swear, it took every ounce of strength I had to keep that small distance between us.

"I'm the one that's jealous," I muttered into her hair. "She gets the next twenty four hours with you while I'll be clear across the country wondering what you are doing every minute of the day."

Benny had quietly made her way back to the front door and was watching us with her arms folded across her chest, "Pillow fights and panties, that's all you need to think about," she said loudly.

Tess jumped at how close Benny's voice was and pulled out of my arms, blushing a deep shade of red that I found out later would cause a whole new set of fantasies to form in my mind… along with the one Benny had just suggested.

"Benny!" she shouted and reached out to punch her friend in the arm, but was evaded at the last second. She giggled, carefree and happy, and the emptiness I felt when she pulled out of our hug filled with hope. Benny was good for her and I immediately formed a plan to keep her close to Tess at any cost.

After saying goodbye and dragging Trevor to the car, the worry had started to poke and prod at me. Would she really come? Would she change her mind and decide she wanted nothing to do with me? Would she finally realize I wasn't going anywhere and let me take care of her without being afraid of what it would do to me?

Honestly, I felt emasculated every time I thought about her being done with me. Worrying wasn't going to help. I wasn't going to let her have nothing to do with me. Trevor said she wanted to wait so she wouldn't distract me, but not having her near me was a distraction in itself. Now, knowing the plane had landed, but she wasn't with me, I lost any hope of concentration.

"Where the hell are they?" I snapped.

Trevor slapped me on the back, "Don't worry too much, man. I'll find them."

"How? Neither one of them are answering their phone. What if something happened?"

Trevor shook his head and ran a hand down his stubbly face, "I'm sure they are fine. I don't think anyone would mess with Benny anyway. You get set up, we have thirty minutes before we need to head downstairs. I'll be back with some information, just focus for now, alright?"

"I should have made her come with me," I mumbled.

"Yeah, then you would have a whole new set of problems. Tess would have ripped you a new one if you forced her to do anything."

He was right, so I just nodded and fell back onto the couch as he walked out the door. Coach and his two assistants fell into the pre-fight routine I had been through hundreds of times before. They started taping my hands and going over technique and everything else I already knew I had to do in order to win. I didn't care to listen to it all over again. I imagined Tess walking through the door at any minute and couldn't for the life of me take my eyes off said door.

Was I pathetic? Most men would probably say yes. After years of waiting, though, I wasn't about to pretend I was some macho jerk who didn't need to put myself out there. I wasn't in a position to be playing games and she wasn't in a position to be played with. If something happened on the way here, Benny would have found a way to contact me. *She's coming, just concentrate.*

Twenty minutes passed before the shrill ring of the suite phone blasted through the room. I dove for it, forgetting everyone else crowding the room around me.

"Hello?"

"Hey, I found them, man. I guess there was a mix up with Tessa's luggage and they got stuck at the airport for a while. Both of their phones were dead and T was too stressed to really take a moment to call." A woman's voice in the background, which I assumed was Benny's, bit out a few choice words at Trevor which made him chuckle into the phone. "They just walked into the hotel and checked in. We are about to head up. See ya in a minute."

He hung up before I could get a word in and I wanted to throttle him for it. I wanted to speak with Tess and hear that she was okay. Now, I had to wait even longer and I only had a few minutes before I had to be downstairs in the arena. I felt relief, though, knowing that she was finally here.

I took a few deep breaths and tried to focus. It was difficult, but I got to the point where I was sure I could face her without overwhelming her with how worried I had been. The door opened a minute later and Trevor walked in with a shit eating grin on his face. Benny followed after him and was laughing at something he said.

When I saw Tess, my heart nearly beat out of my chest and the noise in the room disappeared. She stepped into the room and slowly looked around at everyone standing around the suite. I watched her take in each person and saw her confidence fade little by little. She hated crowds like this and looked uncomfortable, but absolutely beautiful.

Her long dark hair was braided on one side and pinned up into a messy bun in the back. Pieces of hair fell around her face and stuck out a little on the sides. She looked like she had a stressful trip and I felt guilty for putting her through that. Her cheeks flushed a little as she took in the rest of the room and I had to shift on the couch where I sat. When her eyes met mine, the breath was knocked out of my chest. Her chocolate caramel eyes sparkled and she smiled widely. I couldn't get to my feet fast enough.

"You're here."

Not the smartest thing that has ever come out of my mouth, but it was all I could come up with at the moment. A part of me really didn't think she would come.

Benny started talking about the whole fiasco at the airport, but I couldn't force myself to pay attention. Tess didn't seem to be listening either and she kept her gaze on me, but her eyes roamed down as she took me in.

I realized I didn't have my shirt on yet and she was staring at my chest and stomach. I felt a spike of pride for myself for staying in shape and let her stare a few seconds longer before I reached for my shirt lying on the coffee table and pulled it on. Everyone had stopped talking and all but Trevor and Benny were gawking at me and Tess.

"Can everyone give us a few minutes?" I asked loudly.

Coach started to protest along with half of the other people who were worried about making it downstairs in enough time to put down some money on the fight. When they didn't move to leave, I pressed a little harder, "Out, please."

Everyone filed out of the room. Trevor and Benny were the last ones out and when he turned to close the door behind him, he gave me a nod. This wasn't a nod that guys give each other for good luck. No, this was a nod that a brother gives the guy, who is in love with his sister, warning him not to break her heart or he'll have to take care of things himself.

Tess was still watching me and I stepped toward her as soon as the door shut. She stiffened only slightly, but didn't retreat, so I kept moving until I was right in front of her and could breathe in the smell of mint and rain she carried with her everywhere.

Unable to help myself, I tucked a strand of hair behind her ear and brushed my fingers across her jaw. Her skin was as soft as it looked and I wished I could rip the tape off my hands so I could feel more of her in my hand.

"Damn tape," I muttered under my breath.

She giggled softly, then a shiver ran down her body and made it impossible to hold back the groan that rumbled from my chest.

"I'm glad you came, Tess."

She smiled and closed her eyes as I tucked another strand of hair behind her other ear and cupped her face in my hands. "Me too," she breathed.

I pressed closer to her until I could feel the heat radiating off of her.

"Um, are y-you ready for the fight?" she stuttered and her eyelids drooped to half mast when my fingers dropped to her neck.

I was getting ahead of myself, but I couldn't stop if I wanted to. I needed to focus on the upcoming fight, but all I could really focus on was the smoothness of her skin and the sound of her shallow breathing. The fight was nothing. She… she was everything.

Her fingers clutched onto the front of my shirt over my stomach. I was dying to kiss her, but I didn't want to rush it. I wanted to savor every bit of her and I knew that someone would be bursting back into the room at any second so I gathered my control and leaned in to kiss her forehead instead.

"I'm ready," I said roughly. "More than ready now that I know you are okay."

She chuckled and shook her head. "Sorry about that. My bag was somehow lost between the check in and the plane."

"Seriously?"

"Yeah. I have nothing with me except my purse. They said they will call me when they find it, but until then…" She looked down at herself and shrugged. "This is all I got."

I tried not to think about it, but the image of her sleeping in just the hotel robe or even in nothing at all invaded my mind. She must have realized what I was thinking about because she blushed and turned her face away.

"God, I really want to kiss you right now," I whispered.

Her chocolate eyes widened as she looked back at me. Her hands tightened on my shirt and I had to take a deep breath to keep from pressing against her. "Why don't you?" she asked softly.

I was a little surprised by her response, but I wasn't about to complain. If she wanted me to kiss her, I was going to do it happily, but not right now. Not when I didn't have enough time to show her just how much I wanted her.

I would need hours.

"If I start to kiss you… I won't stop. I know what it's like to kiss those lips and I'm not about to overestimate my control right now."

She gasped and closed her eyes as I moved my thumb across her full bottom lip. I pressed my forehead to hers and stayed there as long as I could, breathing her in.

There was a loud knock on the door just then and someone on the other side shouted, "Come on, Mackenzie!"

I took a reluctant step back and smiled at her, "Let's get this over with, shall we?" I kissed her forehead again and her fingers fell away from my shirt.

I grasped one of her hands and pulled her out of the room with me. We stepped out into the hall and I was suddenly bombarded by my coach and a few others that were trying to pep me up. I squeezed her hand and winked at her as I was pulled away and led to the elevators.

I looked over at Jake, the one guy on staff that truly knew what Tess meant to me, and gestured toward her and Benny. "Keep an eye on them for me, Jake."

He nodded and moved to stand with the girls. Tess looked a little nervous, but I gave her one last wink and she relaxed a little more.

"Stick with Jake, okay?" I called as I was dragged away.

She nodded and waved at me before Benny wrapped her arm around her shoulders and whispered something in her ear. The last thing I saw before I was pulled around the corner was the blush on Tessa's face and her mouth gaping open at Benny.

Trevor leaned into me and chuckled, "Benny's the reason why her luggage is missing."

My head snapped over to look at him incredulously and he just laughed.

"She wants to help you out," he said with a shrug.

Yeah, I was going to make sure Benny stuck around. At *any* cost.

Chapter 14

Tessa

"You bitch!" I snapped at Benny. "How the hell could you do that?"

Benny had just told me to thank her for the luggage problems and everything clicked in my mind. When we had gotten in line at the security gate, she immediately left me to go to the 'bathroom'. Apparently, she really went to the luggage desk and got my bag back. I wondered what had taken her so long and why she looked like she had just hit the jack pot when she got back in line with me.

"I just thought it would help things along, that's all."

"How do you figure that? You and I are sharing a room, so how is that going to do anything with Charlie?"

She chuckled and shook her head, "Oh, my sweet little psycho. You still don't know me that well, do you?"

She walked away, following the crowd that had dragged Charlie away from me.

I looked up at Jake who was smiling widely with his arms folded across his chest. He was a very good looking man. Blonde hair that looked like the color could be labeled 'Hollywood', light blue eyes, tall and lean with a noticeable amount of muscles. He looked like someone that would definitely be hanging around with Charlie. You know? The 'Hot Guy Gang'. His smile never faltered even when I scowled at him. He seemed like a guy I could get along with and the flicker of humor in his eyes reminded me of Benny.

"Can you believe that?" I asked, gesturing to where she had gone.

He laughed and nodded quickly, "Yeah, actually. I would do the same thing if I were in her position."

"What? Why? You don't even know me."

He smiled and put his hand to the small of my back to begin leading me down the hall after Benny. "I may not know you, but I know what you are to Charlie."

My brows shot up my forehead and my heart thumped wildly against my chest. "What do you mean?"

"Did you know that I have been working with Charlie since the very beginning?" he asked.

When I shook my head, he shrugged. "He is a tough one. Dedicated. Never let anyone talk him out of doing anything he wanted to do. I'll never forget the first day I met him." He led me to an elevator where Benny was holding the door for us and continued talking, "He came to the gym interested in training and the first thing I asked him was 'what makes you think this is the career for you?' and you know what he said to me?"

I shrugged and glanced over at Benny who was listening intently with a grin. Her blonde curls bobbed when she nodded for him to go on.

"I'll never forget it. He said 'The love of my life ran away and I need something to bury myself in until I can get her back'." He pressed the button for the lobby as if he hadn't just told me something that completely shifted the ground beneath me. "So if you don't mind me saying, it's an absolute pleasure to meet you, Tessa."

I don't remember the rest of the elevator ride, but I do know that I spent a lot of it trying to forget how much I had actually hurt Charlie. Instead of losing his best friend, he lost… well, more. My fault.

***

"I don't think I can take much more of this."

Benny elbowed me in the ribs, "Oh come on, it's only been thirty seconds. This is great!"

Great? Not so much. Impressive? Well, of course. Charlie was amazing at this whole fighting thing, and seeing him without his shirt, covered in sweat with his muscles bulging and strained… I might need to invest in a drool tray if I was going to continue watching these things. Plus, the flash of a tattoo on his shoulder was curious. I didn't notice it in the hotel room and I made a mental note to find out what it was.

Yeah, the whole thing was great in a way, but seeing the other guy, who by the way looked like he could crush half the people in the stands with his thumb and then go to work on them, seeing him hitting Charlie… awful in so many ways.

So yeah, I didn't think I could take much more after the first thirty seconds of the round. I mean, Charlie was seriously covered in sweat already and it wasn't like they fought for a few seconds and one of them suddenly won. It was a grueling amount of time filled with technique and concentration and whatever the hell else you want to call it. It looked harder than I thought it would be and for that, I admired Charlie a little more for taking on a sport like this. It definitely did well for his body and I think it helped to drown out a lot of other things that I now knew had been bothering him.

I had watched him train, but it wasn't anything like this.

"Come on, Charlie! Break his face in!"

Yeah, that's Benny. She obviously enjoys this type of thing which won't help my case at all. Benny will push and shove until she gets us married, which at the moment, isn't freaking me out like it normally would have.

DING! DING!

"Oh, thank God!" I exclaimed and buried my face in my hands. They were shaking and tingling from how tightly I had clenched them together.

"Looks like Charlie may have won that round. Wow! This is so exciting!" Benny shouted over me to Jake who looked like he was enjoying watching us watch the fight more than the actual fight.

I looked back up to where Charlie was now sitting. His coach was squirting water in his mouth and some of it spilled onto his chest and ran a crooked line down to his abs where it was probably turning into a waterfall coming off of those ridges of muscle.

I shifted my legs a little because, damn, the sight was making me ache. I kept staring until the water disappeared into the waistband of his shorts. Yeah, I was that close to him. When I glanced up to his face, he was watching me and his green eyes seemed almost black. Maybe Benny wouldn't need to push anything.

"Holy shitballs! You are in so much trouble, T."

I didn't even acknowledge her comment. I couldn't take my eyes off of him and he didn't seem to be listening to anything his team was yelling at him. When the bell rang, signaling the next round to start, he winked at me and stood to face his opponent. He may have been soaked because of perspiration, but I was now soaked in an entirely different area for an entirely different reason. Benny was right. I was in trouble, but I liked it. For once, I welcomed it.

Jake nudged my arm when they started throwing punches and kicks again. I turned my head just enough to show him I was listening, but I could still see the fight.

"The odds are against him for this fight, you know. The two of them are equally matched, but Jordan is fierce. He doesn't really think about who the other guy is, he kind of just turns into an animal."

I rolled my eyes, "If this is supposed to make it easier to watch, it's not working. I can see the guy is a freaking monster."

"I just thought you should know that Charlie is doing better than any of us thought he would, especially since he is slightly distracted," he shrugged and turned back to the fight.

I kept my eyes on Charlie, but I didn't quite see him anymore. The worry crept up until it was nearly choking me and the breathing exercises I had learned from Dr. G felt like I was just making it worse. Benny saw me panic and wrapped her arm around my shoulders.

"You know? Lydia would be a blast right now, so if a switch comes, keep your mind on her. Camryn would just be a total buzz kill, although… I would love to see what she has to say about all this." Benny waved her hand in the air as if she was conjuring up an image in front of my eyes. "She would probably strangle these two bitches behind us." She tilted her head, gesturing to the two bimbos in the bandana shirts sitting a row behind us and to the right. They did nothing but talk about how hot Charlie was and how they were planning on sticking around afterwards to 'chat'.

I smiled cautiously at Benny's attempt to calm me and tried to swallow down the worry. I focused on Charlie again and saw that he had landed a few good blows, then the other guy, Jordan I guess his name was, did some kind of twirly kick that Charlie tried to evade. He wasn't fast enough this time, though, and the guy nailed him in the shoulder making him stumble to the side.

Then he attacked.

Jordan was on top of Charlie throwing punch after punch and all of a sudden Charlie was on top throwing the same punches, then it looked like they were hugging.

"Good God, I can't keep up with any of it. Who the hell is winning?"

Benny shrugged and Jake just laughed beside me. Then the bell rang and the two sweaty men separated into their different corners.

I watched the men around Charlie patch him up, squirt more water, press his face in awkward ways. His eyes were back on me and I wished he would concentrate because it felt like he was getting his ass kicked out there. I didn't want to blame myself for anything anymore, but if he lost, it would be hard not to.

Then his eyes shifted over to the other corner where the Jordan guy was turned and sneering at me. Not a mean or hateful smile, but probably the creepiest one I had ever seen.

"Ugh, I think maybe you should take a shower after *that* look, Tess. *I* feel dirty now," Benny said and shivered violently.

I frowned at him and turned back to Charlie who looked like he wanted to strangle the guy. He was mad. He was standing before the starting bell rang and Jordan was prepared. He had obviously noticed Charlie watching me and wanted to tick him off a little bit.

There was a blur of movement that I almost missed and then the Jordan guy was on his back, motionless with his mouth hanging open and Charlie standing over him. I couldn't see his face, but I figured he probably wasn't smiling.

"Woooooo!" Benny shouted and jumped up and down.

"What the hell?!" Jake laughed. "Knockout!"

"Probably the hottest thing I've ever seen!" Benny said and reached across me to give Jake a high five.

Next thing I knew, Trevor was running over to us and grabbed Benny and me to drag us with him. Charlie was already walking toward the back rooms with his head turned toward us making sure we were coming.

Jordan was still unconscious in the ring with his whole brigade trying to wake him up and for a split second, I felt concern for him. Didn't stop me from following after Trevor, though.

My heart was pumping rapidly and I felt dizzy with excitement. The crowd around us blurred together as we ran to where Charlie was waiting for us. Benny and Trevor ran past him giving him high fives and congratulations. Jake gave him a slap on the back and a job well done.

By the time I got to him, he was ignoring everyone else and looking down at me with heavy breaths. He was sweaty and bruised and smiling. Absolutely glorious.

"You were incredible out there, Charlie," I said loudly so he could hear me over the cheers and shouts from the crowd and his team.

He didn't say anything, but his smile grew a little wider and his eyes a little darker. His arm wrapped around my waist and pulled me to his side. He kissed the top of my head and muttered, "Are you okay?"

I nodded and took a deep breath. At first, I thought he would smell like all sweaty men smelled, sweaty and gross. Not Charlie. He smelled like him with only a hint of that sweaty smell. It made my head swim and I was grateful he had his arm around me because walking was not going to be easy for me.

We followed after Benny and Trevor to the back room where he could wind down. He kissed my forehead before he was pulled away from me to unwrap his hands and get his cuts and bruises taken care of. His kiss had the same effect on me as it did before the fight. His lips were soft and warm and even though it was a place as regular as my forehead, I felt it in my whole body.

Benny was watching me from across the room where she was talking to Jake and Trevor. She winked my way and I gave her a desperate look. What was I supposed to do now? The fight was over, there was nothing to spend our time doing away from each other. Now was the time to pull up my big girl panties and go forward with the decision I had made.

Just let it happen.

After about an hour and a half of talking about the fight and breaking down everything Charlie did right and wrong, he looked like he was ready to fall over.

Benny and Trevor and Jake left to get ready to go out. Apparently we were all going to have a late dinner and celebrate. I had no clothing options, so there was no need for me to leave with them. My dark jeans and fancy green blouse were going to have to do wherever we ended up.

I kept reminding myself to just act normal and to stop being so nervous about spending time with Charlie. Now more than ever, I knew what I wanted. The ache between my legs and the rush of blood in my head was enough to confirm that every time he glanced over at me.

I didn't realize I was staring at the wall until the voice behind me pulled me out of my thoughts.

"You ready to get out of here?"

I turned to those bright green eyes and saw the anticipation he was feeling. He had taken a quick shower and dressed in jeans and a black t-shirt and even with the bruises on his face and the small cut above his eyebrow, he was gorgeous. I stared at him for a few seconds more before his smile started to look unsure and I saw the Charlie from my past. The teenage boy who always took care of me and always did whatever it took to make me happy. How stupid I was to not realize what we already had and both ignored.

"Yeah, I am," I said breathlessly.

He gently grasped my hand and weaved his fingers through mine, then pulled me out the door with his team murmuring complaints behind us.

"Are you going to get into trouble for leaving with me?"

His laugh was humorless and he shook his head, "No, they work for *me*. They just like to give me a hard time."

I wasn't so sure about that. I looked back to find a few pairs of eyes, that looked anything but happy, following me out of the room and I couldn't help but feel like I was going to cause him some trouble whether he thought so or not.

We met up with the others at the hotel restaurant, which was fancier than what I was dressed for, and Charlie sat close to me in the big booth with his warm hand on my knee and drawing small circles with his thumb.

The words on the menu blurred together and I couldn't for the life of me figure out what anyone around me was saying. My thoughts were on Charlie, his hand, and the smile he kept giving me every time I glanced his way.

"And you, Miss?"

I looked up and realized the waiter was waiting for me to order. When the hell did he even get our drinks? My heart started pounding a little harder as I felt the familiar hum in my head and that disconnection that always made my stomach twist. Charlie squeezed my knee gently and I looked over at him nervously.

"You okay?" he whispered so only I could hear him.

I just nodded, but the look in my eyes must have clued him in that I wasn't.

"Can you give us another minute, please?" he asked the waiter, who nodded and stepped over to the next table.

I looked around our table and saw Jake and Trevor talking heatedly about the fight while Benny looked at me with concern. I took a deep breath and a sip of water hoping my heart would slow down and my head would clear.

"Do you want to just order room service and call it a night, Tess? You've had a long day." Charlie had put his arm around my shoulders and was speaking quietly so no attention would be drawn to us, which I was extremely grateful for.

I was aware that I should call it a night and rest, but tonight wasn't about me and I couldn't let myself be the one to ruin it. "You did amazing tonight and I would feel awful if we missed out on celebrating with everyone. I'll be okay, I just think your hand on my leg really distracted me."

Benny heard me and snorted. "Maybe you *should* call it a night then," she whispered. Well, it wasn't so much a whisper since Trevor's head snapped over to look at her. She just smiled and took a sip of her wine.

"Are you sure, Tess?" Charlie asked when I turned back to him. "I don't care about going out. The only person I care about seeing right now is you."

God, the man sure did know how to make a girl swoon, or at least feel like a million butterflies just took flight in her stomach. I nodded at him with my best smile, "Let's at least have dinner and then we can go from there. I'm pretty hungry."

He grinned, but I could tell he was unsure about staying. I was pretty much holding my breath and doing whatever I could to keep myself grounded for a little while longer. The waiter returned and I ordered the ribs and baked potato. The full rack of ribs. That would keep me busy.

"I'll have the same," Charlie said and handed the waiter our menus and grinned down at me. "Just in case one isn't enough."

I slapped him on the shoulder and laughed. "You know me well, Charlie."

His cheeks turned a light shade of pink and he started to fidget with his glass of water. I wondered what he was thinking, but didn't get a chance to ask. Jake started in on about a billion questions for Charlie about the fight and if he thought it went well.

I tuned out a bit as I caught my breath and calmed down a little more. Benny kept eyeing me from across the table, but I shook my head just slightly, begging her to not say anything. When the boys were deep into their conversation, she announced that we were heading to the ladies' room. Charlie kissed my cheek before I stood and winked at me, then turned back to the conversation.

Benny looped her arm through mine and practically dragged me to the bathrooms. As soon as we were inside she held back while the only woman in the room dried her hands and walked out, then she locked the door and checked the stalls quickly.

I watched her with a confused look on my face until she crossed her arms at her chest and popped her hip out, showing me she wasn't going to take any lip.

"Okay, T. You are obviously having a moment, so spill it."

I took a deep breath and let it out slowly. "I don't know what happened. I was so deep in thought, I didn't even remember ordering drinks or anything."

"Seriously? I argued with you about whether or not you should have any wine tonight and you looked at the list for like a year before just ordering water."

My eyes widened and I shook my head, trying to remember.

"Holy shit! I think you made a switch, T! No way. It's never happened that fast before. In and out like that."

I couldn't find any words and even if I could, they wouldn't get past the huge lump that was now in the middle of my throat.

"You weren't kidding. He pulled you out."

"What?" I was starting to hyperventilate and wondered if I was going to faint right here on this bathroom floor that looked shiny and clean, but I knew better.

She rolled her eyes and walked over to the sink and fixed her hair in the mirror. "At first, I thought you were exaggerating about Charlie bringing you back at your session. I thought maybe you were just confused, but I couldn't be sure. Stranger things have happened. Now, I believe it completely. I was right, babe. He was made for you." She washed her hands and reapplied some lip gloss. "I thought for sure Lydia was going to be here tonight when you switched on the plane, by the way."

That had been a complete disaster for me. I had been so stressed out about seeing Charlie and thought I had fallen asleep. When we were landing, Benny told me that Lydia made quite an impression on the stewardess. The glare I got from her when we walked off the plane made me think otherwise.

She turned back to me and gave me a hug. "Now. Breathe. We are going to go back out there and you aren't going to worry anymore because you already know how tonight is going to go. Charlie isn't going to leave your side and I, being of a great mind and body, just confirmed that he is pretty much your talisman. Let's have fun!"

I nodded and took a final breath before I felt all the tingling fade away. She was right. I had Charlie. "Okay. Yes. Let's do it. I'm good now. I'm not going to worry about it. I'm going to be me. Just me, no one else."

She didn't say anything more, just unlocked the door and pulled me out with her arm looped through mine again. When we arrived back at our table, the food was waiting and Jake and Trevor were halfway through their plates while Charlie was sitting back watching me. He hadn't touched his food yet.

"Aww, thanks for waiting, Charlie," Benny crooned, then looked over at Jake and Trevor. "Jeez, boys. Don't forget that the plate is inedible. I don't feel like taking a trip to the emergency room tonight, so calm the hell down." Benny was giving Trevor a look that made me burst out laughing.

I covered my mouth and shook my head, still laughing, as I sat down and Charlie wrapped his arm around me. "Don't even try to stop laughing, Tess, because it's the most beautiful thing in the world when it happens."

My smile nearly split my face in half and God, did it feel good.

Chapter 15

Charlie

Pretty sure I would give up my right arm if it meant I could read Tessa's mind. On a good day, I can read her like a book. She wears her emotions on her sleeve and is just as bad as her mother at acting. Today has been a good day, but for the life of me, I can't tell what she is thinking.

Maybe it's because I finally feel like she is letting things happen between us and I never thought that would happen in the first place. I'm in uncharted territory here and haven't the slightest clue what direction my first step should be.

After finishing our meals, we all sat and talked for another thirty minutes before deciding to make our way over to a nearby club to dance. My face was throbbing and my side ached. Trevor handed me a few Advil and a slap on the back, which didn't help the pain. Hopefully, I could make it through the night.

Tess wasn't into drinking and I was happy about that. I didn't know what would happen, but having a clear head was probably best for both of us. I didn't want her to do anything she might regret later.

We walked into the club and I immediately took her hand and wove my fingers through hers. The place was packed tight with all kinds of people and I didn't want to lose her in the chaos. She didn't look very comfortable at first in that tight of a crowd, but Benny whispered something into her ear, well more like shouted it just enough so she could hear her, and Tessa's face changed completely. She looked like whatever was said to her was some kind of epiphany. I was grateful to Benny for being the kind of friend that knew what to say and what to do to bring her back down from wherever she was when she got that distant look on her face.

Tess was always up for anything when we were younger, even though she had a lot of the same worries she has now. She had never let that stop her, though. Tonight, I could tell that she was fighting to be that same girl and for some reason, that broke my heart.

She was perfect just the way she was.

We found a table in the back, far away from the bar, and settled in. Benny and Trevor made their way to get their drinks while Jake hung back with Tess and me. She sat close to me and kept her eyes on the crowd around us. When I looked over at Jake, his eyes were on Tess, and boy did that bring out a whole new set of emotions.

"Hey, Jake? How is Jennifer these days?" I asked loudly. His head snapped over to look at me and when he saw the look on my face, he knew he had been caught.

I couldn't blame him really. Tess was gorgeous, especially tonight with her cheeks flushed and her dark hair falling around her face. The skin of her neck looked softer than silk and it taunted me with every passing second. That was no excuse, though. Jake knew from the beginning who Tess was.

"Oh, she uh, it didn't work out."

Her face turned sympathetic, "Were you two together for very long?"

"Nah, just a few months. It never got too serious."

Damn! One more reason to keep my eye on him. Tess and I may not be exclusive right now, or even really in that kind of relationship officially, but for God's sake, this wasn't high school anymore. She was off limits to everyone else and no amount of 'official' was going to change that.

"Oh, I'm sorry," she said to Jake who had the nerve to look crestfallen.

"Yeah, man, that's too bad," I said.

"Thanks. You know? Sometimes things just don't work out the way you want them to," he replied. He was looking at Tess, but I knew where his mind was. I waited for him to meet my stare, but he never did. Sneaky little bastard.

I really liked the guy. He was always good to me and was always honest, but this? He lost points with this.

I wrapped my arm around Tessa's shoulders and moved close to her ear. "You want to dance with me?"

She was watching the crowd again and her lips twitched into a sly grin at my question. The music was loud and rhythmic and the pulse in my chest matched its cadence watching the look on her face turn to excitement. She nodded her head eagerly and started to stand.

I looked over at Jake and he was watching the crowd. Smart man.

Tess placed her small hand in mine while I led her onto the dance floor with my other hand on the small of her back. She had always loved to dance. Whenever we had showed up to a party, she spent 90% of the night on the dance floor and the other 10% trying to convince me to dance with her. That was if she didn't have a boyfriend at the time. I never liked to dance, always felt like an idiot.

Really, though, I didn't want Tess to know how much she affected me and dancing with her would have been like a neon sign pointing straight to the zipper of my jeans. Over the years, I realized how great it would have been to have just gotten over myself and done it. Dancing was like sex, if you fit together well and you moved together well… well? It worked out in the end.

We made our way to the middle of the floor where Benny and Trevor were now dancing happily and laughing at each other. Trevor was the worst dancer I had ever seen, but Benny looked like she couldn't be happier anywhere else but standing there watching him make a fool out of himself. Interesting.

Tess stepped close to Benny and turned to face me as she started to sway her hips and move to the beat of the music. She always took my breath away when she moved like that. I spent a lot of parties trying to cover myself up as I watched her dance with her friends and ended a lot of nights in the bathroom by myself taking care of things.

Now? Holy shit, she was even sexier than before. She had definitely learned some new moves and had no qualms about showing them to me. Benny smiled my way and started to dance next to her while I just stood there like a moron and watched Tess torture me.

I watched her hips move back and forth and up and down and I felt my fingers twitching, urging me to reach out and touch her. Her hands slowly combed through her hair until it fell loose around her shoulders as she pulled it down.

I groaned at the sight of her and felt my heart beat kick up another notch. She kept moving in front of me as I focused on her hips. Then, I stupidly let my eyes move up to her chest. Her breasts were perfect and moved in rhythm with her. I groaned again and licked my lips before moving my eyes to her face. She was watching me watch her and had the sexiest most sultry smile on her lips. I couldn't contain myself any longer and I stepped forward until our bodies were pressed together and I rested my hands on her hips and started to move with her. I couldn't tear my eyes away from hers. Her smile faded, but she didn't look upset, she looked hungry and if my vision was correct, needy as hell.

I suddenly had no desire to be in that club any longer, but I had no desire to stop dancing with her and knew I wouldn't be able to step away from her any time soon. My hands were pulled to her body like magnets and the curves I skimmed over were better than I imagined.

Her hips moved with mine and her arms wrapped around my shoulders. I buried my nose in her neck, inhaling the minty scent of her hair and pressed my lips to her skin. She gasped, but didn't stop dancing. My hand moved across her lower back and slightly downward until it rested at the very top of those luscious swells that fit so perfectly in her jeans. I pressed her closer and moved my lips up until they touched the sensitive spot just behind her ear.

I felt her press her body impossibly closer and grind against me, sure to feel how much I wanted her right then and there. Her chest rubbed against mine in the most glorious way.

I wanted to pour myself into her and tell her how much I needed her until my soul was laid out before her in a pathetic mess. Yeah, I wanted to be *that* guy. The one who got the girl he knew would devour him every day while he enjoyed every moment of it.

"God, Tess. You drive me crazy!" I muttered in her ear and nipped at her earlobe.

I felt her groan, then she was suddenly moving differently. I watched her turn slowly until her back was against my chest and my hand was splayed across her stomach.

Oh God, she is trying to kill me. I just know it.

She continued to dance, but raised her arm up and back until her fingers were buried in the hair at the nape of my neck, pulling my face back down to the crook of her neck.

If I had stopped moving, everyone in the room would see how badly I was trembling. I had to touch her more. I slowly moved my hand to the side of her waist and up over her ribs, lightly brushing the side of her breast. She inhaled sharply and stiffened for a quick moment until my hand continued to her upper arm, over her elbow, and then reversed back down the same path causing goose bumps to cover her silky skin. My lips tugged into a grin at her reaction and I darted my tongue out to taste the skin at the base of her neck that was now damp with sweat. She tasted better than I imagined and believe me, I imagined it a lot over the years.

Her pulse was thumping wildly and I pressed my lips against the steady beat and closed my eyes. She leaned back into me and slowed her dancing. Just when I thought she was going to turn around and face me again, Jake came through the crowd with his cell phone to his ear and tapped me on the shoulder. I guess he was *not* a smart guy.

"Hey, Charlie. Sorry to interrupt, but we've got a problem," he said and gestured for me to follow him.

I turned back to Tess, who was now facing me and standing close, but looking a little frustrated. "Sorry, I gotta take care of something. You want to come with me and take a break?"

She hesitated for just a moment before nodding and grasping my hand. Benny shouted something in her ear that made her already red cheeks redden even more.

I pulled her through the crowd until I found Jake back at the table arguing with someone on the phone. "Yeah, yeah I know. Okay, here he is." He stood quickly and handed me his phone.

I kept a firm grip on Tess, not sure whether he was going to ask her to dance or not, and put the phone to my ear.

"Yeah?"

"Charlie! We got a situation with Rob. He is threatening to quit because he doesn't think you are taking this thing seriously," Phil, one of the guys who coordinates all the fights and schedules gym time, mumbled through the phone sounding like an angry bear. Rob was my coach and had threatened this several times before. He really just wanted more money from me and didn't give two shits about how serious I was.

"Phil, this isn't something I can take care of right now."

"Well, you can get your ass back to the hotel and talk some sense into him or just let him go. Either way, I figured you would want to be made aware."

I looked up to find Jake leaning into Tess and talking in her ear. She scrunched up her nose while he was talking and tried to pull away, but she was already plastered against my side. When Jake pulled back, she shook her head and said, "No, I'm pretty tired, but thanks anyway."

I smiled to myself thinking she could have been a little meaner about it and I wouldn't have cared, but she was nice all the time and it was one of the things I loved about her. I was so focused on her that I completely missed what Phil was saying.

"Sorry, what was that?"

"I think you need to come back, man. He is out of control and I don't think any of us are going to be able to calm him down."

"Alright, I'll head back now. See you in a bit."

I handed the phone back to Jake who was still staring at Tess, but not so obviously now. Tess was watching me and waiting for me to tell her what was going on.

"I gotta head back to the hotel and calm some people down," I said in her ear and noticed she didn't cringe or try to pull away from me. Good to know.

"I hope it's nothing too bad, Charlie. I feel like I've taken you away from stuff you need to do." She was looking at me with a guilty frown and her brow furrowed. I bent and kissed the spot between her brows and felt her relax a little.

"Beautiful, believe me, I would rather be with you than anywhere else."

She beamed up at me and I wanted so badly to kiss her until she was gasping for air.

Of course, Jake had to go and interrupt that, too.

"I can walk you back later, Tessa, if you want to stay longer."

Seriously? Did he really not know me at all? I wanted to punch him in the nose just for thinking that would be okay with me. Then, I realized it wasn't really my choice. If Tess wanted to stay, I wasn't going to force her to leave with me. I wanted her to have a good time and so far, I think she had.

"Thanks, Jake, but if it's okay with you, Charlie," she looked back up at me, "I would like to go back now. I'm pretty worn out and I really could use a shower."

I didn't even look at Jake to see the rejection on his face, I just wrapped my arm around her and said, "Let's get out of here then."

We made our way to the exit while I texted Trevor to let him know we were leaving. He immediately responded to let me know he would keep an eye on Benny. I laughed to myself. Of course he would. I wondered if he even remembered who Ellie was. No matter. I wasn't going to say anything if Tess wasn't. Which she wasn't by the look on her face when I told her what Trevor said. For some reason, I had the feeling she had planned this all along.

We walked hand in hand back to the hotel and talked about the fight. She asked me questions about how things were judged if there wasn't a knockout and how I felt about beating up another guy for money.

I laughed, "It's not really about the money for me. I like the sport and it's definitely a way for me to get my mind off of... other things. Keeps me in shape, too, so that's a plus. The money is just a bonus. As far as beating up a guy, I was nervous at first, then realized they were going to beat me up if I didn't beat them first. It's all a part of the game so you don't really think about it much."

She shrugged and kept her eyes forward, "I just worry about you getting hurt. I mean, you have that cut above your eyebrow and a big bruise under your eye and I have no doubt some bruised ribs or something. I guess I just don't see getting beat up being worth it."

I smiled to myself. She was worried about me and I felt a massive amount of pride in knowing that. I squeezed her hand, "I don't think I'll be doing this much longer. I don't have the same motivations that I used to."

She looked confused, but I didn't elaborate for her. I had gotten into fighting because it kept me busy and kept my mind straight when I thought I would go crazy with worry for her. I needed a distraction so I wouldn't lose my mind thinking about her. The fighting kept me grounded. Now? I didn't need a distraction from anything.

Shit, I was a mess and I wanted to weep from the joy of it. She was back in my life now, a mess was welcomed at this point.

I opened the heavy glass door of the hotel lobby for her and led her through with my hand at the small of her back. Her shirt had ridden up a little and my fingers brushed the soft skin above the waistband of her jeans. A shiver ran down her body which immediately made my entire body light on fire. She was just as affected by me as I was by her.

The elevator ride was crowded so I didn't get a chance to really talk to her more. I didn't mind, though. She leaned into me and rested her head on my shoulder as we listened to the cheesy elevator music playing over the speakers. By the time we made it to our floor, I was just as turned on as I was when we were dancing and her body was moving against mine.

I couldn't imagine ever having enough of her. I didn't want enough of her. I wanted all of her. I had loved her for so long, I don't think I would ever be able to figure out how not to.

She rummaged through her purse as we made our way down the hall to her door. I didn't want to be presumptuous and think that she would stay in my room. Even though I wanted her to. Benny was going to freak if it didn't happen, but I couldn't force her into anything. She had enough things to worry about at the moment. I wanted her so badly, but I had waited this long. I could wait for her forever.

"Son of a bitch! I can't believe her!" She snapped as she threw the strap of her purse back over her shoulder and shook her head before she looked up at me.

"What?"

"Benny! She must have taken the key out of my purse while we were in that room after the fight. I have no way to get into the room."

I think Benny might have become my new best friend. Trevor was no match for her. I wanted to smile, but I had already been punched in the face a few too many times tonight. "What are you going to do?"

She ran a hand through her hair and looked down at her feet. "I don't know. I guess I'll have to go down to the desk and try to get another one."

This was it. She had kept me at a distance ever since she had come back home, except for tonight. Something must have changed since the session with Dr. Geoffrey. She had been more open to me and to being around me. I didn't want to push too far or too hard, but I would be a fool to not hold onto whatever changes she made.

"Why don't you stay in my room?"

Her head popped up and her eyes widened in surprise. *Oh God, you screwed it up. Way to go. Think of a recovery. Quick!*

"I just... " Ah, hell. What am I trying to do? "I have two rooms in my suite. Trevor was going to take the extra one, but I really don't think he would mind if he ended up staying in this suite with Benny. Plus, it's a pain in the ass to go all the way down to get another key." I was rambling at that point, but had no way of stopping it. "I know you probably don't think it's a good idea, but I think it's a great idea and I am not trying to get you to--"

"Charlie."

Deep breath. "Yeah?"

She smiled and put her hand on my arm and squeezed. "I'll stay with you. I don't want to get another key, plus, I don't have any luggage so it's not like I need to grab anything. I was just going to borrow some of Benny's clothes for bed but..."

"I have clothes you can use. Not much, but we can send your clothes down to laundry tonight and then go shopping for you tomorrow." Okay, now my hands were shaking and my heart was pounding against my ribs. Part of me was planning out a way to seduce her somehow. Yeah, the complete dick part of me. Pun intended. The other part, the part where I knew I loved Tess more than I needed the air that I breathe and where I wasn't going to screw this up, that part was telling me to just be cool and take her to my suite, show her to her room, go to fix whatever crap Rob had caused, then come back and go to sleep. I needed that part of me to be strong because Tess didn't need me jumping her.

"Okay, I really need a shower after the day I've had, so let's go now," she chuckled.

I didn't know what to say because now I was picturing her in the shower and having a hard time walking down the hall to my door. Good God, my brain was a winner tonight.

I unlocked the door to my suite and led her through. Ever since I arrived in New York, it had always been packed with people getting ready for the fight. Now, it was completely empty and quiet.

"That door on the right is the extra room. It has its own shower and everything."

She nodded and clasped her hands together in front of her, folding her fingers over each other one by one, unfolding them, then doing it again. She was nervous.

I rested my hand on her shoulder until she looked at me. "I'm going to go take care of this situation. I don't know how long I'll be. I imagine it will be a while, but... if I don't see you again tonight, sleep well."

"Thanks, Charlie," she mumbled with a grin.

"No problem. Oh, and my suit case is in my room. There should be a couple shirts and some extra boxers or something you can use. Feel free to look through it." I backed up to the door and winked at her making her blush all over. "Beautiful."

She smiled again, but looked away too soon. Walking out that door was almost impossible.

***

The whole conversation with Rob took about five minutes. I was gone for a total of thirty. Ten minutes to calm everyone down and find out what was going on, five minutes to talk and find out that the guy was just playing for a bigger paycheck, and ten minutes for the rest of them to calm me down after Rob slipped and insulted Tess resulting in his ass getting fired and me wondering where to find a new coach. That is, if I continued to do what I was doing. I had been thinking about it and thought maybe I could open up my own gym and do some training for other guys who were looking to get serious in this career. It was definitely an option.

I heard the blow dryer going in Tessa's room as I walked into the suite. What I would give to watch that. I know it sounds weird, but watching Tess do anything slightly domestic would be a dream come true.

I knew for a fact that her bedtime routine took a little while. I had spent many nights at her house ready to watch a movie and waiting for her to get her cute ass back to me. I never watched, but I always wanted to. If that makes me a creep, then so be it. I hurried into my room before my thoughts took me any closer to hers.

"Get it together, Charlie." I had to keep saying it to myself over and over.

I stripped down and walked into my bathroom, shutting the door behind me. Quick shower, fix up my face with some bandages, then bed. That was the plan.

I could still smell Tess on my shirt and it took me a few minutes to finally convince myself to take the thing off so I could shower. The shower was incredible for my sore muscles. The bruises on my side were a whole lot darker and the cut above my eye was throbbing like hell.

I always hated patching myself up. I could always let someone else do it, but when I was alone and had no one else to turn to, it was awful. For a guy who sees a lot of cuts and bruises, who *gets* a lot of cuts and bruises, I didn't handle it too well.

I don't know how long I was in there, a while. I had my towel wrapped around my hips and took my time reapplying the few tiny bandages I needed. I sat on the closed toilet for a good few minutes just thinking about all the things Tess was going through and what I needed to do to be there for her.

After her appointment, I decided I needed to get a handle on this thing. I had found a couple of books on dissociative identity disorder and had been reading them religiously. She seemed convinced that integrating the alters was the best thing to do. After reading as much as I could on it, I had been convinced that there was more to it than just therapy.

I needed to figure out what I could do to show her that no matter what, I wasn't going anywhere. She was it for me.

I finally stood, gingerly, and opened the door. I froze after grabbing the frame for support.

Tess was sitting on my bed, dressed in my gray dress shirt and striped boxers with her endless legs crossed and head bent down looking through a book.

Yeah, she's trying to kill me.

Chapter 16

Tessa

I had spent more time in the shower than I originally intended. That time was spent thinking about Charlie and dancing and what his hands felt like at the small of my back when he led me into a room. I couldn't stop myself from thinking about what it would be like to be kissed by him. Then I got upset. I *had* been kissed by him, I just didn't remember it.

I didn't know Charlie had come back and never heard him come in. Probably because the shower was loud, then the blow dryer was loud and I didn't think he would be back anytime soon. By the time I finished drying my hair, I realized that I never grabbed any clothes from his suitcase.

Benny was probably wishing she was a fly on the wall at this point.

At the club, she had reminded me a few times to just let things happen. As a result, I had allowed Charlie to turn me on more than I had ever been turned on before. He was an incredible dancer and his hands… oh, his hands knew what to do. I thought I was going to pass out when he had pressed his lips against my neck and tasted me. I had been about to turn around and just kiss him when Jake showed up on the dance floor. He was a nice guy and all, but he had started to get on my nerves when he wouldn't stop staring at me the whole time. Thankfully, Charlie didn't leave my side.

I wrapped the towel around me and hurried over to his room to find his suitcase on a plush chair next to a nightstand. There wasn't much left in there. A t-shirt and some jeans, which I assumed he would wear the next day, a gray dress shirt and several pairs of boxers and socks.

I decided on the dress shirt and some boxers and quickly put them on. I turned to go back to my room when I noticed the book on his nightstand.

A book about dissociative identity disorder.

Now, I don't know about other people, but this made me smile. I didn't feel any kind of anger or intrusion at all. He couldn't possibly know how much him reading something like this actually meant to me. I opened it up, intending to look through it quickly, but couldn't seem to put it down. There were case studies galore and testimonies from family members, friends, employers, and all kinds of people about living with someone who had multiple personalities. I was engrossed in one particular case study of a young teenage girl who was struggling through school, but receiving treatment and doing well despite her having ten different alters.

I didn't hear the door open, but I felt the warmth hit me from the steam in the bathroom.

Apparently, Charlie was back already and I was sitting on his bed, in his clothes, while he was wrapped in only a towel and holding onto the door frame with both hands looking like a man ready for dinner.

"Oh my God. I'm so sorry. I didn't realize you were back. I didn't hear you in there and… and… holy shit your side is black and blue, Charlie!" My eyes had roamed his entire body, taking in each defined muscle in its entirety. He had an edible six pack that could almost be mistaken for an eight pack and his pectorals were hard and beckoning my hands to run over them. His towel, wrapped low on his hips to reveal that delicious V, was my worst enemy. It was a damn efficient towel. I had continued to let my gaze roam over him until my mind registered the bruises from his fight.

I stood quickly, dropping the book back on the nightstand, and rushed over to him to get a closer look. Stupid men. Why did they think that getting beat up was worthy of a career. I mean, I had seen mixed martial arts throughout the years plenty, and it was fun to watch because I didn't know the guys. But this was Charlie. *My* Charlie. I couldn't let him get all busted up just because it kept his mind busy and had a good paycheck.

I ran my fingers over the bruise on his ribs, he flinched, but didn't move away from me. When I looked up at his face, his expression was still the same as before. His breathing was shallow and the rise and fall of his chest was mesmerizing.

The bandages that were supposed to be holding his cut together were loose and I immediately reached up to fix them. He held still, so stoic, so quiet, but I felt his eyes on me, burning through my skin and caressing me.

I tried to ignore it.

I fixed the bandages and dropped my hand to his cheek and fingered the bruise under his eye. Without thinking, I stood on my tip toes and reached up to place a kiss there, thinking that somehow it would feel better just by kissing it. His eyes were closed when I pulled away and I could see the rapid thrum of his pulse in his throat.

That's when I looked at his shoulder and saw the tattoo I had been wondering about earlier. At first, it looked like a bunch of celtic knots shaped into some sort of design. It was beautiful and elegant. Then I took a closer look and gasped. It was in the shape of a 'T'.

"Charlie…" I looked up into his now open eyes as I ran my fingers over the graceful curves of each knot. "Is this…?"

He looked down at my fingers with heavy lidded eyes and nodded.

"When?"

He cleared his throat and moved his beautiful, bright green eyes back to mine. "After I couldn't find you in Kansas. Since I couldn't be with *you*, I wanted you with *me*."

I caught my breath and kept my eyes locked with his, smoldering and hungry. Mine were probably needy as hell and begging him to take me. I wanted to cry and scream, run and fight, all at once. How stupid we had been. How stupid and ignorant *I* had been.

He slowly bent his head down close to mine until our lips were just a breath away. I took a slow breath and basked in the heat radiating off of him. I wanted him to kiss me, to possess me. I wanted him to erase all the years we had missed together and tell me that everything was going to be alright. I wanted to turn back time and realize what I had in front of me. Right now though, I just wanted him to kiss me until I couldn't breathe anymore.

Then his lips crashed to mine in a soul searing, heart wrenching kiss. The passion of it being built up for years with every thought and fantasy each of us had, with every gutting decision we had made, it was an inferno that could never be tamed.

Oh, he kissed me, and I couldn't breathe anymore. His arms came around my waist and held me against him as he ran his tongue along my bottom lip, seeking entrance.

I didn't hesitate. He plunged his tongue between my lips and moaned when mine tangled with his. One hand clutched at the small of my back while the other made a searing path up between my shoulder blades to the nape of my neck to bury itself in my hair and hold me against him. My hands clawed at his shoulders as he angled his head to deepen the kiss, taking even more of my breath away and causing my knees to knock. He held me up against him when I couldn't stand any longer, locking me in his strong arms.

When he broke the kiss, much too soon, we were both gasping for air. He rested his forehead against mine and looked into my eyes.

"I love you, Tess. I never stopped loving you."

He didn't wait for a response and before I could blink, his mouth was on mine again and he had turned to press me against the wall next to the bathroom doorway, gripping the backs of my thighs with his hands and hauling me up to cradle him between my legs.

His towel, by some stupid goddamn miracle, stayed wrapped around his hips even when I wrapped my legs around him with his encouragement. He never broke the kiss and now that he had me anchored against the wall with his hard body, his one hand moved up to the back of my neck while his other firmly gripped my ass and pulled me toward him even tighter than I thought possible.

I was still clinging to his shoulders and decided it was time for me to do myself a favor and move my hands where I wanted them. I ran my fingers through his hair and tugged his face closer so I could kiss him more thoroughly. He moaned into my mouth before pulling his soft lips away and running them down over my jaw and down the column of my throat.

"Tess. You taste incredible, God, I could kiss you forever."

I couldn't hold back the whimper of pleasure at his words. Forever wasn't long enough.

In the back of my mind, someone was questioning what was happening, whether it was smart or responsible. I ignored the voice and held Charlie against my neck as he devoured me with kisses. It was just me here. No one else.

He kissed down to the open skin just below the collar of his dress shirt, that I was still wearing for some ridiculous reason, and warmth shot down my belly and between my open legs. The heat must have been intense against his lower stomach because he responded with a growl and supported my weight with both hands on my ass as he pulled away from the wall and turned to the bed. I didn't want to let go of him and it seemed he couldn't let go of me either, so we both fell to the bed, still clutching each other frantically and exploring the planes of each other's bodies with our hands.

He kept himself between my thighs and ran his hand down to the back of my knee to hitch my leg up higher so he could grind against me similar to the way he did while we had been dancing. Even though the towel was blocking my view, I could feel how much he wanted me. His lips stayed on the skin at the base of my neck, sucking and nipping until I was dizzy from the pleasurable pulse of blood running through my body. I don't think I had ever felt anything so incredible in my life. He was everywhere, surrounding me with his warmth and filling each breath with his incredible scent.

He finally moved up my neck and jaw and took my lips again, caressing them tenderly, but passionately. His body was a fire pressing me down into the mattress and I had no qualms about being burned. I needed more.

I rolled my hips up and arched my back, telling him what my body wanted. What my whole being wanted from him. He gasped and broke our kiss but stayed close enough so we were still breathing the same air, still able to see into the deepest part of each other as his green eyes looked into mine.

"Charlie."

"Tell me what you want, Tess."

I was suddenly nervous and felt a blush run from my toes to my face. He grinned as he always did when I blushed. I wrapped my hands around the back of his head and dug my fingers into his hair, needing to touch him more. He moved a hand to press into the mattress next to my head and supported his weight as he waited patiently for my directions. The muscles in his arm flexed and oh boy, he was fit. I had no idea what I wanted. At least, I couldn't pin point one specific thing.

I wanted everything.

I wanted all of him.

"You, Charlie."

He leaned in and swept his lips over mine so softly, if it wasn't for the heat coming off of him, I would have never felt it. "You've always had me, love. You own me."

"Then, please. Show me what I've got."

He smiled, baring his perfect white teeth to my eyes, and then tearing it away from me by moving down to the collar of that damn shirt that was still on me. He pulled one side of the collar open and kissed a path over to my collar bone where he used those beautiful teeth to nip me and send lightening down my body. His fingers barely brushed over my still covered breast to find the buttons running down the middle of my torso.

He tugged and maneuvered each button open, leaving the material covering me, the anticipation nearly choking me. His lips followed the same path, branding the inches of skin that ran down between my breasts and over my pierced belly button. He groaned when he saw the tiny jewel dangling over my navel.

"Holy shit, that's so sexy."

I giggled quietly and closed my eyes as he opened the bottom of the shirt to see the piercing more clearly.

"When did you do that?" he asked breathlessly.

I opened my eyes and saw the hungry look on his face, barely able to use the strength of my vocal chords to push the words out.

"Lydia did it a few months after I left. It's the one thing we both agree on."

He smiled wickedly, "Remind me to thank her when I see her next."

He couldn't have known how much his words meant to me. He expected me to switch eventually and it didn't seem to bother him in the least. Even in the heat of passion, my love for him burst out of me. I felt my eyes pool with tears and when his image became too blurry, I let go of my need to hold them back and let the greediness I had to see him clearly, take over. They fell out of the corners of my eyes and down to my hair.

"Oh, baby. Don't cry, please, it kills me when you cry," he murmured and wiped my tears with his warm fingers. He looked worried that he had said something wrong when he had said the one thing that was right.

"I love you, Charlie," I whispered. "I love you so much."

His eyes widened for just a moment before he came crashing down against me, his mouth covering mine and showing me how much those words meant to him.

After a few moments, he tore away from my mouth and kissed down my neck again while his hand slowly moved under one side of the unbuttoned shirt, pushing it away from my skin and revealing a part of my body that hadn't been touched by any man, but longed to be touched by *him.* His lips stopped kissing me as he lifted up to pull away the other side. The rumble in his chest told me he approved and the gleam in his eyes showed his need to possess me.

"Exquisite. Absolutely perfect," he stated and moved his fingers over the sensitive skin at the top of my breasts, making me shiver before moving his touch down to press his palm against the tight protruding bud that ached for him. I gasped and threw my head back. He bent his head and kissed, licked, worshipped one breast while his hand kneaded, caressed, and engulfed the other in its warmth. I arched my back, pushing my breasts closer to him, begging for more.

After ravishing one, he moved to the other and did it all over again, murmuring soft words against my skin and making the ache between my legs grow stronger. I writhed beneath him, moaning at his assault on my breasts and burning each touch to memory.

I had been clutching the blankets so hard, my knuckles were white and now ached from the grip they had. I wanted to touch him. Needed to touch his skin and dig my fingers into the hard muscles of his back, but his touch was almost too much and I couldn't focus enough to move my arms. When I finally broke through and gained control of my limbs, I did exactly what I wanted. My fingers dug into the muscles of his back, hard and twitching at my touch, and pulled his body closer to mine. He pulled his lips from my chest and moved his body down mine until his mouth found the jewel at my navel where he dipped his tongue and sent a whole new rush of liquid heat down my belly. He grasped my hips and pulled them against his chest. I was still in his boxers, but I knew he could feel the heat beneath them, reaching out for him.

God, he was good at this.

My hands could only reach the back of his shoulders now so I moved them to his silky brown hair.

His fingers curled and slipped under the waistband of the boxers to begin pulling them down my legs. I froze when I realized that he probably didn't know I was still a virgin and now my nerves were colliding against each other because I honestly had no clue what I was doing and no idea how to please him.

"What's wrong, love? Do you want me to stop?" Charlie asked, concern lacing his husky voice as his hands paused and he focused on my face.

I hesitated and tried to catch my breath. I didn't want him to stop, but I didn't want my inexperience to ruin anything.

"What is it, Tess? If you want me to stop, just say the word."

I took a deep breath and met his gaze. This man, who loved me despite all my issues, was willing to be pushed away if I wanted to push him, just to make me feel better. I was going to be honest and I wasn't going to let my nervousness get in the way. "I'm... I've never done this before. I-I..."

He stayed silent, but I could see the concern in his eyes soften and turn to understanding. "You're still a virgin?" he asked respectfully.

I just nodded quickly and closed my eyes as I started rambling, "I don't have any clue what to expect. I have never done *anything* even close to this and I mean, I love what you are doing and I know that I can trust you, but I just don't know how to make it good for you or if I should be prepared for it to be painful. I'm sorry, I have no experience with this and I can't imagine the kind of pressure that puts on--"

"Tess, look at me, love." His voice held more than just a trace of amusement and I knew before I opened my eyes that he would be smiling that gorgeous smile that would erase all of my fears.

He didn't disappoint. As soon as I saw that smile, I relaxed.

"You have nothing to be sorry about and you *can* trust me. God, baby, you have no idea how happy it makes me to know that I'm the only man to touch you like this. To love you like this. And pressure? The only pressure I feel is the need to make this good for *you*. I don't want to hurt you and if you still want this, I'll do my best to make sure the pain is minimal." His fingers brushed through my hair and he kissed my face while he spoke. "The only question I have is whether or not we need to use a condom because I don't have any and I don't think I'll live if we get to that point and I can't be inside you."

I couldn't stop my smile. He was incredible and his words turned me on impossibly more. "I want this more than anything, Charlie. And I have been on the pill for a while now, you know, in case one of the alters…"

His brow furrowed and I could see the question in his eyes.

"I made it a point to be checked shortly before I left the facility. I didn't want to *not* know if something like that had happened without me remembering it."

He grinned and kissed me hard. "Then don't worry about making this good for me. It's with you. That's all that matters to me. It will be amazing." He kissed back down to where he had left off and tugged the boxers down while kissing the, until now, untouched skin as it was revealed. "Let me love you now."

No way this could get any better.

But it did. He slipped the boxers over my ankles and feet and leaned back, taking me in. The shirt was still covering my arms and pulled behind my shoulders. I wanted it off. He must have read my mind because he helped me slip it off and tossed it across the room. His eyes slowly roamed over every inch of my skin, causing goose bumps to rise over my entire body. He smiled and even though my mind tried to force me to look away and hide in embarrassment, my eyes wouldn't leave him.

"Fifteen years," he breathed and smiled when my brow furrowed in confusion. "It was worth the wait."

Understanding seeped into my mind. We had known each other for fifteen years. He had waited for me all that time, rarely spending time with anyone else in grade school, only going on a handful of dates in high school, and only God knows what he had been doing since I had left, but he had been holding out for me. I wasn't naïve enough to think that he had saved himself for me. But I knew what he meant. It was the same for me in some ways. I fought against it for so long, but I had always known he was the one for me. The only one I could ever want.

My thoughts were interrupted when his hands moved to the towel around his hips and pulled it off. If I ever questioned if he was a perfectly built man before, I didn't anymore. He was kneeling upright between my legs, gazing down at me, and even knowing what was about to happen, I couldn't avoid taking in every detail of him.

His shoulders were broad and strong, his biceps flexed with anticipation and so smooth I wanted to lick them. His chest puffed out as I perused down his body like he was proud that I couldn't take my eyes off of him. I never thought I would think this before about any man, but his erection was a thing of beauty, so rigid and… big. I gulped, knowing it would fit, but also knowing my luck wasn't the greatest before now.

He made a sound in the back of his throat that was part moan part growl. "Tess, I feel like you are about to devour me, then ask for seconds."

I didn't respond, but the rise and fall of my chest was more pronounced as I tried to find my breath, and the gasps I was making were probably extremely unattractive. "I… you are…"

Slowly, oh so damn slowly, he ran his hands from my knees, up my thighs, then covered my body with his keeping just one hand pressed to the crease at the top of my thigh. He ground his erection against the aching flesh between my legs, sending me soaring, and kissed me deeply. "I love you, Tess."

I kissed him back, giving him everything I had and letting go of all my doubts. His hand moved over my mound and I bucked against him at the shock of sensation.

"Shhh, just relax, love. I'll take care of you," he murmured against my skin and kissed his way back down my body, taking the long way as he licked and kissed my full, heavy breasts again. His finger slipped into my folds and found me wet and pulsing.

"Christ, you're so wet. That's for me?"

"Yes. Oh… Charlie… please…" I couldn't form a coherent thought as his fingers explored my folds and found my opening. I felt a pressure building in my womb and it begged for release.

He continued kissing down my stomach and over my bare mound. The first flick of his tongue sent me spiraling out of control. I cried out his name and struggled to keep my body still for him. He had a hand settled on my hip while his other continued to explore and make me insane. My lungs burned from the effort it took to breathe as I focused on his touch. He found the tiny bundle of nerves easily and kissed me there, pulling it between his lips and gently sucking. I felt a fingertip dip inside me as he flicked his tongue over the tiny bud.

The pressure built and built until I could no longer stand it. That's when I fell apart. My entire body tightened, then blew apart in wave after wave. I don't know what I shouted, but I know I did and when I came back down, he was there to catch me.

His eyes were heavy lidded and his breathing ragged. His fingers were still moving around and he had pressed one deep into my passage when I came. "That was so fucking beautiful," he breathed.

I thought he was going to come back up my body and kiss me the way he had before, but he just settled back down between my thighs.

"Again."

Again? My body could barely move, how the hell was I supposed to do that again? How did it even happen? "Charlie, I don't think--"

"I *do.* One more time, and then you'll be ready for me."

My eyes rolled to the back of my head as he renewed his ministrations on my body. He knew exactly how to touch me and would probably ever be the only one that knew.

The pressure built quickly as he pressed a second finger inside me, stroking me and finding a spot inside that made me forget who I was. He licked and kissed and groaned against me, his warm breath sending sparks up my spine. I was close again.

"There you are, I can feel how close you are. Let it happen, baby. Let me feel you clench around my fingers. Come for me, Tess."

I wouldn't have been able to stop it if I wanted to. My body detonated around him as I cried out, making him groan. Before I could recover, he was on top of me, kissing my neck and rubbing his body over mine. His lips found mine at the same time his thick erection found my entrance. He gave a small thrust and was barely inside of me, stretching me. It wasn't uncomfortable, but I wanted him deeper. I tried to lift my hips, but he steadied me.

"Slowly, sweetheart."

His fingers moved back to that wonderful, sensitive bud and massaged with his thumb in slow circles, making me melt and open wider for him. He pressed in a little further and paused again, waiting for me to stretch around him. His thumb never stopped and I quickly found the precipice once again.

"Oh, God, Charlie!" I cried as my body tightened.

"Again."

I came at his command and he thrust to the hilt. There was barely a moment of pain, a pinch that registered in the back of my mind as he broke through my virginity, then absolute fullness, but the pleasure overpowered everything else.

He was watching me, holding perfectly still as he filled me and his face was rapturous. He kissed my shoulder and I wrapped my arms around his neck. "You okay?"

I smiled and trembled against him, "Yes."

"Good, because you feel so damn good, I don't think I will survive if we stop."

"Please, don't stop," I said and lifted my hips, making him hiss a curse and grind against me in return. He started to pull back and I whimpered at the loss, but it was short lived. Just when I thought he would leave me, he slowly thrust back in, hitting a deep part of me that had waited forever for him. He didn't pause again, he repeated the movement, making me roll my eyes back and sending fire to my veins.

"Open them, love. Open your eyes," he whispered.

When I did, he quickened his thrusts, but held me close, smoothing a hand down over the side of my breast and under me to lift my hips up, finding that same spot from before. I felt the pressure once more, the build up that would probably push me into unconsciousness, but I didn't care about that. I wanted it, reached for it and once again, found it. With a roar, he faltered and his final thrusts were untamed until he stiffened against me and spilled himself inside me whispering my name tenderly.

When he collapsed against me, he murmured words of love, over and over, and buried his face in my neck while we waited for our hearts to slow down.

"Amazing," I muttered and pulled his face to mine to cover him with kisses.

He smiled and did the same until our lips found each other, ending in a tender and emotional kiss that made me dizzy with happiness. "Phenomenal," he breathed.

We kissed and caressed, both sated and spent. After a while, he moved off of me, pulling me with him and holding me in his arms as I rested my head in the nook of his shoulder and stretched my arm across his stomach. His fingers lightly moved across the skin of my arm, back and forth, forcing my eyes to close from the pleasure of it.

I was right about the unconsciousness and I gladly went.

Chapter 17

Charlie

I held Tess for hours, dozing in and out, but wanting to watch her sleep in my arms more than anything else. She looked so peaceful when she slept. It used to be my favorite time to watch her, but now? When she came, I knew there wasn't anything in this world that was more beautiful than that. She didn't hold anything back and she didn't have to with me. I had never felt the pressing need to give all of myself to someone until tonight. She had all of me now and I had no plans to take any of that back.

She loved me.

God, when she said it to me, I thought I would die from the joy of it.

I swept my fingers through her hair and listened to her breathing. The throb in my face and at my side was very noticeable now, but there was no way I was going to move from that spot. I turned to look at the clock on the nightstand, 5:00 AM. Still pretty early. I had to remind myself that Tess had been travelling most of the day before and hadn't stopped until I had thoroughly loved her and she finally drifted off to sleep.

Hundreds of questions kept running through my mind. Where do we go from here? Can I ask her to come move in with me or is it too soon? What is *she* thinking now?

I know I sounded like a girl, but these were questions I needed answers to so I didn't screw anything up. I had waited fifteen years, no way was I going to mess it up now.

Tess stirred in my arms and my fingers froze in her hair. Her eyes flickered open and she laid still for several long seconds seeming to take everything in. Her head was now on my chest and her arm was still wrapped around my stomach. She slowly lifted her head and looked up at me.

"Hi."

"Hi," she replied and if I loved her voice before, the just woke up, scratchy version was sexy beyond all reason. She lifted up and tried to move off of me, "Sorry. I'm kind of smothering you."

I pulled her back against me and held her tight, "I liked it."

She chuckled and relaxed against me while I resumed playing with her hair. She rang her fingers over my chest, back and forth, exploring the dusting of hair I had there and it tickled like crazy, but I didn't want her to stop so I bit the inside of my cheek to distract myself.

"Thank you, for last night," she whispered.

I sat up and put my back against the headboard, bringing her with me. "Why would you thank me for something I have wanted to do for years?"

She smiled and faced me, our noses a mere inch apart, looking in my eyes and finding something there that she apparently hadn't seen before by the look on her face. "When did you know that you loved me?"

"I told you that already, didn't I? That night at your mom's?"

She nodded. "But tell me again, everything. Please?"

I kissed the tip of her nose and moved her to straddle my lap. She wrapped her hands around the back of my neck and pressed close to my chest. I had been hard when I woke up, and her sitting like that only made it worse. Or better, I guess. "Fourth grade, my first day of school as the new kid, first recess of the day. You were playing hopscotch and wearing your multicolored scarf that I swear was brighter than the sun. I couldn't take my eyes off of you. Your hair was braided and bounced up and down… you were beautiful."

She was smiling so wide, my heart nearly leapt out of my chest. "I never saw you until later that year. You were walking toward me during recess and I was so excited, but then something happened and I never got to talk to you. What was it?"

"Amanda. She came running from the playground shouting about how your brother had beat up Michael Stower for spitting on the girls. I remember thinking that I needed to meet him before he beat *me* up," I laughed.

"But, you never talked to me after that. Not until Michael…"

"I was too shy. I never got the chance to do it and every time I did, someone else would get your attention and I was too embarrassed to do anything about it, until Michael dumped the sand on you. I had been watching you play and saw him coming toward you. I didn't get there fast enough, but I think I took care of things, don't you?"

She laughed, a full belly laugh that made me smile and want to ravish her all over again. "Yeah you did. After that, we were inseparable. You were always there for me and I knew that we would be friends for a long time."

She kissed me quickly and ran her fingers through my hair, making my eyes roll back and a moan slip from my lips. She giggled and ran her fingers over my face, studying me as if she had been wanting to for so long, but never got the chance.

"And you? When did you know, love?"

She blushed, but didn't look away, "It might have been that day you saved me, but when I think back, I think I really knew I was in love with you our first day of sixth grade. We were in homeroom and I was assigned to sit next to Jimmy Marshall. I always hated him, but since we had the same last name, I was stuck next to him all the time. You were on the other side of him and when you saw how mad I was, you begged the teacher to switch the two of you so I wouldn't have to sit by him. He was always pulling my hair and drawing on my clothes or tipping over my pencil box. You agreed to stay after school every day for a month and help the teacher clean up the room in order for her to switch you."

She sighed at the memory and seemed like she was looking off in the distance, like she was seeing it all again. "I knew I loved you then. You were always saving me or doing things to make life easier for me. I think that's why Trevor liked you so much and why Mom never had a problem with just the two of us always hanging out. They knew I was safe with you."

I pulled her toward me and kissed her tenderly. All those years of wondering. All the years of being scared to say anything to her about how I felt because I was afraid I would lose her friendship.

"Guess we both should have said something, huh? Seems like we could have saved ourselves a lot of heartache."

She shook her head, "No, I think things would have turned out a lot worse. We might have broken up and torn our friendship apart, who knows? I can't beat myself up about it anymore because I can't change it."

"You are right," I muttered and pulled her close again, this time kissing her hard and long until she was breathless and flushed. "I'm not going to waste anymore time, though." I moved my hand between her legs, finding her already wet. She gasped and kissed me, hungrily. When I pressed a finger inside of her, her hips rolled forward, trying to pull me in deeper. I couldn't wait any longer. I grabbed her hips and positioned her above me. She held onto my shoulders and sank down over me, wrapping me up in her tight sheath. She was heaven.

We moved together perfectly and when I bent to take her breast in my mouth, she threw her head back and moaned. She was close and I could feel her muscles tightening around me. She just needed a little push.

I moved my hand between us and massaged that small bundle of nerves that would send her over the edge. She started riding me harder and faster, throwing away all her reservations. I smiled at the revelation that Tess was even more wild and passionate than I gave her credit for.

I sucked her nipple into my mouth harder and quickened the motion of my fingers.

"Yes, Charlie. Oh, God…"

She came violently and her muscles tightened in waves, pulling my own orgasm out of me as I slammed my hips up against her. "Tess," I cried as I filled her up, pumping into her slowly as the pleasure took me.

Heaven.

Later that morning, Trevor and Benny showed up and forced us to go out. I was perfectly fine staying in bed all day with Tess, but apparently she needed some clothes if she was going to stay with me until Sunday. I thoroughly disagreed, but we went shopping anyway.

Tess was reluctant to let me buy her things, but I wouldn't take no for an answer and with Benny on my side, she had no way of putting up a fight. I did agree to only get her enough for her stay in New York, which consisted of a couple pairs of pants, some shirts that Benny said were an absolute necessity, a little black dress to go out to a fancy dinner that night, and two pairs of shoes. Tess was furious and Benny kept throwing clothes over the door of the dressing room and forcing her to try them on. I loved spoiling her.

At one point, Benny asked for my credit card so she could take Tess to get something 'extra special'. I had no clue what it could be, but by the look on her face, I knew I would like it so I handed the card over and they said they would meet up with us at the hotel later on. Trevor and I hauled the shopping bags with us.

He was quiet as we made our way back to the hotel. I had no idea what to say to him either. I had just been with his sister and the situation was awkward to say the least, so I decided to ask him about Benny.

"So, how long did you guys stay out last night? Benny seems like the all-nighter type."

He smirked and pulled off his sunglasses, "Yeah, she is. We didn't get back until four this morning and what do you know? My sister wasn't in her room when we got there so instead of going back to the suite and finding out that you two had… ugh!... I just stayed in the other bed in their room."

"I figured you would."

"Yeah, well, I had some good company, I guess."

I raised my eyebrows in question, "Did you two…?"

"No! No, man, I'm not a cheater, you know that. We just talked and fell asleep. I was exhausted and she had been dancing all night, so she fell asleep pretty quick."

"She seems like a good catch." We made it to the hotel and I opened the door for him.

He frowned and put his sunglasses back on, covering up what he was really thinking, and looking ridiculous because we were now inside. "Yeah, I guess she is. But I have Ellie, so…"

Yep. He has Ellie. What a shame. Looked like Tess and I would have to find a way to make him see things a little clearer.

"Don't hurt her, okay, man?" Trevor mumbled as we stepped onto the empty elevator. He still had his shades on and was looking down at his feet with his hands in his pockets.

"I won't. You know how long I've waited for her, Trevor. I'm not about to screw things up now. Not when I finally got her back."

"I know. I just worry… you know? About her and what she is going to have to live with for the rest of her life. I worry about you, too. She isn't going to hesitate to leave again if she thinks she should. And she's a worrier, it won't be easy to make her see that you are in it for the long haul. She's stubborn."

That she is.

"I won't give up, Trev. We got her back and none of us are going to let her go." I slapped him on the back and he finally took his sunglasses off, folding them and putting them in the pocket of his shirt.

"Right," he replied weakly.

We were silent as we made our way to the suite and I had a feeling he was going to bring something up that wouldn't be so pleasant. I was right.

"What happened between you two the last time you saw her… before she left?"

I closed my eyes and sat on the couch while I thought back to that day. The day I screwed up. "We were getting some of her stuff ready for college. She had told me about some things that happened over the summer, things she couldn't remember, people telling her she was a liar. She was upset. I couldn't ever stand to see her upset, you know that."

He nodded, "Me either."

"She was worried about having problems in college. Worried about blacking out. Worried that it had happened more often than she thought. She was afraid that her anxiety about college would cause problems. I told her that I was worried about it, too, and your mom. She had no idea that we knew what was going on. I tried to convince her that we were all there for her and wanted to help her, but she was convinced that she had been screwing up everyone's lives. I guess I don't blame her after I told her how concerned we all had been. She said she was a burden to me and her family and she took off before I could argue with her about it. I thought she was just going to blow off some steam, then come back so I went home. I never should have gone home without seeing her first."

"It's not your fault, Charlie. None of us should have kept it from her, we should have talked to her about it long before..."

"Yeah, but still. I shouldn't have made her feel so guilty about it."

"I never thought she would ever take off like that. Not in a million years. We had no way of knowing she was capable of that."

I sighed and stood to pace the room. We both silently agreed that the conversation was over and I was grateful. I felt responsible for her guilt. I never should have let her believe she was a burden. I would make up for it for the rest of my life.

We hung out in the suite for an hour before the girls came back. Tess was only carrying her purse and so was Benny. She handed me my credit card with a wink and turned to talk to Trevor about where we should all go eat tonight.

Tess hurried over to the bags of clothes and pulled out the shoes that I bought to go with her dress and went straight into the extra bedroom after giving me a shy smile. I started to follow after her, but Benny ran to block the door with a scowl on her face.

"Now, Charlie. You are not allowed in this room until she is finished getting ready. She is going to take a shower first while I go get ready, then I'm coming back to help her so give me a room key."

She held her hand out and tapped her foot, waiting impatiently for me to hand over the key. I just stood there with my eyes narrowed while Trevor's jaw was on the floor with his eyes on Benny.

"I thought you were on *my* side," I whined and dropped the key card into her waiting hand.

"I am, silly. I just know the power of anticipation." She started to walk out of the suite, but poked her head around and said, "Trust me, Charlie. It will be worth the wait. You go and get ready to go, too."

Then she was gone.

Trevor was staring at the door she had just walked through and I was staring at the door to that damn extra bedroom where Tess was probably in the shower right then all beautiful and naked. Another fantasy of mine popped into my head and I squeezed my eyes shut tightly and groaned.

"I'm gonna go shower, Trev," I mumbled as I started towards my bedroom.

"What? Why now?" he asked incredulously. We still had a couple hours before we were going out.

I had no intention of telling him that I was going to go shower in the coldest fucking water I could get to come out of that shower. He was my friend, but he was still her brother. I just waved my hand dismissively and hurried through the door leaving him grumbling while he plopped down on the couch and turned on the TV.

The water was freezing and did absolutely nothing to help, especially when I thought about the night before, and that morning, and what would most likely happen tonight, and what I hoped would happen for the next sixty years at least. I had a feeling that she wouldn't be easy to convince, but I'd be damned if I wasn't going to try.

***

I was showered and dressed up by the time Benny came back to the suite and hurried into the bedroom with Tess. I heard her gasp when she opened the door and I tried to lean over the back of the couch far enough to get a peak, but Benny was in the way. Trevor smacked the back of my head when I sat back down.

"Ow! What the hell was that for?"

He smirked, "Not sure, but as the big brother, I think I'm allowed to do that... a lot."

We waited an hour before Benny emerged looking elegant with her blonde hair pinned on top of her head and her green satin cocktail dress hugging her curves. She was very easy on the eyes and I wished that Trevor would pull his head out of his ass, but wishing was all I could do.

"She's just about ready. Did you boys make reservations?"

Trevor was staring at her again with his mouth hanging open and couldn't seem to string together enough words to reply.

"Yeah we did," I said and I smacked him on the back of the head to snap him out of it.

"Ow! What the hell was *that* for?" he snapped at me.

I just laughed and shook my head, "Not sure, but as the best friend's boyfriend, I think I'm allowed to do that."

He frowned when he realized I had thrown his own words back at him, then nodded in agreement. "Touché. Thanks for that."

I didn't get a chance to question him because the door to the bedroom opened and Tess stepped through.

I have had the wind knocked out of me plenty. Getting punched in the gut during a fight is no picnic and in the beginning, it happened a lot. But when Tess stepped out of that room, it was like all those punches rolled into one, without the pain. I couldn't breathe.

Her dark hair was curled and hung loosely over her shoulders and down past her shoulder blades. Her eyes were given just enough of a smoky look that it didn't overpower the chocolate caramel color I couldn't get enough of. It was her dress, though, that really made the cold shower I took earlier even more pointless.

Clinging to her breasts and shoulders and tapering down to flare out at her hips and fall just above her knees, it left everything and nothing to the imagination. The strappy heels on her feet, that made her legs go on for miles, brought up a whole new set of fantasies where those pointy heels dug into my ass as I thrust inside of her.

"Wow… Tess… I-I can't… y-you look… holy shit." I ran a hand through my hair and tugged hard to pull out the images running through my mind.

She smiled so brightly that the air that had been slowly coming back into my lungs was thrust out again.

"Aww, he's been struck dumb by the sight of you, T. And you thought it was too much." Benny shook her head and her finger at Tess like she was scolding a child. "Don't ever forget, I know all about these things. It's pointless to question me."

Tess just smiled and let out a quiet giggle while tugging at the hem of her dress.

I still hadn't said anything smart or even coherent yet and Trevor was still looking at Benny, then darting his eyes over to Tess to scowl, then moving them back to Benny where his expression must have looked like mine. He couldn't decide whether to be upset at Tess for dressing like that, or to gawk at *Benny* for dressing like that.

"You guys okay?" Tess asked.

Trevor came out of his beauty induced coma first, "Yeah, umm, yeah. Hey, T? I don't think it is a good idea for you to… I mean, both of you… maybe we should just stay in tonight."

"What? Why?" she protested.

"Because we are going to spend the entire night trying not to kick the ass of every guy who looks at the two of you," he bit out. "I, personally, do not want to spend a night in jail because another guy couldn't--"

"No! We are going out tonight," Benny said firmly as she raised a hand to stop him from speaking. "Now, you boys can come with us," she said, snaking her arm through Tessa's, "or you can stay here and regret not taking two hot chicks out who, I might add, will have to end up finding other dance partners because you decided to act like morons."

One of her eyebrows had arched defiantly and sent shivers up my neck. Benny was not one to be messed with. Plus, she made a good point. I was definitely going out. No way was I going to let another guy touch Tess.

She started to pull Tess to the door and I realized I still hadn't said anything to her. I reached out and wrapped my arm around her waist to turn her to me while Benny kept going with a defeated looking Trevor following after her. Tess frowned when I still hadn't said anything even after they left the suite.

"Are you okay, Charlie?"

Her voice wavered slightly and I could feel how nervous she actually was even though she looked like a goddess. She started to pull away and her expression fell. I nodded my head to answer her question and cleared my throat. "Tess, you look… there are no words worthy enough. Amazing, stunning, gorgeous, breathtaking. I can't seem to think straight with you looking like this."

She smiled and stepped back into my arms. She was just staring at my chest and I hooked my finger under her chin to tilt her face up to mine so I could see her eyes.

"Just… promise me you won't leave my side at all. Trevor was right. You two are going to keep us busy, but I want you to have a fun night."

She rolled her eyes, but couldn't hide the amusement on her face, "I promise, Charlie."

"Gah, you are so sexy! Don't roll your eyes again unless you want to skip going out and get locked into that bedroom."

She laughed and the sound nearly brought me to my knees. "Let's go then before you change your mind."

***

Trevor was right. The girls must have turned down a million guys throughout the night. Even though we were right next to them the whole time. Isn't there a guy code or something like that? One that says if a girl has her arm wrapped around a guy and he has his arm wrapped around her, she is off limits?

Tess was smiling throughout dinner and laughing with Benny and me while we reminisced about our childhood. Trevor was quiet through most of dinner and kept glancing at his phone with a frown. When I asked him what was wrong, he just said that Ellie wasn't responding to him and he had gotten a text from one of his buddies back home who saw her with her friends. Apparently, there were some guys with them, but his buddy couldn't tell if they were with the other girls or not. He looked like he was about to bolt and go back home to find her, but then I saw him glance over at Benny and he seemed to relax a bit more. He didn't pull his phone out for the rest of the night.

We found a small table in the back of the club and Tess got quiet for a minute. Benny was saying something to her that I couldn't hear and she just kept shaking her head. When she excused herself to go to the restroom, I took the opportunity to ask Benny what was going on.

"Is everything alright?"

She shrugged and took a gulp of her martini, "Not sure."

I narrowed my eyes while she did everything in her power to avoid my stare. "Benny."

"Charlie, you just have to be patient with her. There is really no way to predict a switch or to truly prevent it and with everything going on between you two, her emotions are a little… jarbled."

"Jarbled? What the hell does that mean? She knows how I feel about her. I haven't given her any reason to doubt--"

"That's not what I meant." She took a deep breath and glanced toward the restrooms to make sure Tess wasn't on her way over. "She still doesn't know all her triggers and so far, the only constant she has had is control of her emotions. Any change to that and who knows what could happen. I'm not saying it's a problem. Actually, I think it's the best thing for her."

"What do you mean?"

She sipped her martini again as she tried to think of how to explain it to me. "Okay. Picture a bottle of soda sitting on this table. The liquid has the potential to bubble up and burst out if the bottle is shaken at all. As long as nothing touches it, as long as it's in control, we can assume the soda will just sit in the bottle, right?"

I nodded, not quite sure where she was going with this.

"Tess has all these emotions stuffed inside a bottle, Charlie. She has had control of all of it, on a steady surface with no outside interference to shake her up. Until you. And you are shaking the hell out of her bottle, Charlie."

"So why do you think that's the best thing for her? Won't that hurt her?"

She laughed loudly and gulped down the rest of her drink. "Have you ever drank a soda that hasn't been touched in five years? It's flatter than that stomach of yours, and not as nice looking either. If she doesn't get shaken up, she'll end up emotionless. Flat. Indifferent. And no one will be able to pull her out of it. She's got multiple personalities, so what? I'm manic bipolar. Doesn't mean I shouldn't be allowed to feel anything."

It made sense. Tess couldn't keep bottling everything up inside of her. There had to be a way for her to let go and just feel without worrying about what will happen.

"Problem is, she isn't as in control as she thinks."

My eyebrows raised in surprise. I thought Tess had a good handle on things for the most part. "She isn't?"

She shook her head and widened her eyes at something behind me.

"She's on her way back, but I need to tell you. There's not just Lydia and Camryn. There's no way *that* girl, who has been holding back so much for years, has only two alters to take care of all of her emotions. She's only got stress and anger covered. Don't tell me she doesn't feel anything else. And she needs to start talking to them, Charlie. They need her to. She needs it, too."

"I think maybe I need to go back to the hotel," Tess said from right behind me. She hadn't heard what Benny said, but when I turned to look at her, she looked like she had been put through the ringer.

I stood quickly and wrapped my arms around her waist. "You okay, babe?"

She shook her head and glanced at Benny.

"Has it gotten worse?" Benny asked loudly.

Tess glared at her. Apparently, she didn't want me to know what was going on, but instead of continuing to glare at her best friend, her face softened and her shoulders slumped. "I think I need to get out of this crowd."

I didn't ask her anything else. Benny just nodded at me when I told her to let Trevor know we were leaving and pulled Tess out of the club and got us into a cab. By the time we got back to our room, she seemed a little more relaxed, but a little distant. I wasn't sure what to make of it.

"You want to go to bed?" I asked.

She gazed at me for a while and I couldn't look away. Her eyes seemed lighter than the chocolate caramel I was used to, and looked almost hazel. I didn't get a chance to detail those eyes further because she attacked me the next second. Her mouth found mine and her arms wound around my neck. Mine automatically wrapped around her waist and hauled her into me.

She was so soft, small and fragile in my arms. I felt like I could crush her if I held on too tight. That thought didn't pass through lightly either. I had to hold onto her tightly, I could lose her if I didn't, but at the same time… would I crush her? Would holding onto her the way I wanted make her lose herself?

Benny's words came back to me. I was shaking Tess up more than she had ever been shaken before, but it could be a good thing.

"I'm sorry ahead of time, Charlie," Tess muttered against my lips.

I pulled back, confused and a little anxious. "For what?"

She kissed me lightly before entwining our fingers and pulling me into the bedroom. "For whatever happens tonight that might not make sense to you. I've felt really… off, since this afternoon. Disconnected."

Disconnected.

She had used that word before, but where?

"You seem to keep me grounded so I'm not too worried," she said quietly and kicked off her heels.

I decided not to worry either. Actually, the sight of her hands reaching back to unzip her dress made the decision for me. I stepped into her space and grasped her upper arms, pressing for her to turn her back to me.

"Let me. Please."

Her skin flushed the most glorious shade of pink as she turned around and dropped her hands to her sides. Sliding a zipper down had never been so erotic. I couldn't help but slip my fingers inside her dress and run my fingers down her spine as I separated the metal teeth. She shivered, very noticeably, and that sent a surge of pride coursing through my veins. I affected her and knowing that gave me the confidence I needed to understand how my shaking her up could really be *great*.

I let the dress fall to the ground to pool at her feet and helped her step out of it. She turned back to me as I got a good look at what had been underneath that bit of fabric all night.

"So, I-I was right," I breathed.

One dark, perfectly sculpted eyebrow rose in question.

"You *are* trying to kill me. I know it."

The bra she was wearing was black lace, but just barely. It looked like whoever made it, forgot to sew a couple of things together. I could clearly see the hard peaks of her nipples and the rosy skin surrounding them. Her panties matched perfectly and I suddenly realized why Benny had taken my credit card earlier.

I would have to let her borrow it again for a few hours to pay her back for this.

"Benny forced me," Tess replied with a giggle.

Maybe I'd let her borrow it for a whole day.

I don't know how much time had passed as I took in every detail of her. She was exquisite. Her skin glowed with her bashfulness and it reminded me of how innocent she truly was.

She was perfect.

When she started to squirm under my stare, I realized that holding still was no longer an option. Neither was talking. I pulled her against me and kissed her tenderly, conveying every emotion I was feeling into that kiss. She responded immediately and I was lost.

I made love to her, slowly, savoring the feel of her around me. The scent of her arousal nearly zapped my control, along with the softness of her skin against mine. She was breathless as I thrust into her, holding tightly to the last threads keeping me from consuming her. She was hot and tight as her body gripped mine.

"I love you, Charlie."

I heard the snap of those threads just before I lost myself all over again. Those words coming from her mouth were my downfall. She gasped as I lifted her hips off the bed and thrust harder.

When she came, I crushed my mouth to hers and swallowed her cries as I followed after her.

Disconnected? No. I had never felt more connected in my life. Connected with the woman that I would spend the rest of my life worshipping.

Chapter 18

Tessa

Have you ever woken up from a dream that was so real you felt the effects of whatever happened in the dream? For example, I had a dream once when I was in the seventh grade that I had gone sledding down this giant hill and crashed into a snow drift and went flying through the air and landed in an ice cold river. When I woke up, it felt like I had been run over by a train and my fingers and toes were freezing to the point of pain.

I hate those kinds of dreams. Always have. They always made me question reality. Did it really happen and I was just suffering from some memory loss, or was I just going crazy and needed to see someone about it?

Then I learned that apparently, this was very common. Lots of people have really vivid dreams and feel the after effects of it. It's just part of the whole workings of the mind.

The only difference? It was when they were actually asleep and dreaming.

I never realized until now that my mind was doing this to me more than just at night and being the naïve and unknowing girl that I was back then, I wrote it off to being under too much stress. After all, I was always told that I suffered from anxiety attacks and that I had to learn to manage myself better. Why would I assume any differently?

As I laid there in Charlie's arms, after having been thoroughly loved and sated, I remembered that feeling. Those moments when I 'woke up' and felt strange while immediately forgetting what I had just dreamt.

They weren't dreams, though. It was reality. I would be at school and all of a sudden snap out of some reverie that had taken over. I would be sitting in class and the teacher would be in the middle of a lesson that I had missed half of. Charlie always helped me out back then. I would tell him that I had just dozed off and missed half the class and he would laugh at my supposed laziness and lend me his notes or help me with the material. I could never make myself question it.

Maybe some part of me - a deep part of me - knew that it would open a door that would change everything, and I wasn't ready for that. I could analyze it for days and probably get absolutely nowhere and that wasn't something I couldn't waste my time on at the moment.

I smiled as Charlie ran his fingers up and down my arm, forcing goose bumps to rise at his attention. He chuckled at the full body shiver that ran through me.

I don't know exactly what happened after the sound of his laugh, but it would end up changing everything I thought I knew.

***

Charlie

It happened so fast, so suddenly, I couldn't quite take her seriously at first.

Tess sat up with a jolt, the sheet held to her breasts tightly to cover herself. She looked at me incredulously and for a moment, I thought I might have said something awful without realizing it.

Her voice was normal, but lazier. "Qui diable êtes-vous? Pourquoi êtes-vous dans mon lit?"

"What?"

"Qui êtes-vous?" She ran a hand through her hair and huffed, "Je dois être ivre."

"Tess, what the hell are you saying?" I put my hand on her shoulder and she flinched away from me with wide eyes.

Her eyes.

They were *blue*. A really light blue.

"What the hell?" I shut my eyes tightly and shook my head to clear my mind. When I opened them again, her eyes were still blue. I leaned in closer.

"Pas possible! Partir! S'il vous plaît." She smacked me on the face just as I got close enough to tell that I was definitely not seeing things. Her eyes were definitely blue.

Oh shit!

You know those moments when you realize that something significant just happened that could possibly change the entire course of your life and you are leaning more towards the 'not good' side of it? This was one of those moments.

My stomach dropped and the blood that was coursing through my body sounded as loud as a jet flying directly over my head. This was an alter I hadn't met before and I knew that Tess was going to be furious. I had to think fast before the situation got out of control. If it was even *in* control in the first place.

"I'm Charlie. I don't know any French so if you can speak English..."

She narrowed her eyes and pursed her lips, seeming to take in my face and trying to figure out who I was while making sure I knew to keep my distance.

"Anglais?"

I nodded vigorously, "If that means *English*, then yes."

"I am sorry. I speak English, I just... who are you?"

She spoke English very well for having just spoken like a true French woman. She had an accent of course, and to be honest, it was sexy as hell.

"I'm Charlie. Your boyfriend. Well, I'm Tessa's boyfriend and you are… well, Tess, but I guess you may not know that. Oh God," I dropped my head into my hands and told myself to wake up. This wasn't happening. Tess was already worried about having two alters and I have no idea why or how this one could be missed. I was going to have a serious talk with Dr. Geoffrey. Or Tess was.

"Tessa?" she asked, still clutching tightly to the sheet and starting to move away from me.

I hurried to the edge of the bed and stood, bending to pick up my jeans and pull them on quickly. I needed Benny.

"I will be right back. Why don't you get dressed and then we can talk. Please, don't leave." I pulled open the door and looked back at her. It didn't look like she was going anywhere anytime soon if the lost expression on her face was any indication.

Leaving her in there alone probably wasn't the most well thought out thing to do. I had no other choice, though. I ran down the hall - shirtless and freaking out - and started pounding on the door to Benny's hotel room. I prayed to God they were back from the club.

"Yeah, yeah, just a minute!" I heard Benny shout from the other side.

"Hurry up, Benny. We got a problem."

She opened the door and I almost flew back to the wall behind me. Her hair was an absolute mess and she looked like she was going to strangle me with her bare hands. It was terrifying.

"What the hell could possibly be happening that you need to wake me up--"

I didn't wait for her to finish. I grabbed her arm and pulled her down the hall. She was only wearing a skimpy tank top and the tiniest shorts I had ever seen, but after seeing the look on my face, she didn't protest.

"What the hell, Charlie? What happened?"

I dragged her into the hotel suite and found Tess just stepping out of the bedroom and pulling on some pants. I kept my voice low as I spoke to Benny while closing the door. I didn't know what it would do if I told an alter that she was uh… well, an alter. "Tess switched. But, I don't know who it is. It's not Lydia and it's definitely not Camryn."

Benny's eyes widened as she stared at Tess who was now standing in the bedroom doorway looking confused and a little wary. "I knew it," she said under her breath.

"Who are you?" Tess asked.

"I'm Benny. Who are you?"

I flinched at Benny's no nonsense attitude. Maybe she wasn't the correct person to welcome this new character into our lives.

"My name is Jessamyn Rainier. I am sorry if I wandered in here… I must have had too much to drink tonight."

"She's French?" Benny exclaimed and turned her wide eyes back to me. The disturbing part of it? She was smiling.

"Yes, I am French, but I speak English fluently. I apologize if my accent makes it hard to understand."

"No! No way. You sound hot!" Benny laughed and took a step closer to her. "You have just enough of an accent to seriously make me consider switching teams."

I smacked Benny on the arm and tried to look like a scolding adult. I should have known better than that by now because Benny was her own person and she didn't take to scolding well at all.

"Ow! Fuck, Charlie! That hurt." She rubbed her arm and glared at me. "I'm telling Tess."

"What the hell do we do, Benny?"

"There's nothing we *can* do, Charlie. Except, get to know her." She took another step toward Tess - or I guess Jessamyn - and gestured for her to sit on the couch. "We have a lot to talk about, Jessamyn."

"Please, call me Jessi," she said and smiled widely at Benny while her eyes flickered over to me nervously.

"Don't you worry about him. He is new to this stuff, but he's a good guy. Hopefully you fall in love with him," Benny said with a shrug.

I rolled my eyes. How the hell did Tess get along with this woman?

"I am confused. Charlie said he was my boyfriend, but I do not have a boyfriend."

I leaned against the back of the couch, closer to Benny, as Tess - Jessi - sat down. Scenarios were flying through my mind. The one that was causing the most turmoil, though, was the thought of telling Tess that she had another alter. She had talked to me about the time it would take to find integration with the two she knew about. This was going to make her feel less hope than she already had. How would I tell her that?

"He *is* your boyfriend. Well, he's Tessa's boyfriend. You are Tessa *and* you are Jessi."

Her brow scrunched up and she looked like she was about to bail.

"Holy shit! Your eyes are blue. Physiological changes? Tess is going to freeeeak."

I rolled my eyes again and was starting to get a headache, "That's what I have been trying to tell you."

"Okay, so I will give you the short version and then we can get into details in the morning because I am exhausted. Theresa Marshall has dissociative identity disorder, or multiple personality disorder. Do you know what that is?"

She nodded hesitantly, then shrugged, "A little."

"Good enough. Anyway, the personalities that are not Tess are called alters and you, my dear, are an alter."

"Is this the right thing to do, Benny?" I asked anxiously as I saw Tessa's face twist. She probably thought we were insane.

"Better to tell her now. It could trigger a switch back to Tess if we talk about her and explain the situation." She took a deep breath and turned to me, resting her arm on the back of the couch and crossing an ankle over her knee. "What I am most concerned about isn't that there is another alter, I already knew that. I'm just wondering what the trigger was."

"Trigger?" Tess/Jessi asked.

"Yeah. A switch can be caused by some kind of trigger like stress or fear or an extreme emotion," Benny replied. "Actually, pretty much anything. Everyone is different." She knew more about this than I gave her credit for.

"I think I should leave," Tess/Jessi said and started to stand.

"No!" I cried and quickly stood to block her exit.

"Charlie, calm down," Benny said and came to my side. "Listen, Jessi. You may not believe everything we are saying and that's fine, but we aren't going to hurt you and you have nowhere else to go."

That made Jessi pause. She must have realized that Benny was telling the truth and when she glanced around the room, she looked lost.

"Why don't you go to bed and we will talk more in the morning and figure this out."

She nodded and started to back away to the bedroom we had just made love in not more than half an hour ago.

"I think I will go to bed then. Is this *my* room?" she questioned, eyeing me carefully.

At that moment, the realization that everything had changed finally hit me. This wasn't my Tess that I was dealing with. This wasn't even Lydia or Camryn that already knew me in some way. This was a complete stranger who had no idea who I was and would probably feel threatened by me in some way.

"Go ahead and take that one. Charlie will take the other one and he won't bug you at all. Right, Charlie?" Benny asked.

I stood motionless for what seemed like hours, watching the woman I loved slowly slip through my fingers. No matter how hard I tried to hold onto her, there was no way to know if, some day, she would fall out of my grip. I didn't understand the gravity of Tessa's disorder until now.

She was still my Tess, but her alters were not, no matter how much I wanted them to be.

"Yeah," I croaked. The lump that had lodged in my throat was painful and it took everything I had to keep my expression impassive. I don't think I succeeded, but I tried.

I hurried into the extra bedroom and shut the door softly. Muffled sounds of Benny saying goodnight and Jessi's reassurance that she wasn't going to go anywhere came through the door.

I sat on the bed with shaky legs and a heavy heart. I couldn't give up on her. I couldn't give up on *us.*

Chapter 19

Tessa

I found myself standing in front of the mirror in the luxurious bathroom that was connected to Charlie's room. *Our* room. I had no idea how I got there, but I was definitely there and I was definitely *not* dreaming. The water was running, so hot that it was beginning to fog the mirror in front of me. I quickly shut it off and looked around.

"What the hell?"

The fear that I had switched in the middle of the night hit me with such force that I had to grip the counter top to stay upright. I knew I had experienced this before, finding myself in the middle of something without knowing how I had gotten there, but until now, I hadn't known it at the time. I had always just woken up and realized I had lost a day or so, sometimes a week.

The closest thing to this feeling was what I felt at the restaurant the night before, but I couldn't be sure. The hope that things would get better as I attempted to communicate or integrate with the alters was hanging by its fingernails and screaming for dear life. If anything, things were getting worse before I had the chance to make them better.

I nearly ran out of the bathroom, hoping to find Charlie sleeping and not having any idea what had just happened. When I looked at the disheveled sheets and found them empty, panic coursed through my veins.

"No," I rasped.

I finally looked down at what I was wearing. I was in a t-shirt and jeans. Maybe I lost more time than I thought, but a quick trip back to the bathroom to look in the mirror told me that my hair was still curled the way Benny had done it, although messy from sex and possibly sleep. Maybe it was the next morning and Charlie was getting us breakfast or he was with his team for some kind of meeting. Maybe he had left because I had freaked him out or something without knowing it.

The Maybe's were driving me insane.

I decided to be proactive and look for him or at least find Benny and make sure everything was still normal.

I swung the bedroom door open and stepped out into the living area of the beautiful hotel suite we were staying in. The lights were on and it was still dark outside.

"Okay, maybe I didn't lose much time at all. Maybe I had been sleep walking."

A sound from the extra bedroom made me jump, but I hurriedly closed the distance and gripped the cold doorknob tightly. Was it Trevor who had decided to stay in this room instead of with Benny? He could help me out, right?

I opened the door slowly and peered inside. The only light was coming from the open strip of space underneath the bathroom door. I heard the toilet flush and the sink turn on as I waited to see who was on the other side.

I couldn't move away from the doorway I was standing in. If I had to run, I wanted to make sure nothing was in my way. I flipped on the bedroom light and looked around. There were no suitcases anywhere and the bed didn't look like it had been disturbed.

Maybe it wasn't Trevor.

The water turned off and a few seconds later, the doorknob began to turn.

I held my breath.

It felt like forever before he came into view. His body was unmistakable. The tattoo on his shoulder confirming that it was him. Dressed in nothing but a pair of jeans, Charlie stepped into the bedroom looking down at the ground while a hand tugged sharply at his hair in the way he only did when he was frustrated.

I don't know if relief was the correct response to what I was going through, but that's what I felt. What stood in the forefront of my mind, however, was that Charlie was moving toward the bed instead of the door where he should have been headed to come back to our room.

"Charlie?"

He startled and cursed as his head snapped up to look at me.

We both stood motionless, breathing hard and fast, as if we had both just run a marathon.

"Is it you, Tess?"

Oh shit!

I felt the sting in the back of my eyes and tried to keep myself from crying out in agony by slapping a hand over my mouth.

In three strides, Charlie was standing in front of me and cupped my face in his hands. "Baby, don't cry. Please"

I hadn't realized the tears had already started to fall, and they were streaming out of me faster than ever before. Charlie wrapped his arms around me and I buried my face in his bare chest. I wasn't a crier, but the last couple weeks had been like a dam breaking open.

"D-did I… are y-you okay? What happened?" I asked through my tears.

He took a deep breath and squeezed me tighter. His hesitation was unbearable, like a pair of cement shoes holding me at the bottom of a lake

"You switched, Tess."

I already knew that, but hearing him say it, hearing that he was there during it, made the devastation so much greater.

"Was it Camryn? Did she do something--"

"No, baby. It wasn't Camryn, and there is nothing Camryn can do to make me run off. Got it?" he said firmly and moved back to cup my face again, gently wiping my tears away with his thumbs. He looked into my eyes, almost warily, and after a few seconds he sighed, "You're really back."

"Yes, it's me. Did Lydia make you come in here? Was she a total bitch or something?" I felt a little better knowing that he was only dealing with Lydia, she was easy. Sometimes, I really actually hated not remembering a switch. Co-consciousness was like gold at the moment. Precious and envied.

He shook his head and I paused. Confusion set in as the expression on his face turned more and more anxious. This could not be good.

"It wasn't Lydia either."

At first, I wanted to laugh even though it wasn't a very funny joke. But when he didn't say anything else, I knew he wasn't joking. He was telling the truth, the look in his eyes told me as much, but I couldn't help but feel like he was mocking me.

"Damn it, Charlie. This isn't a game!" I shouted and pushed against his chest to get some distance, but he only held me tighter and didn't budge an inch.

"I know, love. It's not. I just don't know how to tell you."

"Just say it!"

He tugged me toward the bed and we both sat down on the edge, with him wrapped around me as if to anchor me down so I couldn't run. I felt like I was about to snap into a million pieces. If I hadn't switched yet, I know I was about to from all the stress and worry.

"It was another alter, one we didn't know about."

Black spots formed in front of my eyes and I was having a hard time breathing. I felt Charlie's hands holding my face and heard the distant sound of him shouting my name. I even think I felt a tap against my cheek as if someone was trying to snap me out of some daydream. I don't remember if I passed out or if I even responded to anything that was said. All I could think about was the hope that had just been ripped from my soul, shredded into a million pieces and burned into nothing but ash.

I lost everything at that moment.

I knew it was ridiculous to think that I had been okay or even in control of everything. It was almost pathetic. But I couldn't admit to myself or even accept that this life was it, these were the cards that had been dealt and I had bet everything on this hand.

Folding hadn't been an option before. It hadn't even crossed my mind. I could deal with it, right? I could roll with the punches, wing it, stand my ground, and any other idioms that I can't think of right now.

And I *could have* dealt with it.

With Lydia and Camryn.

With the two alters who had been with me for years, protected me emotionally and mentally.

No. Folding hadn't been an option at all.

Until now.

So I welcomed the oblivion, the darkness. The total ignorance that came over me and felt the switch sizzle through my brain. Control was gone and triggers no longer mattered.

Charlie couldn't help me and I could no longer help myself.

***

Charlie

"Tess! Come on, love, answer me."

She hadn't moved since I told her there was another alter. In fact, I don't think I had seen anything hold so still without being dead and I sure as hell hadn't seen anyone dead.

Her eyes had stared straight through me, unseeing and oblivious to everything going on around her. I couldn't get her to respond to anything. I lightly tapped her cheek and shook her shoulders.

Nothing.

It was like she had checked out.

I started to stand so I could go get Benny or call an ambulance. The only explanation was that she was in shock. Her face was pale and her hands were in tight fists that I had no hope of opening. As I stood and slowly released her shoulders to make sure she would stay upright, she blinked several times and finally looked into my eyes.

"Charlie?"

Relief slammed into me. "Tess! Are you okay? You went completely blank." I gathered her in my arms and pulled her into my lap.

"Wow, Charlie. You are like sex on a stick! Look at those muscles. My God."

Every muscle in my body froze as the high pitched voice that was Lydia reached my ears. I remembered the sound of it from the recording Dr. Geoffrey had played at Tessa's last appointment. Plus, Tess would never say 'sex on a stick' out loud. Would she?

I pulled my face out of her hair and slowly met her gaze. Nope. Definitely not in this situation.

She had a shit eating grin on her face and even though it was technically Tess and her smile was always beautiful, this one made me shiver.

"Lydia."

"Yep, how goes it, Charlie? It's been a long time. I see that Tess finally clued in to the perfection that is you." She giggled and licked her lips.

"Why are you here?" I asked, my voice more stern than I had intended.

She huffed and climbed off my lap. "Well, I guess there will be no cuddle time for Liddy, huh? Listen, Tess can't handle the stress. *I can.* That's how this whole thing works with her so you better get used to it."

I wasn't sure how to respond. I didn't realize that Lydia knew what her role was in Tessa's mind. "I don't--"

"Understand. Yeah I know. And you probably never will, but that's okay because that's why I'm here. Tessa Marshall has labeled Cam and me the bad guys. I'm cool with it, but eventually she is going to burst if she doesn't learn to accept us." She closed her eyes tightly and rubbed her fingers against her temples. "Or…"

"Or what?"

She locked eyes with me and frowned. Not a playful, pouty frown that I would probably expect from her knowing what I know. This was her being upset about something and even though Lydia was talking to me, I still felt that protective shove and the need to do whatever it took to fix things for her.

I was wrong before. Lydia was my Tess, just a different part of her.

"She is losing it, Charlie. She's giving up and we all know where that leads so I'm not going to beat around the bush. She needs to talk to us. Or eliminate us."

"Why?"

She laughed. Actually laughed as if I had said the most hilarious thing in the world. "Oh, Charlie. You really think you can handle four different women? And whoever else decides to pop out of her head? This isn't something that you can just walk away from when things get rough. Tess already does that herself." She threw her arms in the air in frustration and pulled on the dark locks falling against her neck like she wanted to rip them out. "We aren't going to go anywhere without causing some serious damage to the already fragile mind she has. She has never really learned to show important emotion or to even handle the shittiest of situations all by herself. This isn't just a phase and it's not going to magically go away or get better. This is the rest of her life."

"I already know that!" I shouted at her, feeling my blood simmer and my fists clench. I wasn't in this thinking that someday things would all turn out normal, I was in this because I loved Tess more than any man had ever loved a woman. I would give my life for her.

"I know that better than anyone else, Lydia. But I also want *Tess* more than anything else. And if that means I get you and Camryn and Jessamyn, or even twenty other people who come with her, I will still consider myself the luckiest bastard alive because I get the moments with Tess that matter. You say I can't walk away from her because it will destroy her, but the truth is it will destroy *me*."

I dropped down onto the bed and held my head in my hands. My mind was racing, frantically trying to find a solution for *Tess*, not me. I didn't care if one of her alters turned out to be a man who wanted nothing more than to put his fist through my face all the time. But she would care and it would rip her apart if she had the slightest inkling that being with her was difficult for me. She had already proven that she could disappear because she felt guilty.

"What do I do, Lydia?" I whispered, feeling a burning sensation at the back of my eyes that I only remember feeling when we had discovered Tess was gone all those years ago.

"That's the problem. You can only be you. There's not much else." She placed her hand on my back and patted softly, trying to comfort me but not really knowing how. "Listen," she demanded, "Tess isn't the only one who needs convincing. She may never accept us, but even if she does, it won't matter unless you can convince the others to accept it. To accept you. Tess sure as hell isn't going to convince them anytime soon."

"What? Like make all you girls fall in love with me?" I scoffed.

"Exactly," she shrugged and then smacked me on the back. "You've got it."

"You have got to be kidding me."

She rolled her eyes, looking so much like the Tess I knew, "I know you may not completely trust me, but there is one thing that you can be assured of. I love you as much as Tess does, so that's two down and two to go… so far."

I gaped at her, completely shocked by what she had just said so flippantly. "You love me?"

She nodded hesitantly, looking only a little wary of my reaction, "Always have. I've spent more time with you than you think, Charlie. And unfortunately, I couldn't tell Tess how stupid she was for leaving at the time, but now I'm glad she did. Benny is good for her and I think she could see that the rest of us are pulling for her, too, if she just held on a little longer."

I dropped my head in my hands for the hundredth time and tried to pull out a solution, one that would be best for Tess. The thought of convincing two other women, besides Tess and Lydia, to fall in love with me, and stay in love with me long enough to live another sixty plus years together, was giving me a massive headache. I had a hard enough time getting it out of Tess. Took fifteen years, really.

I could honestly say that it was worth it, though.

Every minute of it.

And each of these alters was Tess. At least, a part of her that she had created to deal with things that she normally couldn't deal with herself. I didn't have a choice. I loved her so I would love them and hope that they would return the sentiment sooner or later.

Hopefully sooner.

She had been pacing back and forth while I had been thinking and practically wearing a hole in the carpet. Even knowing she was Lydia right now didn't stop me from wanting to pull her into my arms and comfort her. I would have to talk to Tess about that. They were all still her and if I was going to do this - convince them to love me - I was going to have to talk to each of them intimately, be with them intimately. Could I do that without feeling like I was being unfaithful to Tess?

She raked a hand through her hair and tugged.

"Are you nervous?" I asked because from what I had been told and what I had seen and heard, Lydia didn't get nervous.

"Not really," she replied almost too quickly and waved her hand in the air dismissively as if she were shooing away the very idea.

"You seem to know a lot about Tess. Why doesn't she know more about you?"

She shot me a wry smile and finally sat down on the bed. "She doesn't take the time really. Everything she knows about us comes from someone else, her therapist, Benny. She's explained to you about co-consciousness right?"

I nodded and shrugged, "Yeah, but I'm not quite sure I understand it completely."

She smiled and laid down on her side resting her head in her hand. "Tess isn't aware of any of us whether she is in a switch or not. If she wouldn't have wondered why she was losing time here and there, she would have never discovered us without someone else pointing it out to her. As far as she is concerned, she has always only been Tess.

"Camryn and I, on the other hand, are aware of Tess consistently. We have experienced Tess and each other and are aware of everything that happens around us. We aren't aware of Jessamyn, but it seems like she isn't aware of any of us either, just like Tess."

My head was aching more with confusion. It was all so complicated. How could Tess ever keep track of everyone?

"I feel like I need to write this all down so I can remember who is who," I said feeling a little discouragement.

"That's actually a good idea. Dr. G talked to me about that a while ago. Tess should really start keeping a journal or something, writing down her thoughts and feelings about what happens to her and what is going on in her life. Jessamyn will need that. Camryn and I can do it, too. It would help Tess communicate with us. She wants to, but I think she is scared of what it might do. She doesn't want us with her forever, but she can't just kick us out of her head."

We talked about different ways to get Tess to be more involved with her, Camryn, and Jessi. It was after two in the morning by the time we started drifting off to sleep. Neither one of us really wanted to get up and I had no desire to be away from Tess, whether she was aware of me or not. I was still waiting for her to switch back, but it looked like I was going to have Lydia for a while longer.

She had already closed her eyes and her breathing had evened out. I was having a hard time keeping my eyes open, but I wanted to soak her in. I watched her breathe in and out and wondered what she would dream about, if Tess would remember the dreams or if Lydia would.

There would definitely never be a dull moment in our lives, that's for sure.

Chapter 20

Tessa

I honestly don't remember how or why I woke up so suddenly, I just know that Charlie was next to me in bed, on top of the covers, in his jeans, looking like he should be kept locked up and hidden away for looking so god damn beautiful.

I *do* remember feeling awfully freaked out after he told me I had a third alter. The familiar nervous feeling crept up into my chest and my heart started beating faster, but I tamped it down and took a few deep breaths. I didn't need to feel that way anymore.

I know Lydia had taken my place after I blanked out. I knew she could handle the freaking out better than I could. I also know that her and Charlie had a good talk about how to balance myself out and also balance out my life with Charlie.

I know all of this.

I *remember* all of this.

The smile that broke out across my face was probably the biggest one I had ever had since before I left Charlie and my family.

It was the first true hope I had ever felt.

For the few moments after Charlie had dropped the bomb, I had seriously considered ending everything. I knew I wouldn't be able to live my life being so many different people, not knowing if Charlie could truly handle it and not knowing what they were saying and doing with him. My family would struggle. Mom was strong and smart, and she would adapt to everything, Trevor might have a harder time, but they would eventually come to understand me and be able to live with us. I just didn't want them to *have* to.

I felt like I had been dreaming. During the switch, it was like I was a fly on the wall, watching my body and face interact with Charlie. He had looked so confused and almost devastated for me, but as things started to come together for him, he looked hopeful.

Probably as hopeful as I was feeling at the moment.

Benny had been telling me the truth, I was loved by her and my family. By Charlie. They weren't being forced to do *anything*. They were sticking with me because they wanted to.

If you have never felt love like that before… well, let me just say it feels amazing. Like a warmth oozing through your veins. The warm feeling you get after taking that first sip of a good strong Brandy.

Bliss. Happiness. Relief.

I never wanted to let that feeling go. I wasn't *going* to let it go.

I watched Charlie for a few moments longer, raking my eyes over his handsome face, so relaxed and almost boyish. He looked content. I scooted closer to him and gently ran my finger over his brow, passing over the cut above his eye, down along the bridge of his nose, to his soft full lips that could do wonders to me. He had a good amount of scruff along his jaw and the feel of it under my fingers sent tingles down my spine, remembering the sensation of that scruff rubbing along the intimate places on my body. It made the warmth I was already feeling grow into a heady glow.

I moved my hand down his neck to his thick shoulder, then felt the muscles in his upper arm flex like he was on high alert. I looked back at his face and his bright green eyes were watching me. I leaned forward, unable to go on without feeling his lips against mine.

He backed away quickly, his expression confused and wary.

"Lydia, I don't think…"

My stomach fell down through the bed and hit the floor. I didn't like the sound of him calling me another name and the hurt on my face must have shown. I moved to climb off the bed and give him some space, but his hand shot out and grasped my wrist.

"Wait. Tess, you're back?"

"Yeah, I am. Who else would be touching you and attempting to kiss you?" I snapped.

He looked dejected for a split second before understanding crept over his face. "No one else but you, Tess. I wouldn't even put myself in that kind of situation with anyone else."

I knew being upset was irrational. To him, I'm sure that my alters are still me in some way. I would have to learn to be on that same line of thinking, but right now, I just wanted to be mad at him for pulling away from me.

"Lydia told me she was in love with me. I didn't realize how long we had been asleep and I guess I just thought it was still her and she was making a move or something," he said quickly, looking desperate to convince me that it wasn't me he was rejecting.

I took a deep breath and closed my eyes, holding it for ten seconds before slowly letting it seep out. I pushed out the anger and nodded my head.

"I know, Charlie. I'm sorry, I just didn't expect that. Didn't like it either."

He tugged me closer to him, still laying down on his side, and pulled me against his chest so we were face to face with our lips a mere inch apart and our bodies perfectly aligned.

"I think we should talk about that. I don't want to ever pull away from you, Tess. I just don't know what to do with them. It's still you. When I look at them… it's still you. How am I supposed to think any differently? What do you want me to do?"

I closed my eyes. As much as it hurt to think of him with one of the alters, he was right, it was still me. I shrugged, "Well, like Lydia said, make them fall in love with you."

He sighed and nodded before his whole body went stiff and his eyes widened. "You remember?"

I hadn't meant to let him know that I *did* remember the switch. I wanted to wait and see if it lasted. No sense disappointing him if it didn't, but I nodded hesitantly and the look on his face was enough to convince me that it was a good idea.

His smile was breath taking and I think my heart forgot to keep beating for several seconds.

"That's… great. Right?" he whispered.

"Yeah. It is."

When his lips crashed against mine, all thoughts of another alter and whether or not things would work out, left my mind. It was just me and Charlie.

That's all that mattered.

***

"She's French?"

"Pretty sweet, huh?" Benny said with her biggest smile. "I think it ups your hotness score to about one hundred. The accent is definitely irresistible."

I was grateful for Benny's comments, trying to make me feel better that the alter wasn't a freak, but still…

We were on the plane, heading back home, with Charlie in the seat next to me and Benny in front of us with Trevor. Apparently, Charlie had made some calls and gotten us all together in first class on the same flight back. We had all been avoiding the elephant on the plane until the seat belt light went off. Then, Benny immediately turned in her seat and rested against her folded arms on the back of the seat and started filling me in.

She had come back to the room this morning, but Charlie kicked her out in the first five seconds after she barged into the suite. I had just gotten in the shower and Charlie was on his way in when we heard her calling my name. He had poked his head out the bedroom door, told her I was occupied and would be until we had to leave for the airport and not to call or come back until she heard from *us.*

I assumed that she had taken it really well because when we met downstairs at the car, she couldn't stop smiling and winking at me. Charlie hadn't let me leave the room until the last minute and my hair was a mess, my lips were swollen, and my clothes were crooked. Trevor didn't look me in the eye, but his lips had turned up into a smile when Charlie wrapped his arm around me in the car.

The blush on my face hadn't faded until we arrived at the airport.

"So, what else? Is she crazy or anything?" I asked Benny who was looking like a kid who had just unwrapped the coolest birthday present ever.

"Don't know, but she seemed pretty composed, didn't talk too much, but didn't freak out like I expected her to."

"So she isn't co-conscious of any of us. Lydia or Camryn?"

She shook her head and pursed her lips, "Kind of sucks, but it's nothing we haven't dealt with before. It will probably be just like what happened at the beginning with you. Kind of starting over, I guess." She shrugged and looked at Charlie. "Did you tell her the coolest part?"

"I haven't had a chance to talk to her about it much," he said with a wide grin and looked at me, making me blush all over again. He chuckled and kissed my forehead. "Besides, I'm not sure what you think the coolest part is."

"The eyes, duh!"

"Ah," he replied with an exaggerated nod.

"What about the eyes? What happened to the eyes?" I asked with a shaky voice.

"Blue. Her eyes are *blue*," Benny exclaimed. "So freaking cool. I mean, at first, I thought there were some physiological changes with Camryn because, well, you know. She's crazy sometimes. But then I realized that was just because she *looked* crazed. Nothing else was really different except her expressions and posture and stuff like that, but Jessi… she has light blue eyes."

I shook my head. "How is that possible? Did you see them change?"

Charlie responded to this question and his answer was actually not what I was expecting. "I noticed your eyes were a little lighter when we got back from the club, but I thought it was just because you were tired or something. They were more hazel than the usual chocolate color. It wasn't until you started speaking to me in French that I really noticed the change."

"Holy crapballs!"

"Yeah."

"So, tell me what she said."

"She didn't really say much, Tess," he said and squeezed my hand. "We didn't really talk to her much, but she must have been a little freaked when she realized she was in bed with me. Naked."

"Ha! Freaked? No, I think she might have been a little happy about *that*," Benny muttered. "I know *I* would be." The wink she shot to Charlie probably would have pissed me off if it was anyone else. But this was Benny. She was born to make people feel uncomfortable just for the fun of it.

"Anyway," I heard Trevor say from his seat next to Benny.

She rolled her eyes. "Okay, okay. *Anyway...* I was hoping to speak with her this morning, but you switched back. Dr. G will have to fill you in on the rest when he pulls her out."

"I just don't understand how she hasn't come out before now. I mean, what could have triggered her? Am I just going to start turning into a bunch of different people now? A man who only speaks Swahili? Maybe a kid who has a habit of picking his nose?"

Benny laughed loudly and shook her head, "I don't think so, T, but you never know. There may be a lot of things you haven't experienced yet that an alter might be necessary to help you through. I hate to bring it up because it definitely isn't my business, until we have a girl's night in with plenty of wine and junk food and you fill me in on everything, but you just lost your virginity. That's a big deal. Jessi seems to handle waking up naked with a man very well. Maybe that's her purpose."

My mouth had gaped open when she had mentioned my virginity. She was the only person who would talk about that so frivolously and not really care that maybe Charlie and I wanted that to be between *us*. What could I do, though? This wasn't unexpected.

"Benny! My brother doesn't want to hear about that kind of shit."

"Ding, ding, ding! No. I don't," Trevor said, then put in his earphones and turned up the music on his phone to drown us out.

"Well, it's true. Jessi was probably triggered by the sex."

"Okay, that's enough, Benny," Charlie said with a chuckle. "Let's talk about something else." Then he leaned into my ear until his lips were pressed against the skin behind it, "Not that I don't enjoy your blush, but I think that the zipper on my pants might tear apart if you keep it up."

Then his tongue darted out to touch that sensitive skin and I shivered.

Yeah, I definitely think the sex was a part of this. He was just too good and my mind didn't seem to handle it very well. He could make me crazy with only a touch. Only problem was that I didn't want Jessi to pop out whenever I was feeling overly emotional about it. This was *mine*.

Jessi would just have to learn to back off.

***

Mom seemed to handle the news well.

Benny was good at making the strangest things exciting, and *she* was excited about this. She loved Lydia and Camryn and always told me that I was lucky to have such close companions that could 'throw down' when I needed it. Her words, not mine.

Thankfully, Benny didn't tell her that we were assuming that the new development between me and Charlie could be the reason. The way she eyed me when we were all sitting around the table talking and Charlie kept touching me, told me that she knew enough without anyone saying a word. She seemed to be smiling a lot, too.

I had lost track of the time and next thing I knew, it was after midnight and Mom and Benny had gone through a bottle and a half of wine and were laughing at everything that came out of the other's mouth.

Charlie and I didn't have anything to drink and I know he did this to support me. I didn't really like to drink because it made me feel out of control, he didn't drink much because it could affect his fighting, but a beer or two at dinner on occasion was not unusual for him.

Trevor had taken off shortly after dinner to go and find Ellie. We had spent the first hour discussing some kind of plan to get rid of Ellie, but none of our ideas would be possible without the high probability of losing Trevor. Benny was quiet for the majority of this conversation and the look she gave me when I asked her what she thought was enough to let me know she was interested.

If only.

"Well, I'm off to bed," Mom said and stood from the table. "You staying the night, Charlie?"

It took a few seconds for me to actually process her question, and by the time I did, it didn't matter. I was speechless and hoped that Charlie had a response that wouldn't embarrass the hell out of me.

He didn't.

He just squeezed my knee under the table and smiled shyly. That smile was my undoing. He was adorable when he smiled like that and the pink on his cheeks didn't help, so I was instantly turned on, which told me that he needed to leave.

I didn't say it, I think because I actually really wanted him to stay the night. This was my mom's house, though, and with her and Benny present… I wouldn't be able to handle the awkwardness in the morning if he stayed. Unless he slept on the couch.

"I think I'll head home tonight, Sarah."

"You sure?"

He glanced over at me and squeezed my knee again, "Yeah."

I felt a slice of disappointment, but the relief that accompanied it was soothing. I needed a little space after tonight. I needed time to process how I was going to handle a new alter.

"Alright, well, come for breakfast if you can." Then she was gone.

"I'm off. See you in the morning," Benny said quickly and followed after her, leaving Charlie and me alone.

"I better take off, too," he whispered and kissed the tip of my nose.

"Okay," I croaked. Why the hell did my voice give away everything I was feeling? I cleared my throat and tried again. "Okay, see you in the morning?"

He smiled and nodded, then pulled me out of my chair and walked to the front door holding my hand tightly.

"Sleep well, Tess."

He pulled me against his chest and wrapped his arms around my waist with his forehead resting against mine. We stayed like that for a long moment, just breathing each other in, then he dipped down and kissed me, long and soft, making sure I wouldn't dream of anything else but him tonight. I was breathless when he pulled away. He murmured his goodnight and walked out the front door, waving when he got to his car. I watched him drive away before I shut the door and banged my head against it. I wasn't going to get any sleep tonight.

"Let it happen, T," Benny's voice rang out from the stairs.

I turned to see her in her skimpy pajamas, her hair braided, and a shit eating grin on her face.

Let it happen.
"It's already happened, Benny."
"Not all of it," she informed, then hurried up the stairs.
"What the hell does *that* mean?" I shouted after her.
Her response was the sound of her door shutting, then nothing.
"What the hell does that *mean*?"

Chapter 21

Charlie

That had been the longest night of my life.

By the time dawn arrived, I had debated with myself enough to determine that I wouldn't spend a night without Tess from now on and she would just have to deal with it. I know she needed a little time to pull herself together, but she wasn't going to get space anymore. We were in this together and we were going to stay in it *together*.

I had an argument all planned out that I was sure would be a winner, but when she opened the door for me, and she was standing there in her tiny shorts and tank top with her short black robe hanging open revealing that she was again *not* wearing a bra, I forgot what I had planned out and just kissed her. Hard.

"Good morning," she breathed when I finally let her go.

"Yes, it is a good morning. Awful night, but great morning."

She blushed, but rolled her eyes at me. "Don't remind me."

We made our way to the kitchen where the smell of bacon and pancakes made my stomach grumble loudly.

"What time is your appointment?" I asked, remembering that it was Monday and Dr. Geoffrey was expecting her.

"They called me this morning and moved it to two o'clock. Wanted to make sure we would both be there."

I smiled proudly, but felt a little pang of regret that this wasn't *her* decision. "I'll be there. If you want me to."

She sighed and looked down at her feet.

"Hey," I whispered and moved my hands to each side of her neck with my thumbs lifting her jaw so she would look at me. Her skin was soft and warm and I was itching to feel the rest of it against mine again. "I know this isn't what you had planned for yourself, but I won't let you do it alone. Nothing will scare me away."

"I know that."

"Then what's wrong?"

She squeezed her eyes shut and took a deep breath, held it in for a few seconds, then let it out as her muscles relaxed. "What if there is another one?"

"Then there's another one. There could be twenty, but I'll still be here."

"What if another one turns out to be a psycho and a murderer like on that movie with John Cusack?"

I laughed because we had watched that movie together a long time ago and she had always thought it couldn't ever really happen, though she loved every minute of the psychological thriller.

"I don't think that will happen, love, but if it does, I'll still be here."

"Well, what if one of them turns out to be a guy who--"

I pressed my thumb against her lips and she whimpered as if she had a million concerns and no way to push them out of her. Which was probably true.

"Baby, I'm not going anywhere. As long as you still love me and let me love you, I'll be here for the next sixty to seventy years. The others won't have anything to throw at me."

Her eyes widened and the color drained from her face. She wasn't expecting that I guess. How could she not know how badly I wanted to spend the rest of my life with her?

"Don't," I warned her. "Don't freak out. It won't change anything."

I leaned down and kissed her forehead, her cheeks, her nose, and finally her parted lips. I didn't hesitate to slip my tongue through and taste her. She let me, which made me groan and promise myself to be a better man, for her. To be the only man who she *could ever* love.

A part of me hoped that there were more alters, just so I could prove to her that she was stuck with me. As her mouth moved against mine, I felt my determination spike up a notch. This woman was mine and letting her go would be the worst mistake I could ever make.

"Will you two stop sucking face and get in here already? I'm starving my ass off," Benny shouted from the kitchen.

Tess pulled back as she rolled her eyes and turned away. I watched her walk through the door, admiring the sway of her hips and her long legs that had been wrapped around me not twenty four hours before.

I groaned again, and she looked back at me over her shoulder and winked.

Benny wasn't getting my credit card anymore.

***

Trevor was in the kitchen when we walked in and after about thirty minutes of playing question and answer, we all found out that he caught Ellie last night with her maid of honor's boyfriend. They were making out in her living room and he had walked in on him attempting to remove her shirt and her attempting to unzip his pants.

Apparently, she was dumber than we all thought, which was really bad. She tried to convince Trevor that the guy had gotten her drunk and forced himself on her. Instead of giving a response that wasn't worth his time, he tossed her key onto the coffee table, climbed the stairs to the bedroom and stuffed the few things he had there into a bag - along with the engagement ring he had given her that was sitting on her dresser - and walked out the door.

She wasn't happy about it and had been calling and texting him relentlessly. He showed up here at about two o'clock in the morning and crashed on the couch. No cell phone, no extra things, no regrets.

Pissed off, but no regrets.

"I'm sorry, Trevor," Sarah said sincerely and kissed him on the cheek, "But this is good. Better now than when you were married and ended up with an even bigger disaster." I could tell she was fighting a smile. She was ecstatic and wanted to jump for joy and clap her hands. She restrained herself, though.

Benny, on the other hand, said what everyone else wanted to.

"Glad you pulled your head out, Trev. Now you can enjoy life without a demon bitch breathing down your neck."

Tess gasped, then coughed because she was in the middle of taking a drink. I tried not to laugh as I pounded on her back to help her. Sarah just stood frozen to the spot, staring at Benny like she had just grown another head.

Trevor? Well, I think he fell in love with Benny right then and there.

She was bent over her plate, devouring the eggs and bacon, without looking up to see anyone's reaction. She didn't care. She had spoken the truth and no one could chastise her for it.

Trevor was smiling and watching her, then he stood from the table slowly and looked at the rest of us. "Thanks guys, for caring enough to let me work things out on my own time. Benny?"

She looked up at him innocently. Tess snorted and buried her face in my shoulder, shaking with laughter.

"Yeah, Trev?"

"I'll pick you up at seven o'clock tonight. We're going out. Wear pants."

She smiled at him, winked, and said "Alrighty."

Trevor waved to the rest of us and left.

I still don't think Sarah had moved an inch, but when Benny just kept eating without making any eye contact with the rest of us, she couldn't take the silence anymore.

"Someone tell me that really happened."

"It did," I replied.

"Thank God!"

Benny finished up her food and carried her plate to the sink, "Thanks for breakfast, Mom." She kissed Sarah on the cheek and disappeared through the door.

Tess was still laughing into my shoulder. "You see why I love her so much?"

Both Sarah and I responded at the same time, "Yes."

***

Dr. Geoffrey looked like he was about to burst with excitement when Tess told him that another alter had manifested over the weekend. She wasn't as freaked out by the idea anymore and I was proud of her for taking it so well.

"Tell me exactly what occurred over the weekend, Tessa," he demanded gently.

She told him about flying to New York, the baggage stress, the fight. Everything except what happened between the two of us. He knew she was leaving this out, of course, because the look on her face told him so. She was bright red when she answered his question about spending the entire time with me.

"You don't have to give me any details, but I'm assuming you two have… entered into a sexual relationship?"

She nodded as I responded with a firm, "Yes."

"Good. That gives me something to go on then." He picked up his notepad and read through a few notes before looking back at Tess, eyes narrowed. "Have you ever been in a sexual relationship before, Tessa?"

She shook her head and her skin burned redder. I felt awful that she had to answer questions like this and I wanted to slap the doctor for make her feel uncomfortable, but at the same time, I felt pride in knowing that I was the first… and last.

"Alright, let's see what we can find out."

He proceeded to put Tess under and explained to her that we were just going to speak with Jessamyn for a minute and find out for sure if she was co-conscious of Tess and the others or not.

She didn't seem to want to show up, though, so he spoke with Lydia instead.

It would always surprise me to see the changes that occurred as the switch to Lydia was made. Things that would seem so subtle to someone who didn't know Tess were extremely evident to me. She was still Tess, but she sat straighter, arranged her face in a knowing expression - almost mischievous - and constantly pulled at the hair around her neck.

Tess would look beautiful, short hair or long, no matter what, but I really hoped Lydia would cooperate and not chop it off on her own.

"What's up, Doc?"

"Hello, Lydia. How are you doing today?"

Her eyes flicked over to me and a playful smile stretched her lips as she looked down at her hands. "I'm doing amazing."

Her response surprised Dr. G, but he didn't dwell on it. "Do you know anything about Jessamyn?"

She shook her head and spoke very clearly, "Not a clue. I didn't even know she was around until Charlie told Tess. And Tess only knows what I know, so…"

Dr. Geoffrey looked confused for a moment before Lydia clarified for him, "She was aware of the last switch, but I don't think it will stick, although she seems to be handling some things better now that she has a little more incentive."

She looked at me again and winked. I winked back at her and her quick intake of breath told me that made her happy. I liked Lydia. She was playful, blunt, and not afraid to go after something she wanted. Much like Tess, but not as subtle about it and there were only a few people who knew that about her.

"I think maybe it's time to start some form of communication then."

I nodded, "Tess wants that. She has decided that maybe it's time to cooperate with… everyone."

"Good. I'll have to talk to *her* about that, but it's good that she has shared that with you. She is making steps in the right direction and I think it will make things easier to handle."

"What about Camryn?" Lydia asked. "I mean, *I* am very willing to communicate and I know that Camryn wants to, but I don't think she will get much of an opportunity. She gets distracted."

"You are right, Lydia. Maybe we should try talking to her again." He hesitated a moment, then seemed to come to a solid decision after glancing between me and Tess a few times. Guess he felt it was safe for him. "Yes, let's talk to Camryn."

After directing her with a few words, Tessa's shoulders dropped and her face was tight and controlled. Her eyes wary and her hands balled into fists. I immediately moved to sit closer to her. My sudden movement made her flinch, but she stayed in her seat.

Dr. G didn't make a sound until her gaze met his.

"Hello, Camryn."

She nodded stiffly and clenched her fists tighter.

I was watching her closely and noticed the tremble in her lips, the dilation of her pupils that made her eyes look almost black. She was terrified, but was doing her best not to show it. Much like Tess, but much more extreme.

I turned to see what was taking the doctor so long to talk to her, I didn't think she would be very cooperative for much longer. She looked like she was about to burst into a million pieces. He was watching *me*. I was puzzled until he nodded and gestured for me to go ahead.

I looked back at Tess/Camryn. She was still absolutely beautiful even with the anger in her eyes.

"Camryn," I whispered and covered her small hand with mine. She was cold and stiff, but I squeezed gently and she looked at me, cautiously. "I won't let anything happen to you or Tess. We need to talk to you, though. Can you talk to us? It will only help her."

Her eyes softened infinitesimally, and she jerked her head in a nod.

"We need to know if you are willing to communicate with Tess in some way so she can know what exactly you need, what is important to you," Dr. G asked slowly and quietly.

"I don't need anything. I don't want anything but for her to be safe. For *me* to be safe," she said, her voice hoarse and shaky.

I opened my mouth to speak, but she cut me off and glared at me.

"Don't think you can promise *me* anything. *She* is the one you have to promise *that* to."

I paused for a moment, letting that sink in. I hadn't told Tess that I would take care of her. Protect her. Erase the memory of the man who was supposed to give his life protecting her, but instead, hurt her more than anyone else ever had. It took her years to really be herself. To *find* herself. I was there when she finally did and I wouldn't let anyone take that away from her. Not even me.

"You *are* her, Camryn. A part of her that is just as important as the rest," I informed her.

She blinked a few times, in fact, I didn't remember her blinking at all before that. She kept her eyes open, not missing a thing, but my statement seemed to make her question everything she thought she knew.

I still held her hand in mine and squeezed again, running my thumb over her silky skin. Her muscles relaxed and her fingers opened, allowing me to slip my hand under hers and cradle her palm. Her eyes never left mine.

"I'll do whatever it takes, Charlie. If she lets me."

I lifted her hand to my lips and kissed her knuckles. She took a quick breath and closed her eyes.

"She will, Camryn. She wants it."

She shook her head, "No," opened her eyes which were the perfect chocolate caramel that was all Tess. "She wants *you*. Always has."

I smiled and kissed her hand again, pride filling my chest and warmth seeping into my stomach. "And I want her. Every single one of her."

Chapter 22

Tessa

This was the strangest dream I think I had ever had, and I thought I had already had some crazy ones. I was following Charlie around like a lost puppy, clinging to him and he didn't seem to mind.

I remember a muffled conversation with Dr. Geoffrey and feeling like I had woken up and come back to reality, but then everything went back to gray.

Charlie held my hand as we walked out of the office and I tried to speak up and tell him that something wasn't right. He just leaned down and kissed me on the forehead, helped me into the car, and shut the door.

My mind was spinning, trying to make sense of things, but it didn't feel real. I didn't feel like me. At least, not completely.

"Charlie?" I finally squeaked out when he buckled himself in and turned on the ignition.

"Yeah, Cam?"

Cam? Oh dear God, I was Camryn right now. No wonder I felt like I was on the other end of some elastic being pulled gently in different directions. No wonder everything seemed so dream like. This was good, though. I was aware. How I left the office still switched only occurred to me for a moment before Charlie spoke again.

"Cam? Tess? Are you in there?"

I tried to speak, but other words came out instead, other thoughts flashed through my mind and my muscles moved without any commands from me.

"She's here, Charlie."

That voice wasn't mine. It was too deep, too throaty. This was fucked up.

"The doctor pulled you back, Tess, then it was like you didn't want to be there. You looked like you were about to crash. Camryn came back."

How? Camryn wasn't calm like this. Camryn was *crazy*.

"I'm *not* crazy!" she said angrily.

That's when everything cleared up, it was like waking up, but the last few seconds were a distorted piece of reality. Like when your alarm is going off and you are dreaming about it, but then suddenly it's really happening.

"Okay fine, you're not crazy. Maybe it's *me* then," I stated, finally hearing my own voice.

Charlie watched carefully as I faded out again, feeling like I was on the edge of consciousness and about to find the sweet darkness of sleep.

"You aren't either," Camryn's low voice replied. "Just a little lost."

It was like I was in a slingshot, snapping back and forth, being released, then pulled back the next second.

"Yeah, I'm lost. How is this happening?"

Charlie's eyes widened when he realized what was going on. "Tess?"

My voice was shaky and breathless, "Yes, it's me. But Camryn is still here. God, I'm freaking out!"

He reached for me, but my body jerked away.

"Wait," Camryn's voice rang out and I was back to the gray. "Let her do it. Let *us* do this."

He pulled his hand back and balled it into a tight fist. I know he wanted to touch me, hell, I *wanted* him to touch me, to wrap me up in his arms and tell me everything was okay. Camryn was right, though.

"Drive, Charlie. Take me home," I said quickly when everything cleared up again.

He didn't hesitate. In fact, he broke several traffic laws on the way back to my mother's. The entire time, Camryn and I 'faced off'. We didn't speak. We just pushed and pulled at each other. Clearing up, then fading out. I was starting to get really tired from the strain I felt in my mind. It was incredible to finally be present for this, but it was absolutely terrifying at the same time.

Good thing Camryn handled terrified really well.

***

"Shit," Charlie exclaimed when we walked into the house a few minutes later, his arm wrapped tightly around my waist, practically holding me up.

Ellie was standing in the living room, facing off with Benny. Well, trying to. Trevor kept trying to move Benny behind him and she was trying to pull herself in front of him - more like throw herself at Ellie - but Trevor was stronger.

I took this in. So did Camryn. Neither one of us could hold ourselves back.

"What the fuck are *you* doing here," we screamed at the same time. I know. It's freaking crazy to imagine both of us speaking out of the same mouth and maybe no one else really heard it, but I did. Her voice was there with mine, so I couldn't tell which one actually came out.

Everyone turned to face me and Charlie. I noticed my mother sitting on the stairs with her head in her hands. She didn't look up, but her voice rang out loudly through the room.

"Oh, she's just here to try to convince Trevor that he was mistaken and that they are still going to get married. Funny, huh? How stupid can one person *actually be*?"

I laughed, because Mom looked like she felt a huge weight off of her shoulders at finally being able to speak her mind in front of Trevor. No one heard me laugh, though. It was all inside my head. It must have been, because I wasn't *me*.

My feet were moving toward the arguing trio without me actually moving them and I felt every part of me, Theresa, get pulled out, like someone had literally reached inside my head and threw me against the wall behind my body. I felt pinned to the wall, unable to reach out to pull myself back.

The switch was fully Camryn and I wanted to close my eyes so I wouldn't see the massacre actually happen. I watched Charlie try to hold me back, but my arm jerked violently out of his hold.

"I *said*," Camryn's voice was a rumble, dangerous, "What. The fuck. Are you doing here?"

She had stepped right up to Ellie who looked like she was about to pee her pants, but her bitchy façade quickly masked her face. Then her awful voice proceeded to grate on the ears of my friends and family.

"None of your business, *freak*!"

Uh oh.

Camryn didn't like that.

I didn't like it either, but I was too stressed out and fuzzy to do anything.

I saw my body lunge towards Ellie, my mind wondering how it was possible to actually have an out of body experience like this while Camryn's mind screamed things that I would never say out loud.

That's when everything went black.

***

"Get off of me you psycho whore!"

I was in the middle of a peaceful darkness one moment, then thrown back into reality the next, finding myself straddling Ellie with my arms hooked by someone stronger than me and hauled off of her quickly.

Benny was shouting for whoever had a hold of me to let me go so I could finish the job. Typical Benny.

Trevor was trying to pull Ellie up to her feet, so that could only leave Charlie as the one holding me against his hard chest.

"Calm down, Camryn," he murmured in my ear, sending a shiver down my spine and, miraculously, tamping down my anger a notch.

"It's Tess. I'm Tess," I said breathlessly, like I had just run a marathon. My body had just exerted a lot of energy without me really knowing it and the instant adrenaline rush I had felt coming out of the switch, left me just as quickly.

I almost collapsed to the ground, but Charlie caught me with a steel arm around my stomach.

"Get off of me!" Ellie screamed and shoved Trevor out of the way. She wanted my head and she was doing everything she could to get it, but Trevor kept her back.

"I think it's time you left," Charlie ground out.

She stopped struggling and glared at me. Then Trevor turned her shoulders to the door and started pushing her out of the room. We all watched him take her to the door and the look on her face turned smug.

Oh God, please don't leave with her, Trevor.

He didn't. He shoved her out onto the porch and slammed the door in her face.

I had never been so proud of my big brother and the glimpse of shock that had hit Ellie's face right before the door shut was priceless.

Trevor walked back to Benny and grabbed her hand. "I'm sorry about the things she said. She's an idiot."

"That's obvious. She cheated on you. Who the hell would cheat on *you*?" she replied with a roll of her eyes. I knew she thought my brother was hot, she had mentioned it several times in New York, but this must have been the first time she said anything like that to Trevor and he must have really liked it, because his mouth crashed down to hers as his arms came around her and hauled her against him.

It was incredibly hot, even though it was slightly sickening because it was my brother.

It was Benny, though. My best friend, and I was happy for her.

I didn't see my mom until she was standing right in front of me, blocking my view of Trevor and Benny locked together.

"Tess?"

My eyes met hers and the anger and sadness I thought I would see in hers, was missing. She looked happy, amused even.

"Yeah, Mom?"

"Camryn should come around more often," she said.

Charlie chuckled behind me, still holding me against him with his arm around my waist. "That's what I keep thinking, Sarah."

My mom smiled, kissed me on the cheek and headed for the stairs. She stopped halfway up and turned back to me with a huge grin covering her face as if she had just discovered something miraculous. "I knew bringing you home would fix everything."

I wasn't so sure about that. I had a feeling that the unanswered questions I still had would change things.

"Come on, Babe. Let's get you to bed. You look like you're about to drop," Charlie whispered into my hair.

I let him guide me to my bedroom, leaving Benny and Trevor alone, but I don't think they noticed. Once he had me sitting on the edge of my bed, he turned to my dresser and pulled out some shorts and a tank top. It was still early in the evening, but it felt like I had been up for a week.

"Is this still what you usually sleep in?"

I nodded and smiled at his selection. Red shorts and a dark green tank top. "Is it almost Christmas already?"

He looked down at the scraps of clothing and smiled when he realized what he had chosen. "Just for that, you aren't going to wear anything to bed."

I laughed and started to pull off my jacket. He put the clothes back in my dresser without taking his eyes off of me and then knelt down on the floor in front of me, pressing his chest against my knees and spreading his big hands over the tops of my thighs.

"I want to ask you something, but I'm afraid it will freak you out," he said quietly. His voice was so soothing when he talked to me like that and he had no clue how agreeable it made me.

"If it freaks me out, then you will just have to calm me down," I said with a wink.

His breath caught and his eyes dilated, but he attempted to cover up his obvious arousal and the smirk that spread across his face. He looked down at my knees and cleared his throat.

"What if I can't calm you down?"

I slipped my fingers under his chin and tilted his face up to look at me. His mouth was set in a firm line and his brow was creased with worry lines. I knew he loved me, but love can only take a person so far. What happens when one of you just can't do it anymore? I ran my fingers over the lines between his brow and tried to smooth them out.

"What is it, Charlie?"

He lifted up to sit next to me on the bed and took my hands in his. He hesitated another moment, then took a deep breath, releasing it before blurting out his question.

"Will you move in with me? Live with me?"

This, I wasn't expecting at all. I thought his question would be about the alters or finding some other treatment, or even about taking things slower than we were taking them. Any of those things would freak me out in some way. I still wasn't completely confident that he had accepted everything even though he kept telling me he had. I didn't know if the books he had been reading said anything about other treatments that might be a little riskier or lead to a termination of the alters. I didn't think any of those would be good for my already fragile mind.

I was terrified that he felt like we had jumped into something neither one of us could handle either. If he wanted to slow things down and get some space from our relationship, that would freak me out.

Yeah, I had my doubts about how far we would get together, and I would need some space to deal with myself at times, but I wanted him. I wanted him so badly, I always had and I always will. He's my anchor, the only thing that keeps me from giving up. I need that, right? I need to take care of myself first, then the alters. They would understand. They had so far.

He was waiting for a response and I had been stupidly staring at him with a blank expression on my face when everything inside of me was exploding like fireworks on the fourth of July.

I *was* freaking out, but it was the best freak out I had ever experienced.

"Tess? If it's too soon, I completely underst--"

I pressed my fingers against his lips and could no longer hold back the smile tugging on my lips. His eyes widened and he held his breath.

"Yes. If you think you can handle me," I murmured and leaned in closer to him, taking in his scent.

He took my face in his hands and pressed a hard kiss to my waiting lips. "I can handle you," he said through a smile. "God, I want to handle you day and night for the rest of my life."

My heart stuttered thinking about spending the rest of my life being handled by him.

He kissed me again, slow and tender, exploring my lips and mouth like he wanted to savor me. His hands dropped down to the hem of my shirt and his fingers slipped underneath, sending a jolt through me at the touch of his warm fingers. I wrapped my hands around the back of his neck and deepened the kiss.

He growled against my lips and his hands became frantic, lifting my shirt up and over my head. He bent his head to the hollow at the base of my throat and pressed his lips against the sensitive skin, inhaling deeply and murmuring things that I couldn't make sense of because my head was swimming with heat.

He deftly unhooked my bra and his body covered mine as he laid me back on the bed. His lips came back to mine greedily while his calloused hands found my swollen breasts and rubbed over the stiff peaks, sending liquid heat down to my core.

A moan tore from my throat, unable to control myself, and he smiled and lifted his head to gaze at me. "We can't be loud here, baby."

Shit. I completely forgot where we were. My mom was probably just down the hall.

He saw the moment the thought registered and buried his face in my neck as he laughed. I would have laughed, too, but his hands were still roaming over my body, worshipping me and making me crazy aroused.

"I can be quiet," I whispered, shutting my eyes tightly so I could concentrate on getting the words out instead of where his hands were.

"You sure? We can go to my place…"

"I don't think I can wait, Charlie."

He kissed my neck and made a path up and across my jaw to my swollen lips that were aching with the need to be kissed again. I moved my hands down his back until my fingers slipped under his shirt and scored his skin with my nails.

The growl that came from deep in his chest was so sexy, my skin flushed as the rush of blood scorched my veins. No way I could wait now. Not with his taste on my tongue and his perfectly sculpted body touching my skin.

He didn't say another word. He just tugged at my jeans while I struggled to pull his shirt off so I could get my hands on his hard chest. By the time we were both naked, all control had been stripped from us as well.

Our bodies ground against each other and our arms couldn't hold each other tight enough. The feel of his skin against mine was almost too much and I had to close my eyes to compartmentalize the pleasure and keep my head on straight.

He hitched my knee over his hip and pressed the tip of his erection against my swollen core. When he didn't move any further, I opened my eyes to see what was taking him so long. I needed him inside me or I think my heart would burst.

His piercing green eyes had darkened and filled with so much heat, I felt like I was being held against the licking flames of a fire.

"I need to see you, Tess. *All* of you. Don't close off any part of you because it's too much. I'll take care of you." His eyes softened and my body relaxed. "I promise."

He kissed me so softly, if I hadn't had my eyes opened, I wouldn't have known it. When his heated eyes found mine again, he thrust into me slowly, stealing my breath and making the pressure in my core build.

He pulled back, then thrust forward again, going deeper and making my toes curl. He did it again until he was buried to the hilt. His jaw clenched as he fought for control, but his eyes never left mine. I tilted my hips, urging him to move, and he gasped at the movement and pressed against me, pinning me down with a hand gripping my hip tightly.

"Please, Charlie."

He once again buried his face in my neck and ground his hips against mine, not making any move to pull out, just pushing to reach deeper inside of me. He inhaled my scent and groaned, the vibration sending goosebumps across my skin.

Then he began to move. Slowly at first, finding a rhythm that sent me soaring.

"I love you, Tess," he breathed.

This man *could* handle me. He could handle *every one* of me.

Chapter 23

Charlie

I never thought, in a million years, that I would wake up next to Tess in her bed, at her mother's house, completely naked, with her mother standing in the doorway smiling like a cat who ate the canary.

It was very strange.

"Do I need to make breakfast?" she asked quietly, not wanting to wake Tess who was pressed against my chest with my arms around her.

For a moment, I thought I was having a nightmare. Like we were back in high school and I had been caught doing naughty things and needed to jump out of the bed and out the window before I got the shit kicked out of me. The smile on Sarah's face threw me off and it took me a moment to realize that she was just happy and not itching to pummel me.

"No, thank you, Sarah. I'm going to take Tess out for breakfast today," I whispered groggily, shifting to make sure the blankets were covering both me and Tess so maybe she would think we were just in bed in our pajamas and nothing else had happened.

"Good. I'll bring some boxes down from the attic so you guys can start packing up her stuff."

She laughed at the shock on my face. How could she possibly know that Tess was going to move in with me when I had just asked her last night?

"Don't look so surprised, Charlie. I know you better than you think. You aren't one to wait too long to make your move anymore, especially now that you finally got her back," she said with a dismissive wave. "Plus, I know my Tess. She may be slow on the uptake sometimes about you, but she loves you."

With that, she walked out of the room and quietly shut the door behind her.

I looked over at the clock and saw that it was already eight o'clock in the morning. Apparently, we were both exhausted from the last few days. Tess stirred in my arms and I kissed the top of her head and rubbed my hand over the soft skin of her arm.

"Mmmm, ça fait du bien."

I froze.

Shit. I don't think I would ever get used to that.

"Jessi?"

Her entire body went rigid and she slowly pushed herself up.

Seeing her blue eyes looking back at me was like watching a ten car pile-up happen right in front of you and not being able to stop your car from smashing into the fray.

"You? What are you doing in my bed again?"

Okay, but the accent was definitely sexy and I could *possibly* get used to it.

We both sat up and she scrambled to find her clothes, picking them up and scowling at them as she examined them. Watching her move around the room, completely naked, with no shame whatsoever, made me nervous. Jessi shouldn't be comfortable with a stranger watching her.

"Jessi, remember what Benny and I talked to you about last time?"

"Yes, I do," she snapped and jerked her pants over her legs angrily. "We need to talk, no?"

I sighed, feeling the happiness from seeing Tess in my arms after a peaceful night float away to be replaced by that heavy, sinking feeling of anxiousness. This woman wasn't anything like Tess, and I had to get through to her.

"Yeah, we need to talk." I pulled my pants on and slipped the t-shirt over my head. "I'll go get everyone. Come downstairs when you are ready, okay?" I automatically moved to kiss her forehead, but she jerked away from me and I realized what I had done. Still, my heart sank at the rejection and I backed away to the door. "I'm sorry, I just… we'll see you in a few minutes."

I heard her huff of frustration just before I shut the door behind me. I squeezed my eyes shut and pinched the bridge of my nose, trying to chase away the coming headache that was prodding against my eyes.

"It's still Tess," I muttered to myself. "Don't forget that."

***

Sarah did not like Jessi. Benny was still just fascinated by the fact that her eyes changed so dramatically. I felt like my heart was being torn from my chest. Not just because this woman didn't want anything to do with me, but because it would tear Tess apart to know what this woman had told me.

I had been waiting for her at the bottom of the stairs after telling Benny and Sarah what was going on. They were waiting in the kitchen and I felt like my shaking knees were going to fail and my body would crash through the floor.

I was terrified.

After finally getting to a good place with Tess, this was going to force a huge jump backwards.

When she finally emerged from the bedroom, my heart raced impossibly faster. She climbed down the stairs and stopped, inches in front of me, glaring.

"I do not want you interfering in my life," she warned me. "I am happy with way I live."

Her accent was thicker today and she was angry. The two seemed to go together really well.

"I do not commit," she bit out, then walked away from me and into the kitchen.

If Tess hadn't told me she loved me already, that right there would have been the thing to chase me away. Failure would have been the *only* option. But Tess *did* love me. Of that, I had no doubt, and even though her words cut right through me and left me bleeding, failure was *not* an option.

An hour later, after Sarah decided she better make breakfast since we weren't going anywhere, we had figured out who Jessi was. It made sense actually.

Tess had always been worried about giving herself to anyone. Almost every single one of the guys she dated before had broken it off with her because they realized they could get easy action elsewhere. She never knew this of course. Overhearing locker room banter forced my hand a few times and those ex-boyfriends had ended up with a black eye. After that, the jerks stayed away from her. I had never been a concern to them before, I was just known as Tessa's scrawny best friend, but after I first met Camryn without realizing it, I was no longer going to fade into the background. I needed to protect her and that included keeping horny boys who couldn't keep their mouths shut, away from her.

We had spent one night going through the tortuous conversation of why she wanted to save herself - tortuous for me because picturing her with anyone else was like a knife to the heart. I wouldn't have objected to *any* reason, I was just glad that no other guy had taken something like that from her. I wanted to be the one she gave it to, but back then, I *knew* it would never happen. The reason she did give me, surprised me. A lot. And it made me want to pummel those guys all over again for hurting her.

"Giving that up would be like handing over my heart to someone and hoping they see the 'handle with care' label before they dive in to tear it open. I'm not the kind of person that can separate those two things at all."

I fell in love with her even more when she told me that, but I never told her. I just stood off to the side and watched her continue on with her life without knowing how I felt. When she decided to give that away, she was going to give *everything.* I wanted everything from her.

Now, sitting at the dining table listening to Jessi tell Benny the same things, but pointing out that she - after a long line of broken hearts - could separate sex and love, and said that she *had* many times, tore me apart. Benny stole glances at me as we listened, pity flowing from her eyes. I felt my shoulders slump further and further until Sarah grabbed my hand underneath the table and tried to squeeze some hope back into me.

She leaned into me so no one could hear her, "Jessi may be Tess, but Tess isn't Jessi."

It was a good reminder, but it did nothing to help my anxiety. Tess was committed to me. She would never be anything but loyal and I trusted her with every fiber of my being, but… I couldn't trust Jessi. Not just because she had no sense of commitment to me, but because she had no sense of commitment to *anyone*. By the look in her eyes, she would sleep with the first man that she came across just to prove it to me.

I hadn't spoken a word the whole time we had been sitting there afraid it would release the nausea that had bubbled up in my stomach. I couldn't sit there any longer, though. I was slowly losing my mind and my confidence in my ability to keep calm, so I shoved away from the table and made my way to the door.

"Charlie, where are you going?"

"I need to go home. I have some… things to do. Let me know when Tess is back."

I hated leaving her. I hated walking away from her without saying goodbye, without kissing her. But I hated the look on her face more. Smug and heartless.

On Jessi's face. This wasn't my Tess.

I looked at her for several long moments, unable to tear my eyes away from her. She was my life and this woman - this alter - was going to tear her away from me if I couldn't straighten things out and I didn't see that happening anytime soon.

Then something happened that made my shoulders rise up in hope, just slightly. Her eyes flickered with heat as she looked back at me, the smug grin on her face faded to concern and the words that - a few minutes before - I thought I would never tell her, slipped out.

"I love you and I won't give up. Whether your name is Jessamyn Rainier, Lydia Cooper, Camryn Garrett, or John Smith, you are still Tess, and Tess is staying with me whether the rest of you want to or not." My voice came out harder than I had intended, but she needed to understand that I wasn't going to waiver. Tess was mine. Every single one of her was *mine*.

***

My house was a disaster.

I had spent the last two hours ripping it apart. I needed to get to the gym and hit the bag over and over until every knuckle had broken and the pain took over. That kind of pain was better than this kind.

I was telling the truth when I said I wasn't going to give up, but saying the words and actually trying not to give up was harder than I thought it would be. She didn't react when I told her I loved her, but I had a feeling those words hadn't been spoken to her in a long time.

Trevor had come by shortly after I had walked in the door, confirming that Benny had told him everything and sent him over to keep an eye on me. He left five minutes later when I asked him what he would be doing if Benny told him she didn't want him in her life.

He slumped down on the barstool he was sitting at and shook his head. "I'm sorry, man. I can't imagine what that did to you."

"Then get out."

He left, but called an hour later to make sure I wasn't doing anything stupid. I wanted to drink myself into oblivion, but didn't have anything to drink and had no desire to leave the house because I knew I would head straight for Tess and *Jessi* would rip me apart all over again. If it wasn't for that short moment where she looked like she wanted to comfort me, I would have probably stopped at the liquor store on the way home. I needed to keep my head on. I needed to make a plan.

The knock at the door pulled me out of my thoughts and I looked around at my living room. I had thrown anything I could get my hands on across the room. Unfortunately, there wasn't much to break, but the mess I had made was enough to tell anyone I wasn't in a good mood.

Another knock, more insistent this time.

"Go away, Trevor!"

I laid my head on the back of the couch and threw my arm over my face. *How was I going to convince --*

"It's Tess."

Her voice was muffled through the door, but I could tell it was her and my heart slammed against my chest. I ran to the door, flipped the deadbolt, and tore it open. The look on her face told me that she knew. I never talked to Benny about whether or not Tess should know what Jessi had said, but apparently, she would have disagreed with me.

"I'm so sorry, Charlie," she whispered and a tear spilled over onto her cheek before I could pull her into my arms.

"Don't. I'll figure something out. Don't lose hope, sweetheart."

I dragged her inside and pulled her onto my lap as I sat on the couch again. She came willingly and melted into my chest reminding me that I was exactly where I wanted to be and no one was going to change that.

"B-but what if she g-goes and sleeps with someone?" She was sobbing and having a hard time taking in a good breath to calm herself down.

I wanted to tell her not to worry about that, but that would be completely hypocritical. It was what I was worried about, too. So instead of talking, I just held her. Pulled her down closer into my chest and wrapped my arms tightly around her. When her tears finally subsided, I cupped her face in my hands and wiped the last drops away with my fingers. Her lips looked so soft and her chocolate caramel eyes were wide with fear.

I couldn't let her see how absolutely clueless I felt. I promised her that I would take care of her and I would be damned if I broke that promise, so I tried to lighten the mood.

"What? You think that after seeing *me* she would want some other loser?"

She smiled, sadly, but enough to wipe the devastation off of her beautiful face. "I'm glad one of us is thinking clearly."

I kissed her forehead and tucked her head under my chin as I muttered, "We'll figure something out."

She nodded and relaxed against me. She trusted me so completely and that was something to hold on to.

"Let's get some of your stuff together to bring here, then we can stop by Dr. Geoffrey's on the way back. See what he thinks."

She hesitated, but nodded in agreement.

We would figure something out.

"First things first," she said quietly, then crushed her lips to mine.

***

Tessa

At first, I had decided to go back to Boston. After switching back and finding myself sitting at the table with Benny and Mom looking like someone had died, and finding out that Charlie had left shortly before, and what Jessi had said, going back to Boston was the only way to protect the people I loved from being hurt by me. Physical or not.

Mom was completely against it and said if I left, she would never speak to me again. We both knew better, but it made her feel like she got in the last word. Benny didn't say *anything* until I was getting ready to go to Charlie's.

"Don't just disappear this time, T."

I was fixing my hair in my bathroom and met her hard stare in the mirror. She stood against the doorframe with her arms folded across her chest.

"Disappearing will burn the only bridges you have still standing. Don't do it again. You'll regret it for the rest of your miserable life," she said firmly. "And it *will* be miserable."

I bowed my head and held onto the counter, my nerves tensing at the thought of telling Charlie that he was going to have to let me go again. "If I tell him, he won't let me go, Benny."

"Yeah. That's why I'm telling you not to disappear. Talk to him. You need to go back, get some more help? Fine. He needs some kind of closure or reassurance that this isn't the end." She shook her head and looked up at the ceiling in exasperation. "You'll lose him forever, T."

"And what if I stay, huh? What if I stay and Jessi ends up sleeping with some other guy? Then what, Benny? It will be worse." I took a deep breath and looked into her big blue eyes, pleading with me to pull my head out of my ass and see what she saw. "Worse for both of us, but Charlie would be devastated. I can't do that to him."

"So running away and not giving it a chance is the answer?"

"I'm not running away, I'm making a decision that's best for everyone."

"You're making a decision that's *easiest* for *you*!"

"It's *not fucking easy!*" I screamed, my hands shaking as I pushed away from the counter. "It's the hardest decision I've ever made! You think that *I* think leaving him is going to make everything all hunky dory? It's not. Just being away from him for the last little while has torn me up inside, but I don't have a choice. At least, not one that will end well for both of us. I'm making the choice that will end well for *him.*"

"And why would you do that?" she whispered.

"Because I can only live with myself if *he* is happy. And he will be. Eventually."

She stepped toward me, just inches in front of me, grabbed my upper arms and held me in place, obviously resisting the urge to shake me. Her eyes were misty and she didn't look like the carefree, do-it-yourself Benny I had come to know. She looked hurt.

"Eventually, Tess?" Her voice broke on my name and I held my breath. This wasn't the norm. She didn't get emotional, ever. "Eventually doesn't happen in real life. It doesn't happen in fairytales and it doesn't happen in romance books. Eventually means 'the end'. And *eventually,* you'll see that taking that choice from him… it will be the biggest mistake you ever made."

For once, I hadn't started crying after having a heart to heart with my best friend. The look on her faced terrified me. "So… let it happen? The same thing you've been telling me since I came back."

"No, T. You can't *let* it happen anymore. You need to *make* it happen. Take control of your life."

I shook my head and started to remind her that I had no control over the alters and that I never would, it just couldn't happen, but she continued to speak before I could get a word out.

"You don't have control right now? *Take it*! You know exactly what you need to do. Accept it, embrace it."

"I already have."

"No you haven't. If you already had, we wouldn't be having this conversation and you wouldn't be leaving the only man you've ever loved just because some French broad got in the way." She released me and took a step back, running her hand through the mess of blonde curls on top of her head. Her eyes flickered with the mischief she was known for. "The Tessa Marshall I know can keep a bitch in line if she poses a threat. Plus, Liddy and Cam got your back."

The corners of my lips twitched, fighting a smile that I knew would push through, eventually.

"Now, before you dive back into that head maze of yours, I have an idea," she said with a smile. "You may not like it, but just hear me out."

Now, I was sitting on Charlie's lap, kissing him like my life depended on it, which it did. So far, he had been incredible in taking things into his own hands and finding ways to be with me. Now, I needed him to take it a little farther because the problem wasn't Jessi. The problem was Charlie. I know he would do anything for me, but this was a long shot. A long shot for both of us, but I had come to accept that this was the only way for both of us to be happy. I shifted on his lap and he groaned and moved my legs to either side of him so I was straddling him.

"Tess, baby, I need to make love to you," he breathed against my mouth, gripping my hips and pressing himself against me.

"Promise me something first," I replied on a groan, breaking the kiss and resting my forehead against his.

He looked into my eyes, the beautiful green of his, dark and glazed. Right where I needed him.

"Anything," he moaned.

***

"How do you expect me to do that, Tess? It doesn't really feel right."

I kissed him softly and held his head between my hands so he couldn't turn away from me and break eye contact. He needed to know how important this was to me.

After my chat with Benny and a quick stop at Dr. Geoffrey's to confirm that this was a plausible idea, I felt like the only choices I had were to leave or do this, and since I didn't really want to leave Charlie, this was the option I went with.

"But Tess--"

I covered his mouth with my finger and he let out a sigh. Tracing the lines of his face with my index finger, I locked into memory every tiny scar - including the newest one that was healing nicely above his eyebrow - every shape, and the feel of his skin under my fingertips.

"I know it's crazy of me to even be okay with it let alone ask you to do this," I said softly, following the path my finger was making, and watching his eyes slowly close in pleasure at my touch. "But it's still me, right?"

I let my fingertip linger on his bottom lip and his tongue darted out to taste me and pull it in for a kiss. His hand on my hips contracted and I knew he understood what I was asking.

"I had wanted to talk to you about this before, but never had the balls to ask what you thought. Plus, it just seemed like an impossibility. How could I do it and still feel loyal to you?"

"I know deep in my heart that you would never be unfaithful to me, Charlie." I kissed his parted lips and pressed my forehead to his, gripping my fingers in the hair at the nape of his neck. "But they need *your* love just as much as you need *theirs*. And it is still me. Like you have always said. Just… a different side of me that shows up in a… not so conventional way."

I smiled at him, attempting to ease the idea in a way that would make it more amusing than ludicrous. He grinned at me, but it was cautious. And why wouldn't it be? I had just asked my boyfriend to try to love each individual alter the way he loves me, but not just that, I had asked him to make love to each one when the opportunity arose. He had told me that he already loved them in his own way, because they were me. I had asked him to try and love each one for *her*.

Was I sick and twisted? No.

Was I slightly crazy? Maybe, but I had to be.

"And what if they don't want to? What if they freak out and end up leaving because they think I forced myself on them or used them?"

Good questions, but questions I had the answers to, thanks to Benny.

"If they love you, wanting to won't be a problem. It will take time for them to realize that you truly love them, if that is something you will be able to accomplish. I know it's crazy, Charlie, but it's the only way that all of them will be on board." I took a deep breath and steeled myself to give him the ultimatum. It was cruel and manipulative, but it was the only way.

"If they freak out and end up leaving, then it will be for the best. Before I came over, my plan was to go back to Boston."

He stiffened and gripped me tighter, his eyes going wild and his expression turning into something that I never wanted to see on his face. Hopelessness.

"Baby, I'm not going anywhere. Not unless we both agree on it," I said firmly.

He relaxed and looked down at the front of my shirt. I saw his lips twitch, fighting back a smile, before he could hide it from me.

"What's so funny?"

He looked back up at me, smiling so brightly, I was sure the strength of it was brighter than the sun. "Not funny. Just… that's the first time you have called me anything other than my name. Baby."

I scrunched my eyebrows in confusion for a moment before he sat up straight and kissed me quick and hard.

"I *really*, really like it."

I was stunned into silence. Had he been in the same conversation with me? Of all the things to focus on, *that* was what he heard.

"I know you won't leave, Tess. I won't let you. So I'm not worried about that." He raised a hand and tucked a lock of hair behind my ear, still grinning. "I'm just glad you didn't disappear again."

I leaned into his touch and closed my eyes. It felt good to be on the same page and it felt good to have a plan. He still hadn't exactly agreed to it, but I was open to suggestions.

"I'll do whatever you ask me to do, love," he muttered and kissed my chin. "It will definitely take some getting used to." He kissed my throat and I leaned my head back to give him more room to work. "And I can't promise you that I can do it." He kissed the skin where my neck and shoulder meet. "But I'll do it." He kissed my collar bone, then tilted my head back down to look at him. "For you."

Chapter 24

Charlie

It had been four weeks since Tess had asked me to not only make her alters fall in love with me, but for me to fall in love with each one of them. For them. Of course, knowing they were all a part of Tess was a big help, but I found each one of them to have characteristics that definitely appealed to me. It sounds crazy and when Trevor and Sarah found out about it, I think they were tempted to have both of us checked in to the nearest psych ward. How could someone plan to fall in love? It was the only way that made sense, though, and why wouldn't it? Everyone wanted to be loved by someone. I couldn't expect to get each alter on board - neither could Tess - unless they knew their best interests were in mind.

Lydia and Camryn were aware of the plan, obviously, and both were eager to spend time with me, which was weird at first. Benny stuck close to Tess whenever I couldn't, making sure that Jessi didn't show up and try to cause trouble. I had another fight coming up and training was up there on my to do list so Tess made sure I stayed focused, but we made it work.

I had found a new coach who worked well with me and actually had a lot of new techniques that Rob hadn't thought of. I told him not to plan on anything long term because I was in the process of working some things out to get out of the fighting and into the training.

There were always young guys, teenagers really, that needed an outlet. Working out and focusing on something as disciplined as martial arts was something they could get excited about. Tess told me to do what I thought was best for *me*. She didn't enjoy watching me get beat up, but she thought watching me fight was 'beautiful'. Benny gave her a hard time about that. *She* thought it was 'hotter than hell' to watch. Trevor gave *her* a hard time about *that*, but ended up coming to the gym more often and training a bit himself.

I had been training all day, anticipating the fight coming up in two nights, and was wiped out. Sleep had been hard to come by since Tess had been a bundle of nerves the whole week and had been switching more often than usual. Dr. Geoffrey said to just let it happen and take the opportunity to get to know my girls better.

My girls.

I don't know when I had started thinking of them as 'my girls', but I had, and I liked it. I was to the point where I didn't need to hear a word from her to know that Tess had made a switch. The way each one held herself was so unique, I knew who she was as soon as she walked into the room, or woke up, or even looked at me.

Jessi steered clear of me as much as possible. When it was Jessi going to bed at night, which wasn't often, she used the guest bedroom, but I would always wait until she fell asleep and sneak in to sleep next to her. She didn't really speak to me much except for the few times Benny had initiated a discussion with the both of us present. They got along pretty well and Jessi was actually pretty hilarious. She was smart and observant, but in a way that made you wonder what she had been through. She was civil to me, but didn't seem to like me at all.

There were some mornings, though, that I woke up to find Tess gone, but felt her eyes on me. Whenever I found them, they were blue and filled with confusion before they turned away and left the room. She had been watching me and she didn't say anything more about leaving her alone. Just kept to herself around me.

Tess was excited about this new development. She had started keeping a journal with encouragement from Dr. Geoffrey. It was a direct line of communication between her and the girls and because of it, Jessi stuck around when she found herself in my home, which tamped down the amount of drama I had expected. After the first week of Tess writing in the journal, there was a definite change in the way she approached the situation. She was happy.

It was progress.

Tonight, walking in the front door and finding Benny sitting on my couch with Trevor - both looking nervous as hell - I felt the exhaustion deepen. I just wanted to be with Tess tonight and the disappointment at finding them in my house was heavy. Then, their nervousness registered in my tired mind.

"What's going on?"

Benny looked to Trevor, who shrugged like he always does, and then back to me.

"She's making escargot," she whispered harshly. "Do you have any idea what escargot is?"

"Umm, I think it's snails in butter or something. It's a French dish."

"Escargot is a delicacy in my country. Not 'snails in butter'. Mon Dieu!"

Tess/Jessi walked out of the kitchen carrying a white platter with several plates of small shells filled with a slimy piece of meat, glaring at me before rolling her eyes.

"She's trying to *kill* us, Charlie!" Benny shouted and immediately turned green.

"No *kill*, educate," Jessi laughed.

God, she had a good laugh. It was exactly like Tess laughed, but more reserved, and she didn't blush when she realized how loud she had laughed like Tess did - which I absolutely adored. No, she rolled her eyes, like Tess did whenever I teased her. I thought it would take time to really feel anything for the alters, but I found myself deeper and deeper every day.

What would happen if they *all* turned away from me? There would be no saving me.

I was staring at her, and had been since she had walked into the room, until she looked up at me with a smile I rarely saw from her.

"I am to assume you will not try," she said and smirked with her arms folded across her chest.

Another similarity to my Tess. She liked to challenge me, but wasn't as nice about it. Tonight was different, though and she was playful with me. I wanted to point it out, but decided not to, afraid that it would scare her off. So instead, I gave her my best smile, the one Tess always 'swooned' over - her word, not mine - and reached down to grab one of the forks she had brought out. She quirked a perfectly sculpted eyebrow at me, daring me to continue.

Benny was shaking her head at me, begging me not to do it, while Trevor tried to stifle a chuckle. He had become himself more and more since he started dating Benny, which Sarah made a point to mention anytime we were all together. Another thing to thank my Tess for.

I stabbed one of the slimy morsels and twisted it out of its shell. The garlic butter dripped off of it as I raised it to my mouth. She was still expecting me to chicken out, but this wasn't about eating snails - which is disgusting to me - it was about doing something for Jessi. Giving her a glimpse of me that she hadn't allowed until tonight.

I popped the snail into my mouth and chewed slowly. It actually wasn't that bad, a little slimy and rubbery, but not bad. Benny covered her mouth and gagged.

I kept my eyes on Jessi, who was in shock as she watched me. With another smile, I winked at her and said, "Pretty good."

She blinked and her lips turned into a pleased grin, almost as if me praising something she did made her day. "Really?"

I nodded as I finished chewing and swallowed. "Yeah. It's great. Thanks for making it." Then I sat down and stabbed another bite, making Benny turn her head into Trevor's shoulder so she didn't have to watch me.

"Oh. Umm, you are very welcome… Charlie."

My name in her accent was almost as great as my name in Tessa's voice. She hadn't said it in the last four weeks and was rarely very polite to me.

Definite progress.

***

"I think Jessi is starting to like you, Charlie."

It was the morning of the fight and I was helping Tess 'wash her back' against the tile wall of my shower. I had already abandoned the soap and had been running my hands over her slick skin while, apparently, her mind had been elsewhere.

"Am I doing something wrong here? You should be so aroused that your mind is focused on *one thing*. Me."

She giggled and pressed her backside into me, making me groan and tighten my grip on her.

"I *am* focused on you. I just thought you would like to know that Jessi wrote some interesting things about you."

I kissed the spot behind her ear, which drove her crazy, and moved my hands up to massage her shoulders so I could partially listen to what she had to say without getting too distracted. "And what did she write?"

"Mmm, that feels so good," she moaned and dropped her forehead against the tile.

"Baby, you better tell me what you have to tell me, because I'm about to burst here. Plus, you making those little sounds always sends me over the edge."

She giggled again and turned in my arms, not helping my situation at all since now her perfectly rounded breasts were pressed up against me.

"Okay, okay. She wrote about that night she made the snails, which is disgusting by the way, and she said that you surprised her. She said that you looked so tired that night and thought it was sweet that you told her to go to bed while you cleaned up her mess… well, my mess." She kissed my chin and wrapped her arms around my waist. "She also said that you look so handsome every time she sees you come home from the gym."

I felt like a kid at Christmas. "Really?"

She looked up into my eyes and smiled. "Yep, guess that means I have some competition now." She meant it as a joke but frowned when she realized what she actually said. "I'm sorry, I shouldn't have said that. I know this is hard for you."

"Tess." I tucked a wet strand of hair behind her ear and ran my fingers along her jaw. "There's no competition. We are lucky that they are so much like you. Knowing you are in there is what keeps me going."

She nodded warily, but looked straight at my chest and refused to meet my eyes.

"I love you," I muttered and kissed her forehead. "Now… can I please finish what I started when we got in here? The water isn't going to stay hot forever and I'm seriously losing my mind with your wet skin sliding against mine."

She smiled and rolled her eyes.

"Oh, baby, you shouldn't have done that."

I grabbed a handful of her very sexy ass and squeezed, making her squeal and laugh just before I covered her mouth with mine and plunged in to taste her. Even in the shower, she tasted like mint and rain, sending my senses into overdrive. Her skin slid over mine, soft and warm, and the feel of her in my arms got better and better every time.

"Maybe I can just forfeit this fight and we can stay home, in bed all day," I suggested and slid my lips across her jaw and down her neck. She shivered and gasped, but I hadn't succeeded in erasing her common sense like I wanted to.

"Charlie, there is nothing I would like to do more, but you don't really want to skip this fight. You've worked so… hard over the last few… oh God… weeks and I would hate to see--" She was cut off by a very sexy and very feminine growl tearing from her lips as I found the hard peak of her breast and pulled it into my mouth.

"What were you saying, baby?" I murmured against her breast.

"What?"

Mission accomplished.

Now, that she was thoroughly distracted, I lifted her by the backs of her thighs and fit myself between her legs, pressing her back against the cool tile.

She clung to my shoulders and threw her head back as I gently bit down on her nipple, then rolled it across my tongue. She was so damn responsive. She was passionate and held nothing back. She was made for a man to worship, inside and out, and *I* was that man.

She rolled her hips against my stomach and her heat pulled me further and further into her. I couldn't get enough. I would never get enough. She was the prize at the end of the race, the peak of every mountain, the one thing a man would strive for, knowing he would never truly discover all her secrets, but would die trying… die smiling.

She was mine.

Finally, she was mine.

And I was hers.

I entered her in a single thrust, making her cry out my name and finding a place so deep inside her, I knew I would never be able to crawl out. I never wanted to. She made me complete. Pulled every piece of me together and made it fit so easily.

Her name fell from my lips as I started to move and the sounds she made drove me closer to the edge of my sanity. I was too close.

"Baby, I need you to help me out. You're just too damn sexy, I can't control myself right now."

She met my eyes with rapturous confusion, trying to catch her breath enough to respond. "What can I do?"

I thrust hard and deep, forcing a whimper from her, then stilled myself before I lost it. "Touch yourself. I want to, but I don't want you to fall."

She nodded quickly in understanding and her hand slid down my chest and stomach to where we were joined, her fingers connected to that sweet spot that made her fall apart. I didn't dare move, but my cock jumped inside her when she started to move her fingers in slow circles. *Maybe this wasn't such a good idea.* The sight of her pleasuring herself sent electricity shooting down my spine.

At this rate, I wouldn't have to move an inch and I would still burst.

She moaned, forcing me to tear my eyes away from her hand and meet her heavy lidded gaze. She was close. Already so close, and I was desperate to push her over to the other side.

I gathered what control I could and retreated the short, yet grueling, journey back through the tightness of her heat, then thrust forward, finding that perfect place inside of her again. She cried out as her orgasm ripped through her body and her body gripped me so flawlessly. One last faltering thrust was the last I could give before my own orgasm broke through.

Her mouth hovered over mine, sharing the same breaths, as I poured myself inside of her coming face to face with the forces that drove a man to his knees.

God, I loved being that man.

Chapter 25

Tessa

Charlie had nearly begged me to go with him to the stadium. In fact, he had me dragged out to the car where Jake and his new coach, Johnny, were waiting for us, before I convinced him to go ahead without me and I would wait and go with Benny and Trevor a couple hours later. I didn't want to distract him.

That's the excuse I gave him which he thought was bullshit, which it was, but I couldn't tell him that I was worried about switching. I had felt the disconnection shortly after our very long shower and I rushed to write what I needed in my journal before I lost myself.

There were times when I didn't remember a switch with Camryn or Lydia. The co-consciousness I thought I had reigned in was not consistent and it was extremely frustrating. The journal helped, but I knew there were pieces missing that could easily help me understand the girls a little better.

Benny kept lecturing me about being patient and that this wasn't going to smooth out overnight, or really over the next year, probably. I knew that, but my impatience was stemmed from my love for Charlie. He kept reminding me that he could handle it, but that wasn't enough. I needed Jessi on board.

I was sitting in the living room, closing my journal, when Benny walked in the door. Something Charlie had already talked to her about, but she chose to ignore when she knew he wasn't home. I didn't even try to stop her. It was no use.

"You ready?" she asked as she skipped into the room. She was furious about Charlie giving up the fighting. Something about not getting her fix of sweaty, muscled men. Trevor was working on that, though.

"Yeah, just finishing up a few things."

"Do I need to ask who you are?"

I smiled at the familiar question, the one that had kept me grounded for so long. "No. It's me."

Her eyes narrowed and her arms folded firmly across her chest in disagreement. "Honestly?"

I dropped my head in my hands and tried to rub away the detachment that was growing stronger by the minute. "I don't know."

"Shit. You are going to miss the fight?"

"I think so."

I was disappointed, but at the same time, hopeful that I wouldn't have to watch Charlie get hurt tonight. I loved watching him fight, but the nausea that clawed to the surface when his opponent found a way through his careful evasion, was too much for me to take in. Especially tonight. The only thing that kept me from fully embracing that hope was the question of whether or not Jessi would make an appearance.

"Please, Benny. Don't let me out of your sight tonight."

She plopped down onto the couch beside me and leaned forward with her elbows on her knees. "I'll do my best, T. Jake is going to keep watch on you, too, I'm sure."

Panic forced a lump to form in my throat. "I don't think that's a good idea.

"Don't worry. He knows that Charlie will have his nuts if he touches you. Plus, I think he is dating some chick Johnny introduced him to."

My relief was short lived by her next words.

"I don't think she is coming, though, so maybe let me take over the seating arrangements, yeah?"

"Aaahhh," I growled. "Maybe I should just stay home."

"HA! Yeah right. That would make things so much worse, T. Plus, if you stay, I'll just tell Charlie that Jessi had a date which will, therefore, send him running home to you anyway and missing the fight."

"Fine! But I swear to God, if anything bad happens tonight, I am holding *you* personally responsible… and I'll tell Trevor about your week long 'holiday' from the facility."

She gasped, "You wouldn't dare!"

I narrowed my eyes at her in a dare to doubt me. "I would."

During that first three months after Benny and I had met, she had decided to 'sneak out' and go have some fun. She had admitted herself in so there really was no need for her to pretend that she was an escaped mental patient, but she said it added to the thrill. During that week that she was gone, she went dark and ended up in a lot of trouble. She didn't give me all the details, but I do know that she ended up on prime time news channels with her crazy looking mug shot shining for all of Boston to see.

I have no idea who bailed her out of jail and cleaned her up, but whoever it was, she owed big time.

"Touché," she said proudly and stood from the couch. "Let's go then. Mom is coming anyway, so I have back up."

"She's coming? I thought she didn't want to."

"She didn't, but I guess Charlie convinced her to come."

Weird. She had told me plenty of times that she supported Charlie completely, but wouldn't watch him get beat up if she was paid a million dollars. I guess she had as hard of a time saying no to him as I did.

"Alright then. Let's get out of here before I lock myself in the bathroom."

The drive was short. Too short. Not enough time for me to get my thoughts straight, and by the time we parked in the underground garage, a building over from the stadium, I was a mess.

Benny and Mom flanked me on each side, holding me steady as we made the walk to the entrance.

I didn't get to see the inside, though.

***

Charlie

"What do you mean Tess isn't coming?" I shouted after Trevor relayed the message from Benny that he received shortly after they had taken their seats.

"Umm, well, she's heeerre, but not *here.*" He looked nervous, and he should be

"Who is it, Trevor?"

I didn't mind so much that Tess had switched. She was probably a little happy about it as long as she didn't remember the fight afterwards, but the fear that the switch was Jessi, who still hadn't given any indication that she was not going to find some guy…

God, I couldn't even think about it without wanting to put my fist through something.

"Hey, calm down, man. Benny and my mom are sticking with her and I already talked to Jake. He's going to make sure they all stay in their seats and will keep anyone else away from them."

"Jake? You should probably tell Jake that includes *him.*"

Trevor shook his head while I paced back and forth, trying not to rip the door off its hinges and drag Jessi back here to tie her to the bathroom sink.

"Charlie, she's not the same girl she says she is. Benny thinks she might be coming along."

He was right. According to Tess and Benny, Jessi had learned to accept her situation and was making an effort to come to an understanding with Tess, which was great. Marvelous, really, but she hadn't come to any kind of understanding with *me*, yet.

It's selfish, I know, but give me a little credit. Tess was a woman to tie yourself down with. Which is what I had planned to do after the fight. Sarah was here for that reason only. It took some convincing, but after I told her my plan, she had no excuse good enough.

Johnny had the ring in his pocket, ready to hand to me when the time was right. I had planned this for a week. Made sure I had the right words and waited for the right time to ask Tess to marry me.

But Tess wasn't really here.

"Hey! Snap out of it, Charlie, and focus. You don't want to get your ass handed to you out there with her watching. That would kill Tess when she finds out and believe me, she will find out."

I turned to the heavy bag hanging from the ceiling and buried my thoughts with the force of my punches. Johnny walked in a minute later and gave me a warning glare to not exhaust myself.

"If Jessi would just trust me, maybe she could… I don't know," I grunted and started pacing again.

"Maybe that's the problem. She doesn't trust you. You don't trust *her*," he said matter-of-factly. "Give her the benefit of the doubt."

He was right again and it was really starting to bug me. "When did you get so wise with relationships?"

He shrugged and turned to leave, "When I found a real one."

"Charlie!"

I whipped around at the sound of Benny's breathless voice coming from the open door. It looked like she had sprinted back here, she also looked like she was up to no good.

"I have the best fucking idea ever!"

Sometimes 'no good' was the only option.

***

This wasn't going to work because it was ludicrous. It was foolish and immature, but it made sense. After the fight, Benny was going to bring Jessi back, but Trevor was going to bring a couple girls back, too.

"I don't want to do this, B. Tess isn't going to like this," Trevor muttered and ran a hand through his hair.

"Since when do you do anything Tess likes?"

"True."

"It's going to work. Jessi is already looking a little jealous about all of the people cheering for you. There are girls behind us that have done nothing but talk about you, Charlie, and she looks like she's ready to pull a Camryn."

I had been sitting on the couch, listening to her tell me her ridiculous idea, with my head in my taped hands and my knee bouncing a mile a minute.

"We shouldn't even be discussing this. He needs to focus on the fight right now."

"Alright, just leave everything to me."

Before I could stop her and tell her there wasn't a chance in hell that I would leave it all to her, she was gone.

"Thirty minutes," Johnny called from the hall.

I looked over at Trevor who seemed like he was about to vomit. He didn't like this anymore than I did.

"I trust her, Charlie. I just don't want my sister hurt."

And I did? What if this whole thing backfired? The chance of it actually working was slim to none. Bringing in girls that were going to try to hang all over me and hoping that Jessi got jealous enough to admit that she felt something for me… it was desperate.

I just nodded, knowing there was no way for me to reassure him. He knew how much I loved Tess, but I was also in a position where I had no control whatsoever. A man does get desperate once in a while.

"Maybe just leave me alone for a while. I need to get my head straight," I bit out. I didn't want to be so harsh, but I was using all of my energy to stay in this stuffy room and not throw everything that I had worked for away.

"Good luck," he mumbled and shut the door behind him.

I spent the next fifteen minutes inside my head, sorting out the worries I didn't need to hold on to. By the time my team came to haul me to the ring, I was focused enough to get myself through the fight. My eyes roamed over the front row next to my corner and I saw Benny and Sarah clapping and cheering for me. Jessi's head was turned and she was talking to Jake who was sitting on her other side.

I saw red until she turned her head and found me. She grinned at me and damn if it didn't make me puff out my chest like a freaking animal. She felt *something* for me, even if it was just some kind of close friendship or pride. We lived together, after all, so she saw me more often than not. After what Tess had told me this morning, there was hope.

The crowd cheered as I made my way into the ring and waited for the other guy. I was fighting a guy who had only been in the circuit for two years, but hadn't lost a fight, yet. He was younger than me, but just as big and from what I had seen and heard, he could pack quite the right hook.

Didn't matter, though. Whether or not I won this fight had no effect on what happened in the near future. I had enough money put away to live comfortably for a long time and that included my plans to open up my own training center. I just needed to get this over with and move on.

I wouldn't stop training and staying in shape and maybe I could take the occasional fight for a little extra money and the thrill of doing it, but for now, my focus was Tess. I know she wanted to go to school. She didn't get the chance before and she wasn't the type of person to just sit back and be taken care of. I was going to give her the chance to do whatever she wanted. She deserved to live a normal life.

The guy on the microphone announced my opponent. 'The Ripper'. Frankie 'The Ripper' Martelli. I hadn't told Tess his name and I felt guilty for the relief I felt knowing she still hadn't heard it. She wouldn't have been able to keep herself calm. I glanced over to where she sat… where Jessi sat, and saw her watching me carefully, but her gaze was almost blank. It was more of a pensive stare. She was thinking about something and looked like whatever it was, ticked her off. I glanced over at Benny who had her hand over her mouth and an amused look in her eyes. She saw my confusion and pointed her thumb to the row behind them.

Two women sitting behind them, dressed for more of a swim party than a fight, were glaring at the back of my girl's head. I glanced back at Jessi and she had slouched back in her chair with her arms crossing over her chest and an angry expression. Benny leaned over and said something to her that made her glance up at me and shift in her seat.

Our gazes locked and her blue eyes hooded. She wanted me, I know she did, so what happened next was like a right hook to the face.

She leaned over, closer to Jake, and muttered something in his ear. He smiled at whatever it was she had said and then shook his head and started a conversation with her. I wanted to jump down there and throw him out of the chair and across the arena. He was clearly flirting with her and I saw red again when I realized she was flirting back.

Johnny was yelling something to me, but I didn't hear him. The roar in my head was deafening. Jake's eyes flickered over to me, obviously wondering if he was getting away with the stunt he was pulling, and his face paled when he caught my glare. It only took a few more seconds of speaking to her before he scooted farther away from her in his chair and focused on the announcer.

What had seemed like hours, had only been minutes. Frankie was already in his corner loosening up and glancing around at the crowd with a grin. He was a good looking guy, dark hair and eyes, bronzed skin showing his Italian decent. Unfortunately for him, I was now having a really bad night. He looked like a nice kid and like he really enjoyed the attention and the career. I almost felt bad that I was going to mess up that baby face of his.

Next thing I knew, we tapped gloves and the fight began. We circled each other for several seconds, measuring the other up and waiting for the right time to strike. He still had a slight grin on his face. Confidence. Good thing to have.

He struck first. A left jab that I narrowly avoided. He was quick and I felt the slight breeze hit my cheek from the force of it. I swung my leg out to drop him but he was quick to jump away. His grin got a little wider and it looked like he was having the time of his life.

My eyes flickered over to my girl. She was watching me with a heat in her eyes that I hadn't seen before. She tried to cover it up, but I saw it. I winked at her then charged.

Poor Frankie never saw it coming.

Chapter 26

Jessi

How Tessa did this was a mystery to me.

Charlie was a force to be reckoned with. He was beautiful, the way he moved, so graceful and so… powerful. I couldn't take my eyes off of him.

Neither could all the other women in the room.

The two sluts behind us were talking louder and louder the more they saw me fume. Mon Dieu! What a pain in my ass. They had no respect for themselves or Charlie… or anyone that was sitting around them that might be a little protective of him.

Protective?

Yeah, definitely.

I wanted Charlie. I didn't *want* to want him, but I did anyway and after fighting it for a month, I couldn't think of a better time to just give in. Even if that meant changing the life I thought I knew, completely. I had nothing to lose anymore. The life I thought I had, actually didn't belong to me. It was surreal.

But I had everything to gain.

I had Tess, Benny, Charlie, and everyone else that came with them. I had never felt that kind of closeness before. My life had been filled with meaningless relationships that were only pursued for personal gain, not always on my side of it, though. I had spent the majority of my time proving to myself that I wasn't fragile, while I tried to keep the pieces of my soul together.

Now, with these people who loved Tess more than anything and therefore loved me, I could breathe a little.

That first time I saw Charlie, I thought I had made a mistake. I never attempted to pursue a man who I could see myself with in the future. I stayed away from them because I didn't want to be disappointed when they ripped my heart out from being unfaithful or uncaring. The way he looked at me didn't help in my effort to keep my distance. I was drawn to him and he to me.

At least, that is what Tess had communicated to me. She wrote about the friendship they had years ago and how she knew there was no other man on earth who could love her the way he did.

I wanted that, too.

So, tonight, I decided that I would give this whole thing a chance. He was a loyal man, a strong man who fought for what he wanted.

I needed to be like Tess. I needed to fight for what *I* wanted.

Tess would keep me safe.

Charlie wouldn't break my soul.

He wouldn't break my heart.

***

Charlie

The fight only lasted one round.

The first hit I connected stunned Frankie and after that it was over. He couldn't defend himself once I got him to the ground. His fist did connect with my bottom lip, though, and it was split open and bleeding as I made my way to the backroom. The kid was a good sport. He gave me a weak hug and that same cocky grin.

"Thanks for that, Mackenzie," he had said.

After looking at him in confusion for a few seconds, he laughed, "Or is it *you* who should be thanking *me*? Guess you're night is going as well as mine."

I didn't stick around much longer. I needed to stop Benny from carrying out her ridiculous plan and I just had to pull Jessi aside and talk to her.

Unfortunately, Benny and Trevor were quicker than I thought. The two bimbos that had been sitting behind them were sitting on the couch waiting for me looking like predators about to make their next kill. When they saw me walk in with my team in tow, they launched themselves at me.

I felt bile rise up as their scent hit me. I think they may have bathed in nothing but perfume and the strength of it was nauseating. That headache I had been fighting back was now the only thing I could focus on.

"What a fight. You were so incredible out there, like, totally insane. Watching you… wow! It seriously is like, so hot."

"Umm, thanks." I looked around frantically for Benny and Tess… or Jessi, I guess, but they weren't in the room. Trevor was, and he looked like he was about to run. "If you even think about it, you take these with you."

He shook his head and started toward me. By then, the girls had latched themselves onto each arm and were plastered against me. Hands were roaming over me as I struggled to get away without hurting them.

"Please, don't. You ladies need to get out."

They both laughed like I had just told the funniest joke and pressed closer. "We were told that we could hang out with you. Looks like you need some company anyway. We are available and will take really good care of you."

I tugged harder to get my arms out of their vise like grips. They were surprisingly strong for how skinny they were and their bony fingers were sure to leave bruises.

"Get off of me and get out," I said firmly.

"What the hell?"

I jerked my head to the door at the sound of her voice. Blue eyes were looking my way.

"Jessi."

She was glaring at the two hyenas attached to my sides, but when she looked into my eyes, I saw pain.

Trevor finally came to my aid and pulled one of the girls off of me as I pushed the other away, making her fall onto the couch. I saw the decision in Jessi's eyes before she took the first step. She flew towards the girls with a fierceness that I had never seen before.

She was going to kill them.

I stepped in front of her as she careened towards the one in Trevor's grasp. She crashed into my chest, but pushed and shoved as she tried to claw her way to the woman. I wrapped my arms around her tiny waist and lifted her off the ground before she could get away. She was screaming in French so I had no idea what she was saying, but from the sound of it, it was filthy.

I hauled her out the door and into the room across the hall, kicking the heavy door shut behind us and turning the lock before setting her down.

"Let me go! I need to teach those sluts a lesson!"

Her cheeks were flushed and her brow was scrunched in anger. The fire in her blue eyes was blazing, much like the inferno in Tessa's eyes when she got mad.

It was gorgeous.

"After I'm done, you can do whatever you want. Just let me go out there and--"

I silenced her with a hard kiss and pulled her into my arms again. She went stiff for a few seconds until I swept my tongue over her bottom lip, then she melted against me and started to move her lips against mine.

My cut lip stung with the force of the kiss, and I knew it was going to start bleeding again, but I ignored it. The pain was nothing.

I slipped my tongue into her mouth and she made a whimpering sound that sent electricity coursing through my veins. I pulled her tighter against me and she wrapped her arms around my neck, tugging on my hair to get me closer.

I felt myself starting to lose control and realized that I had completely forgotten that this wasn't Tess. I tore away from her leaving both of us panting.

"Charlie. What… why did you do that?"

I took a few deep breaths, willing my body to calm down, before I answered her.

"Why wouldn't I?"

She shoved a hand through her long hair and turned away from me. I knew what I had to do. Tess would want me to do it before I lost her completely.

"I love you, Jessamyn. You may not know why and I don't know how to explain it, but I do."

"You do?" Her eyes were wide and frightened and I could see the beat of her pulse in her slender neck. I wanted to feel that rhythm with my lips, but I didn't move. I stayed in front of the door so she couldn't leave before I was finished.

She looked down at her feet, wringing her hands together nervously. She spoke so quietly that I almost couldn't hear her. "You are the only man I feel safe with. The only man I could ever see myself…"

"See yourself what?"

She changed her mind about whatever she was going to say and turned away from me again. "How is this possible? How can you love Tess and still love the rest of us?"

"Because that's what Tess wants. She doesn't want to live her life as four different women. She wants all of you to be able to live that life *with* her. I don't want her to be afraid, though, if that doesn't work out."

"I'm sorry, Charlie. I don't understand what you say."

Her accent was getting thicker as her emotions started to crash around her. I could tell that she was about to lose it and I wasn't sure why.

"You are a part of Tess. A part she created to deal with the worry and fear she has about being with me for the rest of her life. You are her strength in her love for me. Without you…"

She stepped closer to me as I thought about my next words. My heart raced and my fingers twitched with the urge to grab onto her and never let her go.

"I don't want to lose *any* of you. I see how each of you are a piece of her. A strength for her that she may not believe she can have herself." I stepped toward her, close enough to feel the heat radiating off of her. "That makes her strong in ways other women can't be all at once. Therefore, Tess is the perfect woman because she has all of you."

Her lips twitched, fighting a smile. I lifted my hands and held her face between them.

"I've got a lot of holes in my soul, Jessi. You all make up the perfect woman to fill them."

Her blue eyes pierced through me as she looked into my eyes, like she was reaching into the missing pieces of my soul and mending them together.

"I have never been in love before, Charlie. Is that what this is?"

I kissed her lips softly then pressed my forehead to hers. "This is so much more than just being in love, but since there isn't a word strong enough to describe it, then yes. That is what this is."

She closed her eyes and sighed. This was the moment Tess was telling me about, the moment she asked me to take advantage of when the time came, but watching her open her eyes and seeing blue instead of my favorite chocolate caramel, I felt doubt. I loved them all, but Tess had my heart completely.

"Can we go home?" Her usual sharp voice waivered and I knew she had come to a decision. What that was, I had no idea, and it terrified me either way.

I kissed her again, because I just couldn't help myself, and nodded. "Of course."

An hour later, we were sitting in front of my house, *our* house, with the car turned off and silence surrounding us.

"Is it difficult for you to identify with all of us?" she asked shakily.

I entwined our fingers together and kissed her hand. "Not anymore. Your blue eyes give you away, but you all hold yourself differently."

"I wish I could meet her, Charlie. Really speak with her and find out why she needs me."

"I do, too. She occasionally gets to be with Lydia and Camryn. Maybe one day she will with you."

She didn't respond, but smiled shyly.

We walked hand in hand through the front door and up the stairs to our room. She paused just outside the door, looking unsure. She glanced down the hallway at the guestroom before turning back and walking into the bathroom while I changed into some sweats and a t-shirt. It was late, and I was exhausted, but not knowing what was going to happen was going to keep me awake.

Tess wanted me to treat the girls like I would treat her. If it was Tess in that bathroom, I would storm in there and take her on the counter. Instead of doing that, I sat on the bed with my head in my hands. I know she was okay with it, but it still felt like I would be making love to a different woman.

I grabbed my pants off the floor and reached inside the pocket, pulling out the small velvet box encasing the ring I had gotten for Tess. Obviously, with everything that happened tonight, there wasn't a chance to ask her to marry me. I wasn't sure how long before she switched back, but when she did, I wasn't going to wait any longer.

I strained my ears to hear what she was doing in there, but there was complete silence. I looked around the room, smiling when I saw her touches on the dresser and the pictures on the wall. All of them were of the two of us from different times in our lives. When I looked at her nightstand, I saw her journal lying there, opened. It wasn't necessarily her journal, but it was where she spoke with the alters and told them her deepest thoughts and feelings. She told me I was welcomed to read it, but I never did so myself. She had always just read pieces of it to me.

After hiding the ring in the drawer of my nightstand, I stretched across the bed and lifted the book into my hands. It was opened to a place in the middle of all the entries. One page was written in tall, elegant handwriting, while the other page was written in short letters with sharp edges. So different. I knew the short letters were Camryn and the tall was Lydia. I read a few lines from each page, all explaining what had happened during the switch. I flipped through a few pages until I got to Tessa's writing.

Her letters were wide and curvy, much like a typical woman's handwriting would be. What caught my eye was the large letters in the middle of the page spelling out my name.

CHARLIE,

I know one day you will read this on your own without me forcing you to. I hope by then, you haven't decided to leave all this craziness behind, but I can't force you to stay.

I love you more than anything, Charlie, and I know you love me. I know it in the deepest part of my heart and soul.

The girls love you, too, in their own ways. Each one of them can love you in ways that I would never be able to on my own. Which seems impossible to me, but I know it's true.

Love them back, Charlie. Show each one of them why I can't let you go. Show them why they *should never let you go.*

Other people may think we are insane to pursue this. I understand how it looks, I even understand how you might feel about it and I won't force you to do anything you don't want to do. But I love you enough and want to be with you enough to not ask you to constantly be waiting for me to show up.

Do whatever makes you happy because no matter what that is, I'm happy with you.

I love you.

Every one of me does.

I read over her words again and again, thanking God for letting me have her.

The sound of the bathroom door opening caught my attention and when I looked up, Tessa's chocolate caramel eyes were looking back at me and she was smiling so brightly that I had a hard time taking in a breath at the sight.

"Tess?"

She stepped toward me, cautiously, like she was approaching a frightened animal, but she was still smiling.

"Baby?"

"Yes, Charlie. It's me."

"I missed you."

She hurried over to me and looked at what I was reading before tossing the journal aside and sitting herself down on my lap. I immediately buried my nose in her neck and wrapped my arms around her.

She kissed the top of my head and ran her fingers through my hair. "Tell me everything."

***

Tessa

Charlie told me everything that had happened, including Benny's ludicrous plan to get Jessi jealous enough to reveal her true feelings for Charlie, which apparently worked, but not the way she thought it would.

I'm just glad it didn't backfire like it would have if Charlie had played along. No way would Jessi put up with that. She had been burned too much in the past.

It was Charlie's kisses that fixed everything. Knowing that he saw *her* and *her alone* was the deciding factor. She loved Charlie, deeply, but she had no intention of taking it further than that kiss, which was a relief for me. I had the asinine idea that Charlie needed to treat all of them as he would treat me, which meant making love to all of them, too. I wanted him to love them and I wanted them to love him, but I didn't realize they would respect me enough to leave it at that.

I felt Jessi when I came to in the bathroom, staring at myself in the mirror. I even saw the blue of her eyes fade into the brown of mine. I felt her relief and I felt her love for the both of us. She wasn't going to interfere with that in any way. In fact, being in love and being loved back was all she had really wanted.

Charlie and I ended up lying down facing each other while we talked. He didn't stop touching me the whole time and ran his hand over my body, gradually pulling me closer until we were pressed against each other from chest to thighs with our legs entangled.

"I don't think I can do what you asked of me, love."

I knew what he was asking, but I didn't respond. I wanted to hear what he had to say before I told him that he didn't have to do what I asked, because it wasn't the solution. The girls didn't have any intention of being anything more to him than what they already were.

"I love Lydia and Camryn. I love Jessi. I love all of them so much, but I love my Tess more. You are everything for me, baby. I know they are a part of you and that's why I *do* love them, but they aren't… you. You are the only one I want to give myself to in every way."

I smiled at him and ran my fingers over the worry lines on his forehead. He moved his lips against mine in a gently, barely there, kiss. A kiss that told me he would do *anything* for me, but that he couldn't do this. It wasn't right.

"They don't want that from you, Charlie."

"What?"

"They don't want that part of you, baby. They want that to be mine. I have taken care of them and lived the last few years sacrificing for them. They don't feel right coming between me and the one man they all know was made for *me*. Especially Jessi. She's not against you kissing her…" I smiled at him to let him know I wasn't either. "She just wants to protect herself, and me."

His relief was palpable and the look in his eyes told me I had just made a horrible night the greatest of his life. "Thank God. I wouldn't have been able to go through with it."

"I know."

"Listen, it's not a big deal for me to wait for you, love. I'm willing to wait however long it takes to get you back to me. I waited fifteen years to have you as my own. I can wait a few days here and there, if it comes down to it."

He kissed me again, a little harder this time, and dipped his tongue against my lips before pulling away again. "Right now, though, I can't wait another minute."

He rolled away from me and opened the drawer on his nightstand. I was a little confused at first. I was expecting him to rip off my clothes and go for it because I couldn't wait another minute either. He closed the drawer slowly after picking something up and closing it in his hand. He knelt down next to me on the bed and looked like he had broken out in a sweat and I was too busy watching his face to see that he had placed something between us.

When I looked down at the black velvet box, my heart pounded against my chest as if it were trying to escape my body to jump into his. I looked back up at Charlie, feeling a warmth cover every inch of my skin and a sting behind my eyes.

"I know that we haven't been *together* for very long, but I've spent the last fifteen years of my life loving you and hoping to make you mine some day. I'll wait another fifteen years if you want me to, but it will always be you, love. I know I'll spend the rest of my life being yours, but I'm asking you to spend the rest of your life being mine."

He reached for my hand and it shook as he covered it in his.

"Will you marry me?"

The tears I had been holding back spilled over and my cheeks ached from the strength of the smile on my face.

"Yes, Charlie. I'm yours forever."

His mouth came down on mine and his body covered mine. He groaned when I wrapped myself around him and kissed him with everything I was worth. I heard the tiny box fall to the floor, but didn't stop kissing him.

"You want to see it?" he asked as he moved his lips down my neck to my collar bone.

I did, but I didn't want him to stop, yet.

"Maybe later?" I said breathlessly as his lips touched the sensitive curve of my breast.

I heard him chuckle, then felt cold air as he pulled himself off of me and grabbed the box off the floor. He wasn't gone long. He covered me again and slipped the ring on my left hand.

"You can look at it later," he mumbled and returned his mouth to my chest, "but I want to make love to you wearing it for the first time. Proving your really mine."

He slid up my body and kissed my deeply.

I forgot about the ring immediately when his hands lifted my shirt over my head. All I could focus on was the feel of him against me. The thought of him loving me for the rest of my life.

Every one of me.

Epilogue

1 year later

"So, what now?" Benny asked as she tapped her pen on the back of her chair.

"No idea," I replied. I stuffed the last of my clothes into my new duffel bag and shrugged. "I guess I'll just take it a day at a time."

She scoffed and quirked an eyebrow. "Really? You are one week overdue, T. Can't they go in there and pull her out or something?"

I laughed and looked down at my swollen belly, feeling my little girl kick hard against my ribs. It was still so amazing to feel her moving inside of me, even when I felt like my ribs were going to break.

"Charlie looks like he is about to snap any second, T. I think his hair is falling out. He keeps pulling on it and he's going to be completely bald by the time you deliver."

I laughed again, harder this time because she was telling the truth. Charlie's hands were pretty much glued to his head, constantly worrying about whether or not I was going to go into labor, or if I was moving around too much, or if I wasn't completely packed and ready to go to the hospital when the time came. Therefore, the reason I was zipping up my bag and setting it by the front door. I had been packed and ready for the last two weeks, but Benny kept switching out my comfortable clothes with things that were extremely impractical. Like lingerie and a tight black dress that she had found to wear to our rehearsal dinner and wanted me to wear when I left the hospital. She didn't understand that my body wasn't going to fit in any of that stuff for a while.

She thought I was being negative.

I thought I was being normal. I was also confused at how she even got to my bag in the first place. She must have been sneaking in while we weren't home.

"Hey, babe? Do you know where I put that onesie? I thought I packed it in my bag, but I can't find it anywhere." Charlie burst into the room with his arms full of pinks and yellows. "It's not in any of her drawers either. That's the one I wanted her to wear when we came home. I just can't find it."

Benny was shaking her head and palmed her face in exasperation.

I just giggled and unzipped by bag, pulling out the tiny onesie that said 'Daddy's Little Fighter' in bright pink letters on the front and pink boxing gloves on the back.

He had it made after the first time he felt her kick hard. He was holding me in his arms with my belly pressed against his when she kicked against him. He had been glued to me for the remaining months of my pregnancy, not wanting to miss a single movement from her.

"I'll keep it in *my* bag, Tess. Otherwise Benny might replace it with something stupid."

"Excuse me?" Benny sneered.

"Not now, you two," I laughed. The two of them were constantly bickering at each other, but they loved each other. Charlie said his love for her had something to do with that first time I saw him fight in New York. Benny said her love for him had something to do with his credit card.

I didn't even care enough to figure it out.

We were married two and a half months after he asked me that night, neither of us wanting to wait very long, and he had convinced me that it was a good idea to go off of my birth control. We both wanted kids, but I was still worried about being a good mother. He convinced me and the girls that we would never know unless we tried.

So now, I was a week over my due date, feeling like a balloon about ready to pop. Benny and Trevor were still together, but both of them were worried about taking the next step. Mom kicked Benny out shortly after the wedding hoping to speed some things along with them. Nothing worked, but they seemed happy.

Charlie had opened up his gym and stayed busy training a couple of fighters here and there, but he focused on the young kids who came there to stay out of trouble. It was a huge success. I helped him with paperwork since he wouldn't let me get a job anywhere else that he couldn't keep an eye on me. I didn't mind so much and lately, we were all just anticipating the baby's arrival so everything else fell on the back burner.

I walked into the bathroom to make sure I hadn't forgotten to pack my deodorant and felt a gush of warm liquid run down my legs.

"Well, what do you know?" I muttered to myself.

I felt a pull in the back of my mind as I looked down at the floor.

"About damn time," Lydia's voice rang out from my lips.

"No kidding. I'm tired of feeling like a balloon," Camryn rasped.

"Okay, girls. You keep quiet. I'm not missing this," I replied.

"Nous resterons à proximité, Tessa," Jessi whispered. "We will stay close."

"Thanks girls."

I felt the disconnection fade, but the euphoria of what was about to happen was welcome.

Charlie walked into the bathroom mumbling about his little girl being restricted from ever wearing mini-skirts when he saw the look on my face.

"Tess?"

"Yeah, Charlie, it's me."

He looked down at the puddle I was standing in and his face paled as he realized what was happening.

"I think I'm going to pass out," he said and scrubbed his hand through his hair.

His bright green eyes started to water and I couldn't stop myself from cupping his face and kissing those perfect full lips that were mine forever.

"Time to go, love."

He wrapped his arms around me and kissed me hard, then pressed his lips just behind my ear, in the spot that drove me crazy, and whispered to every part of me, "Let's go ladies."

###

The End

About the Author

I live in Morgan Utah with my husband, daughter, and dogs, Kolo and Keena. I write as often as my active daughter will let me and my husband has the patience of a saint. I find inspiration from dreams, people I meet, and life experiences. When I write, I usually end up drinking one too many cans of Peace Tea, eating three too many Fruit by the Foot fruit snacks, and accidently kicking my pup and best buddy, Kolo, too many times since he loves to sleep under my desk at my feet.

I started writing as a teen, but my fear of the unknown won out every time and I threw everything out. After becoming a mother and deciding to stay at home to raise my beautiful little girl, I tried again when I couldn't stop thinking of ideas. I loved every minute, every hour of sleep lost, and every character that came to life in my mind.

It's strange, but my favorite moments are when I have writer's block because I can turn to my husband and find inspiration through him by just doing what we do best together. Talking, laughing, and just being in love. He doesn't like to read, but he never stops encouraging me to keep going.

Writing has become an important part of my life and every book has a special place in my heart.

Connect with Jessica Wilde

Goodreads: https://www.goodreads.com/author/show/7373464.Jessica_Wilde

Facebook: http://www.facebook.com/AuthorJessicaWilde

Smashwords: http://www.smashwords.com/profile/view/Jessicawildeauthor

Twitter: https://twitter.com/JessicaWilde9

ACKNOWLEDGEMENTS

There just aren't enough words to express how grateful I am to all of you. To my family. To my friends, both old and new. To the readers and bloggers who have been so willing to spread the word and opened their hearts to my stories. To the readers that have reached out to me to tell me how much they have enjoyed reading about my characters. To those who have seen Tess and Charlie for who and what they are.

Love can truly conquer anything. Pure love is the most powerful thing in the universe. Love is every light, every smile, every trial overcome, every bit of peace that has ever been felt, every happy child, every family created and so much more.

When I first started this journey, I had no one to help me and no idea how to even start. But because of love, I am where I am and I look forward to the future.

Thank you so much!

Thank you for your kind words, your enthusiasm, and your love.

I will cherish it all.

Find other titles by Jessica Wilde

Our Time

Print ISBN13: 978-1494310219
ASIN: B00H1AJCTC
eBook ISBN: 9781311364517

Jocelyn White's only priority in life is her daughter, Olivia. As a single mother, with no family and the only friends she had now hours away, life isn't easy. But the last several years taught her what is truly important and she plans on spending the time she has loving her little girl and keeping her safe and happy. She doesn't plan on her new gorgeous, blue eyed neighbor turning out to be the one thing her and Olivia have been missing.

Andrew Carter has been waiting his whole life for a woman like Jocelyn. After his parents died years before, leaving him to care for his little sister, Madison, he spent years patiently waiting for a family of his own. When Jocelyn and Olivia completely steal his heart, he knows his patience has finally paid off and it's time for his life to finally start.

What he doesn't know is that Jocelyn is keeping something from him. Something she learned a few years ago.

Life is short and sometimes, time isn't on your side.

Leverage (The Brannock Siblings, #1)

Print ISBN-13: 978-1495276989
ASIN: B00J8766O0
eBook ISBN: 9781311640024

Adventure. That's all Aislinn 'Ash' Brannock wanted in her life. Her dad and two brothers - all cops - got to see it all, but their over-protectiveness made her feel like she had been locked away in a tower with three fire breathing dragons watching her every move.

Yes, it was that bad. The only silver lining? Lucas Shade. Her brothers' best friend growing up, and apparently the only man she will ever love because let's face it, none of the others even come close. After an unfortunate mistake lands her back in her father's home, her world is turned upside down and Lucas is there in a tightly wrapped package of serious with a big red bow on top. Life just got interesting, but it comes with a price, one she never wanted to pay.

Detective Lucas Shade never had a real family, but the Brannocks took him in as one of their own and he never took it for granted. Ash was a big reason for why he stuck around, but in order to save himself the beating of a lifetime from her two older brothers, he kept his feelings for her hidden. When the case he has been working on for months takes a turn, Ash could become the leverage the bad guys have been waiting for, but keeping her invisible may destroy everything Lucas has worked so hard for. Good thing Ash is the only person he would give up everything to protect.

Conned (The Brannock Siblings, #2)

Print ISBN13: 978-1499363180
ASIN: B00L2FQE9I
eBook ISBN: 9781310302473

Conall Brannock takes his job seriously. He doesn't get attached, he doesn't ask questions, and he protects his family at all costs. Nothing will change that. Not even the sweet, green eyed witness that just burst into his life and shifted his world. He has one job to do; protect Emily until she can testify. He can't let his interest in her get in the way, but the more he finds out about her, the more he can't help but wonder how the beautiful broken girl got into this mess in the first place. And the longer he takes to learn the truth, the deeper he falls for her.

Emily Dawson has a job to do. Stay off the grid, testify, and hopefully get her brother back. He's all she has left of the family she struggled so hard to hold together and she would do anything to keep him safe. Even if it means she has put herself in harm's way or that she has conned everyone into believing she saw something she didn't. She knows where her loyalties lie, but her stoic yet gentle protector and his crazy family makes her question everything she once knew.

Loyalty can be one sided.

Family isn't always blood.

And honesty can destroy everything she has come to love.

Missing (The Brannock Siblings, #3)

Print ISBN-13: 978-1500858032
ASIN: B00N505Q06
eBook ISBN: 9781310343186

There are two things in this life that Gus Brannock truly loves; his family and his job. His family is growing and he wants what his brother and sister have before the job he's worked so hard for takes its toll. The woman he's got his eye on, however, isn't interested in being with a man who risks his life every day. When the unexpected friendship with the sassy red head he used to hate turns into something Gus just doesn't want to live without, he will do whatever it takes to have her. The hazards of his job as a detective for missing children may end up proving to be too much, but there's a reason Aiden was brought into his life and nothing will stand in his way to keep her there.

Aiden Murphy used to hate the handsome jerk next door until a surprising discovery spun her world in another direction. Her life of devotion to her sister and niece has been her biggest strength with the exception of her art. That is, until Gus turns out to be the one thing that has been missing from that life all along. Aiden must decide if the unknown is worth the risk of loving the dedicated detective or if being pulled into his world is more than she can handle. When Gus becomes the only way for her to keep the people she loves most safe, will she understand why he treasures her untried strength or will she let her fear of the unknown decide *for* her?

Ricochet (Rise & Fall, #1)

Print ISBN-13: 978-1507574621
ASIN: B00SJ2A8MQ
eBook ISBN: 9781311230010

Fear.

It's the last thing I remembered.

I was afraid.

Afraid to fight, afraid to run… afraid to breathe.

Then, everything had gone dark. As if life was finally hearing my pleas, my cries to end the torment. To end the fear.

But even in the dark, I still felt it.

I always felt it.

My life had been a ricochet of one event leading to the next. Bouncing back and forth from good to bad. Happiness to despair. Hope to fear.

My name is Arianna West. I'm stronger now. Steady. Alive.

I can find a way to survive on my own. I can see what is coming for me. I can channel my fear into strength.

Except… I didn't see Jack.

And Jack changed everything.

38981629R00154

Made in the USA
Charleston, SC
21 February 2015